"Imagination is everything.
It is the preview of life's coming attractions."

~Albert Einstein

"The past can be cleansed.
The present can be made fruitful.
The future can be what you decide it shall be."

~Raymond Charles Barker
The Power of Decision

"Your thoughts become things!"

~Rhonda Byrne
The Secret

Beyond the Last Horizon

BEYOND THE LAST HORIZON

MARY DE GROAT

BEYOND THE LAST HORIZON

Windy City Publishers
2118 Plum Grove Road, #349
Rolling Meadows, IL 60008
www.windycitypublishers.com

Published in the United States of America

ISBN:
978-1-941478-19-6

Library of Congress Control Number:
2015953175

WINDY CITY PUBLISHERS
CHICAGO

To My Son

ACKNOWLEDGMENTS

The journey of writing this book began with one idea that took on a life of its own. It's proof that anything imagined can be realized. I couldn't wait to get out of bed each day to see what would happen next to the diverse cast of characters. It took three months to write. The story unfolded to the end quite naturally and with little effort. Then the hard part. Seeing if it accomplished the intention: to inspire and entertain.

I have been blessed by the wisdom, encouragement and great edits of many friends and strangers who read the manuscript. Whether we've met or not, my sincere thanks go to each and every one of you.

To Cathi Lincoln, who out of friendship and her generous heart, read and proofed the book countless times. To Dennis Lincoln, (AKA 'Bob' because he says he can't spell) who shared a guy's perspective and corrected a couple of critical facts. Genine Barker who gave me the greatest compliment by saying, "The story inspired me to get off the pity pot." Tim O'Dahl for another guy's opinion and Jan O'Dahl for her objectivity. Dr. Carell Zaehn for spiritual guidance; apt, pithy and witty comments. Melanie Bretz for her time editing and suggestions for a title. Carol Goozé and the San Jose, California book club members for their candid feedback. To my fellow Algonkian New York Writers Conference attendees who provided the toughest, most constructive, yet optimistic input.

Thank you to my Windy City Publishers team, Dawn, Lise, and Kristyn, for taking on and believing in the project while patiently guiding me through my publishing debut.

Thank you to my husband, Justin Thornburg, who gave me the time, space, and support to the end. And, for asking, "How is the next book coming along?"

And, to my son, Sean O'Sullivan, on whom I've always relied for his unfiltered opinions delivered with love regarding my ventures (and adventures). Thank you, sweetheart, for your unwavering encouragement.

SATURDAY NIGHT

Hank Johns was finally getting used to a new life. Moving through the foyer and expansive living room filled with art and thick colorful rugs, he joined the other guests on the terrace. There, the one person he knew channeled him to the bar. Accepting a cold beer, Hank turned to survey his surroundings. Three women stood together laughing. He'd known David for years, but had only heard of the others. The men interrupted the animated trio and David introduced Hank to Sara, Gina and Carrie.

It was a balmy summer evening. Gossamer layers of the ladies' dresses fluttered in a light breeze. Low lights of amber lined a meandering pathway to an oval pool of cobalt blue. The sweet scent of cut grass mingled with jasmine in the day's fading light.

Sara raised her glass of Chardonnay in welcome. "All together at last. Cheers!"

"Cheers!" echoed the happy group.

"And, Hank, thanks for coming tonight. It's great to finally meet you," Sara said.

Gina was the first to lean slightly toward the tall black man and extend a slender hand, "I'm Gina."

For an instant, Hank noticed the brilliant blue eyes, fringed with long lashes. They glowed like lighthouse beacons; contrasted with the smooth golden complexion Gina had inherited from her Peruvian mother. He shook off the glimmer of attraction. Releasing Gina's hand, he returned Carrie's strong handshake and smiled at her words of welcome, followed by David's embarrassing accolades for a job well done. To escape being the focus of attention, Hank checked the time on his watch. Though he'd only just arrived, he wanted to make a call.

Sara offered her office. "It's private, go ahead. Just off the living room."

Hank sat at Sara's desk, ignoring the labels on the pile of files and the contents of the loose scattered papers. His call was answered on the first ring. Hank's voice was soft and deep.

"I just called to say good-night again…yeah, I know I just got here. I miss you, though. You get a good night's sleep and don't worry. I'll see you in the morning. I love you very, very much." A minute later Hank hung up and read the message scrolling across Sara's computer screen.

Imagination is everything. It is the preview to life's coming attractions.

The decision that changed everything came to mind.

In a reflective mood, Hank returned to the terrace to find the others watching the dawning glow of the full moon rising over the horizon. The growing light illuminated the silent group. Like Hank, Carrie, Gina, David, and Sara were also recalling the turning point in their pasts.

CHAPTER 1
CARRIE

Growing up, Carrie's home life was nothing like her friend Gina's. Where Gina had more loving attention than she could stand, Carrie's mother, when home, was usually raging over some detail forgotten by the household staff. Carrie was the only child of very wealthy people. Her father was a vice-president at Kendall Innovations Incorporated, a massive enterprise founded by her maternal grandfather, Justice Kendall. Justice Kendall was a visionary with an imagination beyond the wildest dreams of most other entrepreneurs and business moguls. Several times a year, Carrie stayed at her grandparents' house while her parents toured the world with friends. Their home overlooked the glorious Golden Gate Bridge and the San Francisco skyline beyond. From the hilltop perch, she could watch tankers and other cargo-laden ships passing beneath the towering icon, leaving a wake in the cold, white-peaked chop.

Carrie spent a lot of time watching the activity on the bay waters by day and the river of light pouring across the bridge at night—a solid red flow from southbound traffic, neon white heading north. This was the view from her bedroom there; a little girl's dream in pink-and-white frills. A private toy land dominated by a fluffy bed covered with stuffed animals. She loved her room and was allowed to wander freely throughout the mansion and its gardens, but grandfather's impressive office was off limits. Carrie visited that room only by invitation. It was where her grandfather spent most of his time. To a small girl, everything in it seemed huge. A floor-to-ceiling bay window with a southern exposure brightened the room's rich dark mahogany wainscoting. A fireplace that Carrie could stand in was set for a warming fire on chilly, foggy days. The black walnut desk positioned in front of shelves of first editions was matched with a soft leather chair big enough for Carrie and her grandfather to sit in side by side. One wall was covered with paintings by people named Monet and Turner. Carrie's favorite place was a cushiony window seat upholstered in an ornate gold and sage-green fabric.

One afternoon, while sitting cozily next to her grandfather at his desk, Carrie jumped down to cross the room and sit in the bay window.

Not realizing what had drawn her attention, her grandfather asked, "Do you like the view, Caroline?"

Sounding older than her six years, Carrie said, "Yes, but I love this." She traced the window seat's swirling pattern with tiny fingers.

"Do you like the colors?"

"I want a princess dress of this to wear to a party. Then everyone would love me."

Justice Kendall recognized the loneliness in his only grand-child's voice.

"Come back here."

Carrie slid down and went to stand in front of the imposing man.

"Caroline, I want you to know something and always remember it."

"Yes, grandfather." Carrie was thinking he was about to tell her something special. A secret that only she would share with the person she loved most in the world.

Unused to talking to little girls except the tall-for-her-age skinny one with knobby knees and slightly protruding tummy standing before him, Justice Kendall knew Carrie well. She was smart and already conjuring up ideas about how her life would be when she grew up. But Kendall, a man of few words who spent most of his time generating great profits in global markets, struggled to come up with a simple statement that condensed what he wanted his granddaughter to understand.

They stared at each other for a moment. Little Carrie's gaze never leaving his, waiting.

Finally he said, "You will grow up with everything you could ever want, Caroline. But toys and princess dresses won't make you happy for very long. There will always be another wish you'll want to come true. A simple idea is the seed, one that with care, reaches its full potential: start with an idea for making anything come true. But to be happy, really happy, I want you to remember that people come first...not things."

"What do you mean, grandfather?"

Pausing for thought without answering the question, the great man posed one of his own. "Do you know what it means to 'imagine'?"

Carrie nodded.

"Whatever you can imagine can come true. My company is built on imagination. Whatever you think about—whatever you can imagine—*can* happen. You have the power inside you." He gently tapped a long, thin finger on the center of her little chest.

Carrie's expression showed she was listening intently, but didn't understand.

He continued. "You have a strong mind and can make anything that you want happen. The secret is to trust what's inside. Sometimes there's just a whisper of a feeling, or an idea that comes so fast you might miss it if you're not paying attention. If there's something you really want and you keep thinking about it, feel what it would be like to already have it. Does it really make you happy? Does it make someone else happy? The secret is not really a secret at all, but it can be hard to remember. Help people when you can, and you will have everything you could ever imagine for your own happiness."

Some of what her grandfather was saying made sense, but most of it was mysterious, and she was intrigued by two words, "power" and "secret."

Carrie stepped into her grandfather's waiting open arms.

He gently kissed the top of her dark blonde head. Smiling, Justice Kendall sighed and held her tight while Carrie murmured against the crush of his soft sweater, "I'm going to imagine living with you forever." Then she asked, "Will you tell me how the secret power works?"

Pulling Carrie's arms from around his shoulders, Justice noted the inquisitive expression on the pale angular face just inches from his own bearded smile and said, "Anyone can do it. There's no magic to it. Considering how smart you are at six, I expect you will understand soon enough but we'll talk again later. Now my little dear, I need to make a phone call."

Carrie left her grandfather's office and went directly to her room. Sitting at the antique school desk, Carrie lifted the top to find a piece of drawing paper and took her favorite colors from her pencil set. She drew pictures of what she thought about most. And that included one long stick figure, her grandfather. Sensing the importance of their talk that afternoon, Carrie vowed to find out how something imagined could come true.

≈≈≈

Three days later, Carrie was crawling around on her hands and knees in the sprawling country garden, spying between the bushes on the workers who were trimming and weeding the lavish flower beds. Her grandfather loved the gardens. He would tell her the name of each plant whenever they walked there together. She would listen carefully and try to remember: Yerba Buena, Hummingbird Sage, Monterey Manzanita, Iris, Sugar Bush, California Fuchsia.

It was a quiet, sunny afternoon in September, the time of year for the best weather in San Francisco, when the morning fog disappeared early in the day and the temperatures grew comfortably warm. When she tired of spying on the gardeners, Carrie sat cross-legged on the just-mowed grass, imagining good things for her grandfather and waiting to feel happy. According to him she thought that's what should happen. The sounds of birds chirping, the gardeners' low discussion of which plants needed attention and the soft clicking of stones in Carrie's small hands blended together until suddenly interrupted.

"Miguel! Andre! Mister Kendall is sick!" The housekeeper's shrill call pierced the drowsy afternoon. Carrie's head jerked up to see Marta flying out the back patio doors, nearly tripping while screaming in Spanish.

Miguel instantly dropped his rake and raced up the winding path to the house, followed by Andre. Carrie watched without understanding what Marta had shouted, then jumped up to follow both men. By the time she ran inside, an ambulance had arrived and three paramedics were being directed upstairs by Marta.

Carrie's grandmother stood still as a statue, just inside the massive front door that had been left wide open.

"Marta," Carrie's grandmother whispered as more staff gathered in the grand foyer, "Tell everyone to go back to work. We will let them know what's happened when we have all the facts." The elegant woman was still in charge of her household, but Carrie could see the clasped, bejeweled hands shaking.

Carrie went over to her. "Grandmother? What's wrong?"

"Not now, Caroline."

"But…"

"NOT NOW! This is not a time for children to be in the way. Go to your room and Marta will see to you."

Carrie trudged up the back stairs leading to her bedroom on the third floor. She instinctively avoided the main staircase where those men in blue uniforms had gone up. *Where's grandfather?* She wondered. *What's going on?*

"Miss Caroline?" Several minutes later, Marta walked into Carrie's bedroom, at the same time knocking lightly on the door. "Miss Caroline. Do you want something to eat?"

"Marta. I want to see grandfather. Where is he? Why is grandmother so upset? I want to see my grandfather! He loves me! He's the only one who loves me!" Carrie was scared and didn't know why. Without getting an answer about dinner, Marta turned and left Carrie alone watching the rush hour traffic clog up on the bridge without a word of explanation or reassurance.

కకక

The ambulance had left hours ago with its siren screaming. A deep silence weighed down the huge house. Carrie left her room and tiptoed down the stairs. Reaching the kitchen door, she saw Marta bent over the sink, one elbow flailing, furiously peeling potatoes. Carrie moved on. Passing the great room where she had last seen her grandmother, passing the dining room where twenty people had sat for dinner two days before, passing the library with another fireplace where grandmother could usually be found. Wandering farther down the wide hallway, Carrie stopped in front of the tall double doors that opened to her grandfather's favorite room, his office.

Carrie knocked. "Grandfather?" She called quietly and then a little louder, but didn't want Marta or anyone else who might still be in the house to know she was about to enter the forbidden room.

With a slight push, the door swung open and Carrie walked in. She made a full turn, looking at the high ceiling and windows overlooking the gardens she had played in earlier that day. *I wonder if grandfather saw me watching the gardeners*, she thought. She touched nearly everything she could reach before crossing the room to the desk. Carrie sat down. The chair was on casters and swiveled. Curling up on her knees, Carrie scooted the chair forward. She sat up very straight and folded her hands on the desk top. A moment later she addressed an imaginary audience of very important people who had come to ask her very important questions.

She was careful not to move anything on grandfather's desk while pretending she was the one in charge. When she closed her eyes to picture people sitting in front of her, Carrie felt a presence, a warm pressure, as if her grandfather was sitting next to her in his chair.

Don't be scared my little dear. I love you very much.

Her eyes popped open. Looking around the room she called out, "Grandfather?"

Footsteps snapped her back to attention. Carrie quickly left the desk and ducked behind an over-stuffed chair by the fireplace as the office door opened. Carrie didn't dare peek out from her hiding place, but she could hear a desk drawer being pulled open. Then she heard a slight scraping, followed by a light ticking. Dialing the combination and opening the thick door to the safe, someone pulled out a box and unlocked it. Then Carrie heard a rustle of paper. The visitor departed, leaving the office door ajar. Carrie escaped to her bedroom unnoticed.

Carrie's mother arrived the next day and told her that her father would be coming, too. Carrie still didn't know what was going on, and badgered Marta with questions. "Why is mother here? Where is grandfather? What's the matter with grandmother?"

"Shush bambina," an exasperated Marta chided. "Your mother wanted to come see you and I don't know anything about your grandmother. Shush and go play."

When her father arrived the following day, he took Carrie into her bedroom and sat her down on the big bed. "Carrie," he said taking her onto his lap, which he never did unless it was really good or really bad news. "Grandfather died. Do you know what that means?"

Carrie didn't blink, but felt her heart tighten. "Yes, I know."

"He got sick and went to the hospital. The doctors did everything they could to make him better but he was too sick and they couldn't help him. He won't be coming back and that's why your grandmother and mother are so sad. They loved him very much."

"I love grandfather too, Daddy. Why didn't he say goodbye to me?"

"He couldn't, Carrie. He didn't know that he wasn't going to come back home. I think he would have said goodbye to you if he could have," her father added. He only now realized how attached Carrie had been to the renowned, brilliant and intimidating Justice Kendall.

❧❧❧

Not only did Justice Kendall leave his little granddaughter with a message that seemed mysterious to her at the time, she would also receive a significant portion of his estate. His wife, the second Mrs. Justice Kendall, received millions and the house in Marin in recognition of their ten years of marriage. Carrie's mother inherited enough to continue living in the manner in which she had grown up. Everyone at the reading of the will got something. But the lion's share went to Carrie. In addition to liquid assets, Carrie received her grandfather's majority ownership of Kendall Innovations Incorporated. Should she choose to do so after successfully fulfilling all stipulations, Carrie could take command of the company. Ownership would be held in trust and released to her control upon completing a master's degree in business and serving as an intern at the company for five years.

Carrie wasn't in her grandfather's office that day, as the lawyer sat at his client's desk to convey the last wishes of a wealthy man. But her mother and father were there and were as stunned as everyone else. "How could he leave his company to a child?" was the most common reaction, followed by, "That's outrageous." Several even asked, "Who is Caroline Marie Jeffries?"

Contesting the will was out of the question. Anticipating hard feelings and chaos among his family and those business associates known to assume they were in line to take over Kendall Innovations, including Carrie's father, Carson W. Jeffries, III, the will was not to be contestable; it was airtight. Justice Kendall had engaged one of the best estate attorneys in California to manage the complex job of legally sorting out his empire.

The company's stock dove by fifty percent when the news broke that the founding principal had died. Kendall had a succession plan in place and the appointed individual took charge as interim president the day after the owner's death. The first emergency board meeting included an hour of collective shock at the news and bantered suggestions of getting around the ridiculous idea of a young girl taking over. They speculated that it would be about twenty years before Caroline would emerge to claim her inheritance. Anything could happen in that length of time, so they turned their attention to the urgent business at hand: protecting stockholder interests as well as their own.

Carrie left her grandfather's home with her mother and father right after the reading of the will. She wouldn't see her grandmother or the view from her pink-and-white bedroom for many years to come.

Carson Jeffries never accepted the fact that his daughter had been given what he felt was rightly his, and ignored his little girl more than before. Carrie's mother embarked on a string of affairs, and her father stayed away for longer and longer periods of time. Carson eventually left his position at Kendall Innovations, after having worked for his father-in-law for nearly ten years. He took a new job on the east coast, leaving Carrie and her mother. That was when the house a few doors up from Gina's on Bainbridge Island in Seattle became Carrie's new home.

೪೪೪

While growing up, Carrie enjoyed being purposefully obtuse to gain power over others if they didn't challenge her quick and ready wit. She was decisive and knowledgeable, but habitually treated other people as intellectual inferiors. She headed off to Europe for a year after high school and found a sexy Frenchman to pal around with, but never lost sight of her intention to take over her grandfather's company. When the time came, Wharton University challenged her, and after years of driven, concentrated effort, Carrie received her MBA. Her next step was to walk into the corporate offices of Kendall Innovations and claim the first phase of her inheritance: as an intern starting in the mailroom.

CHAPTER 2
GINA

In the beginning, Gina was a happy, well-adjusted child, capable of being an 'A' student. Her parents were proud of each one of their children: two athletic boys who loved soccer and baseball, and their baby-doll girl with silky black waves and lively blue eyes. A perfect complexion and slender limbs even at ten years promised a great beauty in the making. Gina was sheltered from the harsher side of life. Lavished with love and what her parents could afford, Gina was consequently naïve and susceptible to being taken advantage of.

The day the moving van parked three houses up the street, she watched the tall, skinny girl with fly-away hair standing in the driveway while the movers carried heavy furniture into the house. Gina wondered who she was. During their first encounter, Carrie and Gina debated the arguable beauty of each other's favorite Disney princess and whether Barbie dolls were cool or not. But Gina acquiesced to Carrie's opinion. A provocative influencer, as the girls got older, Carrie became Gina's mentor in delinquency and taught her how to smoke a cigarette; that parents were annoying; and uncles will touch you in nasty places. Gina had grown up in an insular family circle. After meeting Carrie, she hid behind a tough can-and-will-do-anything attitude to win the prestigious position of being Carrie's favorite best friend. Gina didn't realize for a long time that she was Carrie's only friend.

When her two older brothers went away to college, Gina had her parent's full attention, and it was more than she could stand. Feeling suffocated and envying Carrie's unbridled freedom, Gina surprised and scared everyone.

念念念

"Gina?" Antonella, Gina's mother, called out for the third time before heading down the hallway to the girl's bedroom. "Gina!"

By the next morning Antonella was hysterical. Her husband, Tom, took over the questioning while standing in the front doorway of Carrie's house on a drizzly Seattle morning.

"Carrie," he said, "do you know where Gina is? She's been gone all night."

"I haven't seen her, Mr. Severns. I saw her three days ago. I haven't been home," Carrie explained. "She's been talking about feeling overwhelmed lately...maybe she ran away."

"Dios Mio! No, no, no!" Antonella cried out.

"Carrie, look at me," Tom Severns commanded. "Where would she go? Do you have any idea?"

"I don't know, maybe San Francisco? She asked about what it was like there last time I saw her. That was right before you called, Mrs. Severns. It was like she didn't want to go home."

Carrie told them about the last conversation she and Gina had had about their parents and the argument over which of them was worse off.

Three months went by with no word. Gina's parents called Carrie nearly every day, hired an investigator, and haunted the San Francisco police stations. Gina had vanished.

For weeks, Tom Severns struggled to focus at work and stayed home as often as he dared, risking the health of his business while his wife refused to leave the house at all.

Mid-afternoon on another dreary day in Seattle, the phone woke a much thinner and grayer Antonella. "Every time that phone rings, I jump. I can't live like this any longer...that's probably one of the boys again," Antonella said, while reaching for the phone. "Hello?"

"Mom, it's me."

‌ৰ৵৵

Tom and Antonella took the first flight out of SeaTac to San Francisco, snatched their waiting daughter, and took her home. Avoiding her parents' questions for the time being, Gina went right to bed and slept until nearly noon the next day.

Then, gathered around the kitchen table with cups of tea and warm, buttered blueberry muffins, looking all of her sixteen years, Gina bravely admitted everything to her parents."I had sex, tried drugs and snuck into the clubs…as long as I didn't drink inside; I thought it would be okay.

"I went to San Francisco because that's where Carrie used to live. She talked about living there at her grandparents' house all the time. I know you guys love me, but I need freedom. Just like Carrie."

Gina's parents looked at each other and silently made a decision. Carrie was about to leave for Europe, and until she left, Gina wouldn't be allowed to see the girl who had so negatively influenced their daughter.

"There was a guy," Gina continued, "who had a place where people could stay. He didn't live there but visited the apartment a lot. There were three of us. In return for letting us stay for free, we slept with him."

Gina watched her mom and dad for a reaction. "That guy was such a sleaze. I don't know his real name…he told us to call him John. He always used a condom, but the other girls said that he knew the number for the pregnancy center at Planned Parenthood by heart."

She paused. Talking about what she'd done now sounded so bad and wrong that she felt ashamed and sorry she'd scared her parents.

"Most afternoons, I'd spend a lot of time in a bookstore. There was one book I wanted, but I had no money. It was small and fit in my coat pocket. I read it a couple of times before smuggling it back into the store. The manager didn't even notice it had been gone. The main thing the book said was something like, 'what you think about all the time will happen.' Something about that made sense, but something else got me to call home."

Antonella and Tom waited for Gina to continue telling her story without barraging her with questions.

"An old guy, at least he seemed old, walked up to me one day outside that bookstore. I thought he was going to bust me for taking the book, but he got in my face and said, 'Life is what you make it. It's up to you.' He had a long gray ponytail. And I'll never forget his scary face. His eyes bored into mine for what seemed a long time but it was probably only a few seconds before he gave me a card and shouted, 'read it!'"

Her father asked, "What did it say?"

Ignoring her father's question, Gina went on, "I watched him walk away and do the same thing to another girl. What he said and what was on the card made me realize just how far off track I'd gotten and where I was headed. I ran to a coffee shop and asked a waitress if I could use the phone because I really needed to call home. I didn't tell her that I was calling Seattle!"

Oliver, the family's golden retriever, got up from under the table and nudged Gina's arm to be petted.

"What did the card say, honey?" Gina's dad asked again.

Having memorized it, Gina spoke deliberately.

"I gave my life to become the person I am right now. Was it worth it?"

The silence around the kitchen table was profound. Oliver's tail kept a soft beat on the slate floor as Gina absently stroked his smooth head.

Gina finished her story. "Standing in that coffee shop, waiting for you to answer the phone, I thought, '*NO, this is not worth it*.' And, thanks to that guy with the ponytail, I decided to quit all the stuff I'd been doing to make my life miserable…and come home."

Antonella gently brushed the tears away from her lovely daughter's cheeks and said quietly, "I don't understand. Why would you leave us? Why didn't you talk to me?"

"Mom, you don't get it. You left your family in Peru to marry dad. I'll bet Nana never asked you why you left them, did she? At least I didn't leave for a boyfriend—I left for me!"

"But you're only sixteen, Gina," Antonella answered. "You don't know anything about the world."

"And that's *your* fault, Mom! I can't do anything without asking you and explaining everything…"

Gina's father spoke up. "Okay, baby. You're home safe. That's what mat—"

Antonella interrupted, "We were so scared—you could have been dead. My God!"

"It's over now. Antonella, we have to let our daughter grow up."

∼∼∼

After high school, Gina left the family fold to attend Washington University. There was enough distance between home and campus to give her the breathing space she needed. While relishing her independence, she floundered around, changing her mind about various degree programs until she landed on Communications. But even then she was aimless, unfocused, and lacking ambition. Gina shared an apartment with two other young women, one from Oregon, and the other from Utah. They were happy, goofy girls enjoying freedom from parental grasp.

It was there that Gina found herself in a new role. As a leader. Oddly, it was her looks, and not any strength of character, that gave her influence over her roommates. What Gina felt like doing, the others would want to do it too. Struggling along, fitting studies in between parties and dates, Gina was becoming a negative influence on her new friends. She even persuaded them to leave their classes for a week in October for a little diversion in Los Angeles.

"Let's go! We'll fly down and see the Viper Room, the bar Johnny Depp used to own, and have lunch at Spagos and watch for celebrities. We might even get to see a movie being made."

They packed their bags and took off. The girls found a somewhat affordable motel on the outskirts of Beverly Hills. After three days of haunting Rodeo Drive, restaurant bars and nightclubs, the count for celebrity sightings was up to ten. The top score went to Gina, who had noticed Anne Hartford going into Gucci's with Jake Harris. Anne was hot news in Hollywood right then for her break-out role in a tragic story of a young stepmother challenged by her new husband's two terrorizing teenage children. Jake was a new face in the modeling industry, recognizable from billboards and fashion spreads, and as the handsome romantic interest in an international perfume campaign. Gina and her friends ran down the sidewalk and composed themselves before entering one of the Drive's intimidating shops. Normally, a high-profile celebrity would book a private appointment and the store manager would keep the general public at bay for as long as the famous one was shopping. This day, the girls were allowed in. The three squeezed through the front door together. The slight ruckus drew attention inside. Anne had a pair of shoes in hand when she turned toward the noise. Jake slouched in a leather chair watching Anne shop.

Gina forgot all about keeping cool. Walking up to the actress, she stuck out her hand and smiled. "I'm so pleased to meet you. My name is Gina Severns and I'm a huge fan. I love your work." Using every cliché flustered fans say when they meet a celebrity, Gina settled down and boldly asked Anne if she would join them for lunch.

Anne was graceful under the barrage of adoration from the threesome. The store manager had hustled toward Gina when she approached the celebrity, who seemed ready to drop $5,000 on the shoes with silver-leaf stilettos, but was flagged off by Jake. He watched Gina's eyes sparkle. Her smile as wide as it could be. Her shimmering hair danced with every bob of the head. Jake noticed everything about Gina and got up to join the conversation.

"I'm ready for lunch, Anne. How about you?" Jake said.

"Can't," Anne replied, then turned to Gina and explained, "But it's always great when someone can be themself and just be friendly. I enjoyed meeting you."

Gina's friends had stood just behind her, gazing stupidly, starstruck. They hadn't said more than hello, while Gina babbled on.

"Tell you what, ladies. There's a private party tonight at Hard Rock Café in Hollywood. It's a closed pre-premiere party for Anne's next movie. Do you mind, Annie?"

Setting down the shoes and checking her watch, Anne said, "We'll leave your name at the door as my guests. But I've really got to go."

Jake gave Gina the address and went to catch up with Anne.

The store manager was furious at the lost sale and extended his own invitation to Gina and her friends.

"You may leave now," he said, while rounding them up and herding them toward the front door without a touch or another word.

Outside, the girls bent over gasping at the exchange with one of their favorite movie stars. "We have to get new dresses!" Gina shouted. "And haircuts and manicures. New shoes!"

"We can't afford all that," countered the others.

Heading back to the motel by bus, Gina was silent. She was quiet throughout the rest of the afternoon, while doing her own mani-pedi. She played with her hair in front of the small mirror over the bathroom sink, trying out different ways to push it into some new shape without benefit of a professional cut and style. She agonized over the few choices of what to wear presented by the clothes in her suitcase. "I'm going tonight. With or without you guys," she told her friends.

She went without them.

Gina decided to stay in Los Angeles after discussing it the next day with her roommates for all of thirty minutes. She had told them about the party, about Jake and his friends. "Oh my God, it's amazing here," she'd said. "I even got to talk with Anne for a few minutes again."

The roommates left her in Los Angeles, disgruntled that they now had to find someone to take over Gina's share of the rent.

There's always interest in the next new character in the world of make-believe, and Gina's face was her ticket to "stardom." It was the right choice at the time for someone who didn't know what she wanted. She was close to flunking out of college, something that didn't matter to her anyway. At nineteen, Gina was headstrong and becoming self-reliant. With Jake's help, she got an appointment with a modeling agency.

"Gorgeous, but too short for runway," was one agent's comment.

"Lose ten pounds then come back," was another.

Gina left the last agent's office unconcerned about her future. She had found something that finally interested her. It was a month later, weighing the suggested ten pounds less while living on salad and rice and beans in a studio apartment off Sunset, when Gina's costly headshot got noticed by a photographer looking for a fresh, unusual look for ELLE magazine.

Entering the photographer's studio for the first time gave Gina direction in her aimless life. Only weeks after making the spontaneous decision to stay in L.A., Gina was awarded a contract with La Vie Modeling agency.

Though he rarely left her thoughts, Gina refused to pursue Jake until she was sure Anne was out of the picture. There were lots of other men and always lots of parties to attend. "Life in the fast lane" didn't come close to describing everything that kept Gina busy. She was learning about clothes, how to walk, sit, stand, smile, not-smile, strike-a-pose, and to look perfectly groomed every minute of the day. Exhausting, exhilarating and expansive is how Gina summed up her new life to her mother.

Gina never visited home, but her parents made sure they saw her once a month. They couldn't believe the change in their daughter since leaving college. She was still sweet and naïve, but too skinny, they thought. They also observed a new self-confidence. Eyes followed Gina when she entered a room. Her parents noticed their daughter seemed to expect the attention, especially from men. And there was one man who now had Gina's full attention.

CHAPTER 3
DAVID

"Not interested! You're just a big frog in a small-town pond. I want bigger things. I want the world." David yelled.

It was a verbal slap in his father's face. All through his senior year, David's parents had pushed him to attend the nearby state college and take a job at the neighborhood bank. They dismissed their son's "unrealistic" dream of going to Harvard and getting rich.

But David moved out of his family home exactly one week after graduating from high school and found a room in Boston. He also found a job at Stockyard Medical. It was no coincidence that William Stockyard, the company owner, was an alumnus of Harvard's School of Business. He also happened to serve on Harvard's Board of Directors. David made friends with the matronly gatekeeper in the executive office by applying his endearing smile and tenacious charm. It wasn't long before Stockyard's executive assistant persuaded the boss to meet with David for ten minutes about getting into Harvard.

Impressed by the eighteen-year-old's focus and passion for business, and obsession about attending his alma mater, the old man began treating David like a son, without realizing he'd been sought out and used for his connections to the university.

It didn't take long for David to persuade his mentor to forward a recommendation to the student selection committee and loan him enough money to cover the first two years of college. Once in school, it was do or die for David. The "die" being to flunk out, swallow his pride, and follow in his father's shallow footsteps at the bank in Kansas. The "do" was to leave Harvard with a MBA.

Since leaving home eight years earlier, David succeeded in earning the degree he'd set his sights on and met his parents at Logan International on a bright, late-spring afternoon. They traveled for the first time in their simple lives to attend David's graduation. It was a highlight for everyone. To celebrate with the entire family of aunts, uncles and cousins, David's now proud and boasting father had booked a private dining room at one of the best steakhouses in Boston. Their server's name was Lindsey, a tall blond with big brown eyes.

"Pretty girl," was all David's father said when Lindsey walked away with their orders. David noticed her, too.

"David," one of his uncles called from across the table, "where's Cindy?"

David's mother kicked her husband to intervene in case the subject was a sore one for David, but it wasn't. After the graduation party with his family, David found he was asking himself the question his father had asked so often over the years: What do you want to do with your life? The answer didn't include his girlfriend.

He had several job offers and accepted an opportunity to step into an executive position at a start-up company with plans for global real estate development. He was ready to go to work, but hadn't forgotten the pretty waitress at the steakhouse. In fact, her sweet face came to mind more often than David would have liked. He didn't even know her, yet she had become a distraction.

It was several weeks later when David walked back into the steakhouse before it got busy for the evening.

"Can I help you?"

Turning toward the voice, David asked, "Is Lindsey here?"

Lindsey and David married ten months later. The young couple moved into a high-rise apartment complex in Baltimore near the Heritage Global Development offices.

They were in-lust for the time being and looked perfect together. David made a senior executive level salary and Lindsey didn't have to work, nor did she want to. She had completed high school and waitressed full time until David came along and married her. She loved her financial status as a young executive's wife and David would show her off at business dinners. She was attractive and could joke around when appropriate with the bosses. The one annoying thing about Lindsey was her habit of making sure David knew when he had had three glasses of any kind of alcohol. It was her presumed cut-off point before drunkenness would set in. Her father had died when she was fifteen years old. He had been a pathetic alcoholic who left Lindsey with hyper-sensitivity to what and how much anyone around her drank, especially David. His drinking was the only thorn in their otherwise rosy marriage.

When David and Lindsey spent nearly three weeks in China, Lindsey came back pregnant with twins. It was a business trip under the guise of vacation. Lindsey wanted to see Italy and Greece. David wanted to fuel his knowledge of Hong Kong and major cities in China as part of his plan to run HGD's Asian division. Lindsey was promised they'd go wherever she wanted another time.

The new father was fascinated by the opportunities that lay before him in commercial real estate. He gleaned every possible ounce of knowledge from the men who had hired him. David was soon promoted to vice-president of development in North America, an important stepping-stone toward even greater responsibilities and money. David knew he should spend more time with Lindsey and the kids, but he was ambitious and made his career the top priority. Nearly every evening at home, David would head to the wet bar for a double of something relaxing before saying hello to his family. Lindsey saw the signs of a drinking problem and tried to get David to cut back, but he would accuse her of being paranoid.

"I'm not your father!" David roared one night after being nagged into a state of frustration and anger.

The intensity in David's voice scared Lindsey and she backed down to keep the peace. Her state of silence about his drinking would last for a few weeks, even months, if there was a special project that kept her busy beyond chasing after the boys. Such as trying to convince David they needed a house with a big yard.

"For a dog and so the boys will have a place to play outside," she reasoned. "We've outgrown this place and you need a special room to yourself when you get home. Wouldn't you like that?"

It would be inconvenient for David to move. His downtown office was several blocks away from their apartment—walking distance for someone who liked the exercise— but David usually drove his silver Mercedes with the top down in the summer. When Lindsey got pregnant again, the boys were three years old. The anticipation of a third child excited Lindsey and annoyed David. His guilt for feeling that way, and the reasoning that they would certainly need more room, caused David to give in about buying a house. Lindsey had been secretly house-hunting for months and immediately narrowed her choices down to two rather spectacular places. She knew David would appreciate the prestigious addresses. The location of one house was closer to a private school, but she let David decide which house he liked better. It happened so fast David couldn't believe he was signing papers a month later. He was now a first-time home owner and had to admit that he liked the feeling.

Just weeks after getting the boys settled in pre-school, Lindsey was using her time alone to unpack the final few boxes and complete the move to their home on a lake. She bent down to cut open the last box when a sharp pain shot through her belly and a sticky wetness filled her panties. Lindsey called David at work in a state of panic.

"I have to speak with my husband! Now!" Lindsey screamed when she noticed the hesitation in the assistant's voice.

"Mrs. Hendricks, he is with clients from Toronto. Can he call you back in maybe an hour?"

Lindsey hung up on the woman and punched in David's cell number only to get his voice-mail message. She called his assistant again.

"Look!" Lindsey said without an apology for hanging up earlier. "I shouldn't have to explain this, but it's an emergency! I'm pregnant and may be losing the baby. Now get my husband on the phone."

"Of course, Mrs. Hendricks! I'm so sorry. I lost a baby last year…"

"Are you an idiot? Get my husband!" Lindsey had never talked to a stranger like that before and didn't realize how desperate she sounded.

"Lindsey! What the hell is wrong?" David had finally excused himself from persuading his potential clients to invest in his renovation concept for their city.

"David, you have to come home immediately! I think I'm having a miscarriage."

"Are you in pain? You sound all right except for the hysterics. Why didn't you call the doctor or an ambulance?"

"I hurt—I'm scared I'll lose the baby. Come home…please?" Lindsey had regressed to sounding like a ten-year-old child.

"Lindsey, listen to me. I can't do anything for you. If you don't want to call an ambulance, call a friend to take you to the hospital. I'll meet you there later."

"But what about the boys!" Lindsey slammed the phone down when she realized David had hung up.

A neighbor Lindsey had only recently met knocked on the door minutes later and took control of the situation. Lucy stayed with Lindsey at the hospital for as long as she could before leaving to rescue her own husband, who had picked up the Hendricks's boys at school and was babysitting them and their own two children. Never thinking about calling a cab, Lindsey waited five hours for David. He found her alone in the outpatient waiting room.

Lindsey was silent on the twenty-minute ride home. Curled up in the soft-leather bucket seat, she stared straight ahead.

David didn't understand her earlier hysterics. *Things like this happened all the time*, he thought. Without a reassuring hug or even a pat on the hand, all he could finally come up with was, "It was probably a deformation, anyway that caused this."

He missed the look Lindsey gave him. Tears of sorrow and anger poured down her pale cheeks while David calculated the commission behind the Toronto project he'd been awarded that afternoon.

As his career continued to build, and David's earning power escalated, their marriage sputtered. David drank more. Lindsey spent more. David traveled more. Lindsey's whining about his drinking diminished, and David suspected that she might have something going on with someone else.

*As long as it or **he** keeps her off my back, it's fine*, David thought.

David's lack of interest in his family was apparent to their friends and family. He never socialized unless it was business-related. Lindsey went everywhere alone. The boys saw their father briefly at night a few times a week. David would pretend interest in their childish world, but the play never lasted long before he waved them off, yelling for Lindsey to get them ready for bed.

Since joining the company during its start-up years, David had proved to be the right choice when they hired him. In the final years of his marriage, David and his business colleagues found Las Vegas to be the place to go to reward themselves with mutual admiration and back-patting as, year after year, the company's stock exceeded projections. They were self-made millionaires and arrogant about it.

In their opinion, the Bellagio was the best hotel with the best suites on the Las Vegas strip: the most beautiful women, the best casinos, and the HGD executives were treated royally. Drinks were on the house for gamblers, and the drinks were served by certain females who would do much more than hand over a tumbler of top-shelf whiskey. That was the ace-in-the-hole for David. He became a regular, with and without his business colleagues. Over a short time, he learned who to go to for anything he could imagine. Whatever it was, it was usually expensive, and worth it.

David met Hank Johns for the first time after an evening in the casinos and fifth-row center seats for an Elton John concert. David's newest distraction, Shanti, was an exotic beauty with black eyes, black hair, red lips, dark complexion and a figure that he couldn't keep his hands off—qualifying her to be in the expensive-but-worth-it category.

After the concert, David maneuvered Shanti through the hotel lobby and left her to wait for him at a bank of elevators. He doubled back to the bell desk.

"I'm looking for something to keep the evening lively, Julio," David said, having read the bellman's name tag. He hoped the man with the knowledgeable expression would understand. Julio happened to be one of few men in the hotel trusted by Hank Johns. Julio nodded and pocketed the hundred dollar bill that had been placed in his hand. It wasn't a guess on his part. He could read the man with the money who already had a beautiful call girl going upstairs with him. Cocaine was the second most common reason people secretly pressed large bills into his hand without explanation, so Julio called his connection.

Normally, Julio would have made the delivery to David's suite, but soon after getting Julio's call, observant eyes shifted as Hank strode through the crowded hotel lobby. Hank knew how to dress well: expensive, traditional and classy without being obvious.

Hank knocked quietly on the door. Shanti opened it. Over her bare shoulder Hank could see a man sprawled on the white leather couch. The picture window revealed the magnificent city view and below, the Bellagio waters danced in sync with music that couldn't be heard in the suite. The flash and brilliance of the famous neon strip brightened the room's low, ambient lighting. Hank followed Shanti and sat directly across from David without giving her a second glance. It was a difficult thing to do for any man, considering she wore nothing but a black lace thong and bra.

Hank efficiently conducted the business transaction and left with $1,500 in cash. Few words were spoken during that first meeting. What Hank provided that night started a new habit for David and the beginning of conjuring reasons to return to Las Vegas several times a month.

Chapter 4
Hank

Hank had been born poor and struggling. He had stopped breathing right after birth. One of several foster parents had cruelly explained to their eight-year-old charge what a one-night-stand meant and that his father had disappeared the morning after. Hank was also told that his drug-addict mother died minutes after delivery while the doctor was reviving *him*. Upon hearing about his mother and being the unwanted son of a hooker, Hank wished they had let him die, too.

Hank learned his way around the streets of Las Vegas while bouncing from one foster family to another. He was the odd boy out. Never part of a family, while waiting for someone to adopt him. No one did, and social services moved him around so much that twice he forgot where he lived and took the wrong bus home from school. He was independent and smarter than he would let on, which meant he was sneaky. By the age of thirteen he had wandered the seediest downtown streets of Las Vegas, miles away from the comfortable bed he was given as long as he behaved. "Behaving" in parental terms was not Hank's strong suit. He learned how to deal cards from a burned-out old man on a street corner. Sitting on a plastic crate alongside a busy street with the beggar was Hank's preferred place to be. Occasionally a man the beggar seemed to know would stop to talk while scrutinizing Hank.

Weeks went by, and one day the man asked Hank, "What's your name, kid?"

"What's yours first?" Hank answered sarcastically.

"Alluicious."

"That's a bullshit name."

"Then call me Al if you can't pronounce it."

"I won't call you nothin' 'cuz you nothin' to me."

"I might be if you listen to what I have to say. It might be worth your while. How old are you?"

Instead of giving a smart-ass answer, the boy turned his head and pretended interest in something down the street. The glare of the sun reflecting off the hot sidewalk and shop windows nearly blinded him, but still, Hank stared away from the man in the white suit and shiny shoes towering over him.

"Look. I know a way for you to make some money. A lot of money, in fact. Are you smart enough to pay attention to my proposal?"

The beggar spoke up. "Leave 'im be, Al. He don' wanna hear nothin' from you."

Hank interrupted, squinting up at the man. "How much money?"

A week later Hank found himself in front of a video camera with two adult men and his pants down. He was sickened by what he had to do and suffered through nightmares of struggling against the other actors. He had sold out and, young as he was, knew what that meant. But he figured he was being paid more money than the hookers would ever make in a lifetime. Then the day came when the man named Al patted Hank on the head and said affection-ately, "It's time to go kid. You're too old now. Get out of here."

With more than seventy thousand dollars locked in his clothes trunk inside a closet at his current foster home, Hank started won-dering what he should do next. He bided his time, finishing high school, and then his mentor on the street said he knew someone who was looking for help.

After sizing up the now sixteen-year-old Hank, Jimmie Benigo hired him to run drugs to customers. By then Hank was old enough to drive. He got his license and a sharp-looking black Miata on the same day. He paid cash, and the private seller asked no questions.

It was several years later while working his runs one afternoon that he noticed a girl walking his way. Hank was about to unlock his car when he happened to glance up and see a familiar face. It was Althea, a girl he'd known in high school. She didn't see him wave, so he jumped in front of her before she could walk past.

"Whatcha doin' babe, besides lookin' so good?" Hank asked.

"Hank! What are *you* doin'?" Althea liked what she saw. Her glance dropped to below his belt then roamed slowly back up to the sexy smile and narrowed eyes.

"Are you hooked up?" He asked. "Want to have dinner sometime?" Hank drew her off the crowded sidewalk to stand next to his car.

Althea took a minute to think. Her cheap, provocative outfit didn't match Hank's natural elegance and expensive clothes. All that and his nice car appealed to her.

"Come on, babe. You dodged me in high school…you gonna keep that shit up? Are you married or what?"

Althea liked having the upper hand, and so she coyly answered, "No, I'm not married. I guess we could get together."

Three months later in the tiny guest bedroom of her mother's apartment Althea put her candy-red panties back on and pulled her black leather mini skirt down from around her waist. "How about we get married, Hank? I want to settle down."

Hiding his shock at the sudden proposal, Hank answered, "I guess we could do that," and walked out the front door. He returned an hour later with an engagement ring.

Nearly fainting with relief that he'd come back, let alone with a ring, Althea called her mom out of the kitchen and said, "Momma! I'm getting married to a rich man!"

They were married the following Saturday. Althea's mom and two sisters attended the ceremony at the famous Little Chapel of Love in Las Vegas. Althea wore a white gown and veil that she had rushed to find the afternoon they decided to marry. Hank wore a black silk shirt with gold cufflinks, black slacks and custom-made boots. The ½ carat diamond in his ear was one-quarter the size of Althea's engagement ring, and then there was the weight of the diamond-encrusted gold wedding band he slipped on her finger while saying, "Yes. I do."

After the ceremony Hank went to meet with Jimmie, his boss of nearly nine years, and Althea returned home with her mother and sisters. Going right back to their daily lives without taking a honeymoon was a let-down for Althea that didn't bode well for the couple. Hank now found himself responsible for a wife and keeping his new mother-in-law off his back. They got married so fast, it was decided they would live with Althea's mother until they found an affordable apartment that suited Althea's expensive taste. That meant little privacy in the small two-bedroom, one bath home, ten miles away from Hank's primary territory on the strip.

His used Miata was in good shape, so transportation wasn't a problem; however, Althea's expectations for elevated financial status as Hank's wife emerged immediately.

"Hank, I'm gonna need a car now. I can't rely on using Momma's car all the time or waiting for you to get home to use yours. Especially since you never know when you gonna get home."

"Sure. I'll find you a car, baby. What color do you want?"

That kind of response out of Hank would assuage her demands for a while. It seemed that he could afford the things she asked for herself and for her mother and sisters until their first fight erupted.

While looking for their own apartment, Althea wanted to surprise her mom with new bedroom furniture for Christmas.

"We've done our share of helping your mom. It's time to concentrate on us," was Hank's response. "Come on Althea, be fair. I only make so much."

Althea's way of pouting was to give Hank the silent treatment. Though Hank didn't miss the conversation, there wasn't any sex either. When Hank gave in to Althea, which was every time, it was like training her to withhold sex whenever she wanted anything, and she came to expect to win every fight. She also expected a make-up gift. Jewelry usually did the trick.

Other than those occasional fights, they were married for five uneventful years, until one afternoon Hank tired of watching Althea's favorite chick flick with her. Sitting on the couch together he looked over at Althea's profile and said, "You're so pretty, baby." He reached under her tank top to find her bare breasts.

"Knock it off!" Althea pushed away his hand.

"What's wrong?" Hank was confused. Unless mad, Althea hadn't stopped him before.

Obviously not happy about the news she was about to give her husband, Althea announced in one breath, "My breasts hurt. I think I'm pregnant."

While Althea watched his reaction closely, Hank laughed nervously, then smiled at the idea. "I never thought about being a father."

"Well, if I don't go get an abortion, which I'm thinkin' about, you're gonna be a daddy whether you like it or not."

"Abortion!" Hank was stunned that she'd even consider the idea. "Oh no you're not, Althea! This baby is mine, too, and I'll take good care of you both! I've never had a family. This is my shot at it and you're going to be good momma."

"Shush! My favorite part of the movie's on." Althea had already removed herself from the discussion.

Alone later that evening, Hank wondered what kind of father he could be, and then vowed to be a good one. It was a revelation. *I'm going to be a father*, Hank thought to himself, knowing he'd never felt this happy about anything before.

Nearly eight months later, Althea said she had a feeling that it was a boy and told Hank she had decided to name him "Thomas Jefferson." Saying, "Isn't that cute?"

Thomas Jefferson Johns was born with little more than the usual drama. Althea called Hank when her water broke. He rushed to complete a drug drop, then met Althea, her mother and sisters and their husbands and all their little kids at County General, the same hospital where Hank had been born thirty years before. That night, a beautiful, healthy boy was born, and everyone called him "TJ."

Holding his son for the first time, Hank was struck by the realization that he'd never known the depth of love he was feeling. While Althea's family talked noisily around the hospital bed where the new mother lay propped up against three pillows, basking in their attention, Hank's eyes welled with tears for the first time in his life. He could physically feel his heart expanding as he watched the newborn stare blindly up at him. It was a moment stopped in time for Hank, when everything went silent and everyone else in the room disappeared. It was a moment of love at first sight, a moment he would never forget. He held his son gingerly and tucked the end of the light blue blanket around the perfect little toes. Someone's camera flashed, startling Hank out of his reverie, but the baby's gaze didn't waver from his father's face.

The following night, Hank saw that his wife was comfortable in bed in the master bedroom of their own home. He kissed her and the baby good-night and said, "I've got to meet the boss. I'll try not to wake you when I come in."

"Bye," Althea replied without looking up from her celebrity tabloid while the newborn nursed.

CHAPTER 5
SARA

While growing up, Sara's mother would preach what she knew to be true. "Thoughts are powerfully creative," her mother would say. "If you think about being sick and tired all the time, that's exactly how you feel." Sara remembered her mother's faith. She could still hear that firm voice of experience. "Imagine the best outcome. The future is yours to decide." Sara had grown up being told what others typically had to learn over the years on their own. But being handed the golden goose of wisdom about the power of decision didn't give Sara the gift of making every decision the right one. Married three times, she bounced out of four jobs, and lost three years of her life wallowing in a pool of self-pity and lethargy. Sara was focused on taking without giving, and on all things negative. It took her months to get over the blow of losing the last job, which she had loved, before waking up to the fact that she needed to do things differently. When that happened, she made the best decision of her life.

In college, the only event that stood out in an otherwise ordinary university experience was her marriage to Stephen.

Sara met Stephen and two of his friends by flirting across the community room. The guys were sitting at a table discussing the redhead sitting alone with her books and coffee. Glancing up, Sara saw three sets of eyes watching her from several yards away. She went back to her reading for a few minutes, then gave up and took a peek to see if they were still there. Yup, they were. They were all interesting looking in good and very different ways. Back to her reading again and after five minutes of rereading the same paragraph, Sara gave up. She stood up, gathered her books and coffee cup, and walked across the room. Stopping in front of their table, she looked each man in the eye for five seconds, said nothing, and then walked away.

Days later Stephen told her that she had charmed each of them that day with her pretty eyes. None of them had looked away from the pools of dark green that sparkled with challenge. After giving them the full treatment and walking away, it was Stephen who said it first, "She's mine." The others groaned but stuck to their friendship policy to respect each other's "territory." Stephen took on getting Sara's attention with a hurricane-five force. They dated for a year while still in college. Stephen's friends found girls of their own and, one by one, got married. It was a year of weddings. Sara was twenty-three and desperate to join the ranks of wedded bliss.

"Don't you love me?" she whined. "What's the problem? Everyone else is getting married and we're not even engaged."

Stephen resisted so hard that Sara would break into tears as she tried to challenge his inability to deal with his mixed feelings about getting married but not wanting to lose her.

He finally proposed in a Denny's diner over the Thursday night special of meatloaf and mashed potatoes. The poem he had written that day was handed to her with a kiss. Sara opened the envelope and read the missive quickly. The last line was, *Will you marry me?*

Sara's tearful outburst of, "YES!" and "Oh My God YES!" made it obvious throughout the restaurant what had just transpired. An elderly couple sent dessert to the newly betrotheds' table. It was the happiest few minutes of Sara's life.

The wedding date was set, honeymoon plans were made, and every so often Stephen would try to back out. Each time, Sara would cry and lock her arms around his neck. Her kisses would always lead them to sex and all would be well again.

The wedding day came, the honeymoon went, and one month later, Sara began to ask Stephen what was wrong. Two months after their wedding, after telling Sara innumerable times that everything was fine, Stephen finally admitted, "I'm in love with someone else."

The words slammed into her like shockwaves. Sara's heart pounded in her ears and before she knew it, her hand went back and swung forward fast and hard, catching Stephen perfectly across the jaw. He hit her back. She landed on the bed, a deep bruise forming across her cheek and eye.

"I hate you for what you've done!" she screamed. "Why did you put me through this? Who is she?"

Without a word, Stephen threw his clothes together in a bag, boxed up the stereo equipment, jumped into his twenty-year-old truck, and drove to his lover's house.

It was months before Sara's depression began to lift. That was when husband number two showed up and accelerated her recovery from heartbreak. This time the marriage lasted four years, until one warm summer evening at their favorite restaurant, watching the sunset over the harbor, enjoying their favorite wine, her husband decided to bring up his innermost thoughts.

"Tell me your fantasy. What do you dream about?" he asked.

Lulled by the intimate trust a husband and wife should share, Sara opened her heart and said, "I want a family, don't you? Maybe two or three kids. And this may sound silly, but I hope to run a business, do work that would be fun and be meaningful at the same time."

Sara's husband smiled. He took her hand and said, "I think I like men."

As that bit of new information flooded her brain, Sara stumbled through the restaurant into the ladies' room, slammed open the door of a vacant stall, and threw up. When she finished, her first thought was, *I have to divorce him.*

A year later, she met husband number three. It was all fun and laughter for a while. Once married, everything went great as long as Sara was working. But she was laid off from one job and then another. Each time that happened, he would leave for days to punish her. When Sara didn't work, neither did the marriage. She was the stable one. He was an unpredictable man, a trait Sara had found exciting at first, but later her feelings turned to anger over his lack of responsibility. Sara worked; he played and overspent on frivolous things they would never use. When Sara discovered that she was pregnant, he was absolutely beside himself with joy. Sara, on the other hand, was scared and wondered how she would be able to work full time, take care of a baby, and deal with her husband's irresponsibility, increasingly volatile temper and their skyrocketing debt. The question was moot. At six months along in her pregnancy, Sara went into labor and delivered a one-pound baby girl. The baby was stillborn. Shortly after losing the baby, on Valentine's Day and the day of their seventh wedding anniversary, her husband called it quits. Sara was relieved when he left.

After closing the door on that chapter, Sara asked herself, "What could possibly be next?" She thought: *I'll never marry again. I'm not capable of choosing the right man.*

With no one to distract her, she threw herself into her job of three years as a senior manager at Main Events, a special events management company.

Sara called her colleague, Erik. "What are you working on today?"

"I ordered the ice sculpture to arrive at four o'clock, lighting is coming at three o'clock, and catering should already be there."

Brandy, their new boss, had stepped into Sara's office, and hearing what they were discussing, spoke up while Sara was still on the phone with Erik. "Catering is there, Sara. I just confirmed that they arrived on time and have everything they need to begin setting up and cooking."

"Oh. Good. Thanks." Sara conveyed the information to Erik.

She had been wary of her new boss from day one. The woman was everywhere and didn't trust anyone to do their job properly. It was irritating. When Brandy arrived, everything changed.

One day Brandy called Sara and Erik into her office and said, "I think you two will work better together if you share office space," "Your communications have to be completely coordinated."

Looking at each other in exasperation, Erik spoke up. "Brandy. Sara and I have been working together for three years without having to sit right next to each other. It will be distracting when we're both on the phone or trying to meet with someone at our desks. Clients come in person sometimes, and it's good to give them some private space, too."

Erik made sense. Pointing out client comfort nearly persuaded Brandy to allow them to keep their respective offices, but then she said, "You can take our clients into the conference room. I want to consolidate your space and you'll need to get used to it. You don't need those big offices."

Sara began to speak when Brandy answered her ringing phone and waved them away.

"This is stupid. It's a silly power trip and we're the pawns," Sara complained to the other two event managers, who had not been told that they had to share an office. "I think she has it in for me."

"That's because you're a threat," Erik said.

"If I was a threat why didn't I get promoted to the job of running this business? Instead, the owners looked outside the company and brought in Brandy. I could have done it and so could you, Erik. Aren't you pissed about not at least being considered?"

"I didn't want it," Erik said without thinking. "I mean, I didn't go for it."

Sara wasn't deaf. She heard the meaning behind Erik's first words. "You mean they offered it to you?"

"Uh, yeah. They did, but I don't want the responsibility. It would have taken up too much of my personal time."

Oh yes, Sara thought. *Don't want to miss any precious time with Gary*. Gary was the latest and most wonderful new lover Erik constantly talked about.

"Well, lucky you, that you at least were given a choice. The owners never approached me with an offer."

"Don't fret it, sweetie. You're wonderful and you should know that for yourself without validation from some job that will only keep you awake at night. I think Brandy is just testing you to see what you're made of," Erik continued. "You're the best, most creative event planner I've ever worked with, and after thirty years in this business, that's saying something."

"I'll get over it. I like it here, but I'd better keep my eyes open."

Brandy didn't let up on Sara. For months, Sara was questioned about everything she did; every decision and idea. Sara tried to be polite and professional while keeping her head down and working hard. But even a high-profile wedding that went off perfectly, thanks to Sara, didn't dissuade Brandy from her next move.

Calling Sara into her office the day after the big wedding, Brandy began with a curt, "Sit down, Sara. This is your last day and I want to explain the severance package."

It was a cold-hearted boot in the butt with no preamble, no "I'm sorry to inform you," no chance to hear why she was being fired. Sara simply stared at Brandy with hatred, without giving the woman any satisfaction by responding in anger or tears. Sara stood and held out her hand for the envelope that included her last paycheck and one month of severance.

"You can clean out your office now."

Sara turned and left without a word. She packed up her few personal effects and walked out with a smile on her face, nodding to those she passed as if she were simply heading out to meet a client.

When she got home, Sara pulled out a box of Oreo cookies and called her mother for support and further comfort.

"You've been complaining about that job for a year now, Sara. Aren't you glad it's over? I know you tried to work things out with your boss, but some things are beyond our understanding. Now take some time to relax and discover what's next for you. Something better will come along—I just know it! God has a plan."

Sara had been crying when she called her mom, but the soothing words of faith and trust that everything was all right made her feel better.

Now, rambling around her apartment, worrying about how to pay the bills in the coming months, Sara finally took her mother's advice and did a little soul-searching. Sitting on her couch, petting Buster, her little Maltese, Sara took a deep breath, closed her eyes and said out loud, "The question is, what do I want?"

Immediately words came rushing in so fast that Sara jumped up, startling her four-legged pal, and ran to find a notepad and pen. When she returned, Buster forgave her and snuggled back onto her lap. Sara began listing whatever came to mind.

The word "Love" came first. *I want to share love with someone wonderful*, she thought.

"Happiness." *Everyone just wants to be happy. What makes me happy?*

"Sharing," *sharing time with people I love makes me happy.*

The connection was obvious right away. *Love equals happiness; happiness comes from sharing with people I love. That's kind of cool.*

Sara closed her eyes again to see what else would come to mind.

Sharing what...? Laughter. I love to laugh.

Sharing...good food. I love to cook.

Helping people...like sharing, but doing something that will make a difference.

Good health...I need to get more exercise.

Money...a creative way to make lots of money, which will enable me to help people I love and live the way I choose to live.

Creative...I love to throw parties. I loved my event-planning job. I was good at it. Why couldn't I have kept it? Sara let out a loud sigh.

What's my next step?

Sara stopped writing and tried to listen to her intuition. It was a simmering thought at first, then a wave of enthusiasm, followed by an energizing sense of joy. Sara smiled. She knew she had the answer, but worried about the financial risk.

"Hello?" Sara's mother answered.

"Mom! It's me again. It's time I start my own business. I'm sick of being controlled and at the mercy of other people. I know enough about event planning to make it work. What do you think?"

"You can do it if you put your mind to it. How will you get started? How much money will you need?"

That's when Sara's idea went a little farther. "I'm going to start gradually. I'll consult first. I have contacts. I'll do one event, then ask that client to tell a friend or give me a reference to get another, then another. Baby steps, one at a time. It's going to work, Mom. I can feel it. I'm going to make people happy and help them by making their special events everything they've ever wanted. I'll work with them on a very personal level to discover their dreams and make their wishes come true."

Sara's mom was all for it, and said she'd keep good thoughts about the idea.

After talking with her mother, Sara felt sure her idea would work, and began making a list of everything she needed to do. She combed her address book for names of friends and business acquaintances to call and tell about her service. Brandy had neglected to have Sara sign a non-competition agreement, so she was legally free to call on people she had worked with in the past.

≈≈≈

It took Sara six months to get her first event planning job. She stuck by her decision and pushed past discouraging thoughts by keeping busy. Sara had made calls to people she knew and had worked for in the past. She kept telling herself that the holidays were around the corner and someone would ask her to arrange a party. Waitressing at a nearby deli kept a small amount of income flowing, but she held on to a lifeline of hope that surely her idea to start her own business was a good one. She was right. The first call came in October, two more followed on the same day, and another came in the following week. Her first three jobs took place in December, all on the same weekend. After making two milestone birthday parties and a golden wedding anniversary extraordinary for her first three clients, she began the planning for one very large non-profit event that was scheduled for January. Sara was on her way. She incorporated and called her company *Dare to Dream Events*.

CHAPTER 6
HANK AND DAVID

Hank became a regular source of cocaine for David, and Shanti became a different kind of habit, while Lindsey stayed home with the kids. Lindsey was still trying to keep it together with David in spite of his cold, uncaring treatment of her and their sons, Josh and Tim. Nearly every time David returned home from Las Vegas, she would ask, "Why don't I get my mother to take the boys and come with you next time?"

She never suggested traveling to Calgary or Vancouver or even Mexico City with him, all places David also frequently visited to work through the politics of development deals or begin new projects with the local officials and design teams. Oddly, it was Las Vegas Lindsey was most interested in seeing with David.

"It's not possible. I'll be too busy to worry about you. Go with a girlfriend sometime." David was clear. His wife was not welcome to join him in Vegas.

One night before turning off her bedside lamp, Lindsey ventured into territory that she knew would lead to another fight.

"David, why did you marry me? You don't love me. Sometimes I wish you had never walked through that door at Harvey's Steakhouse. You barely know your own children. You wouldn't recognize them if you had to pick them out in a crowd."

David's response was to put down the report he'd been reading with a sigh. He gently placed his hand over her mouth and moved to lie on top of the squirming woman. She hated it when he maneuvered out of the discussion by trying to fuck her. Sometimes she let it work, but not this time.

44

She was a neglected wife who loved the financial security, but wanted her husband's attention even more.

❧❧❧

David would come and go to all points throughout North America, always with a stopover in Las Vegas to check on the new resort/housing complex that Heritage Global Development had on its books. He was addicted to the excitement of that city. He even found a little time between gambling, drugs, and Shanti, who had by now achieved mistress status, to actually work. He had everything he thought he could want.

Hank was beginning to hang around after their usual transaction was completed. Both men were smart, quick-witted, and good at business; even though one was older and expensively educated and the other was educated on the street, they were finding a friendship neither could have expected.

One evening, in their usual places around the glass coffee table, comfortable on soft burgundy leather with Shanti curled up next to him, David ventured, "We're self-made men, Hank. We're business associates who know what we want in life."

"Business associate, yeah, that's exactly what I am," Hank had said thoughtfully when David first mentioned that's how he would be introduced if ever necessary. Without revealing why he was so adamant about it, Hank added, "And I'm gonna have my own business someday. No more bullshit and watching my back in Vegas."

Watching the men and quietly commenting if they spoke to her, Shanti would read David's coke-induced highs and lows. Hank would occasionally pop open a beer and relax until his pager went off and he'd leave to make another delivery.

Shanti didn't accept any harsh words from David. She simply didn't care enough about him to let him take her for granted. She enjoyed her life, but protected her sense of self-worth by never allowing anyone to treat her with disrespect. Odd for a high-priced call girl, but it was a lucrative living and she enjoyed the work as long as she stuck with her own rules. She may have had loose morality when it came to her profession, but Shanti was a sweet, smart, and responsible twenty-three- year-old woman. She had intended to go to college when she arrived in Los Angeles from New Deli, but had been swiftly surrounded by celebrities and shysters alike. Well-meaning people advised her to go into modeling or to use her dancing talent somehow. To dance professionally sounded appealing, but waiting for a break in Los Angeles that would pay the bills leveled her funds to nearly zero before she found her way to Las Vegas by bus. Dancing in shows did not turn out to be what she expected. She wasn't in Las Vegas for more than a few weeks when she was offered an invitation to a party and got paid for it. In one night Shanti made $3,000, and that was the beginning of a career her parents would never know about.

She observed David and Hank in their own battle to find happiness while fast-tracking to self-destruction. Month after month she watched David indulge in high-priced activities while Hank drank beer. Her part in the play was to make good money and send most of it to her parents and brothers and sisters. She would constantly remind herself that her current life experience was temporary, and that she hoped to one day return home to her family.

Shanti pretended to love the gifts David brought her from Prada, Tiffany, Chanel, and Victoria's Secret. It was difficult not to enjoy beautiful clothes and particularly the clear-cut diamonds and deep blue sapphires. Blue and gold were her favorite colors, but any bright color would bring out the luster in her skin and contrast with her rich, dark hair and eyes. What David didn't know was that she would sell the jewelry after wearing it once or twice. David's generosity meant money for her family's escape from poverty. Her client never noticed what she did or didn't wear after he bought it for her. As long as David didn't tire of her, she would feign interest in him. It was business, her business, and treating David like a king was how she kept her most generous, well-paying client happy.

♦♦♦

The North American division of Heritage Global Development had grown quickly under David's leadership. By his fourth year with the company, David had two vice-presidents reporting to him and a total staff of 400 people in four offices located in Toronto, Mexico City, Baltimore, and Los Angeles. His primary residence with Lindsey and the boys was in an exclusive neighborhood a few miles outside of Baltimore. David leased an apartment in Los Angeles and was looking for another in Las Vegas. He was confident that his boss would understand the need for a company apartment, since he was spending more time trying to get something going on the strip. That was the rationale. David's idea was for an entirely different housing and resort complex that would attract clients from all over the world. It was a sound proposal.

However, David still had his sights on the ultimate prize: to run the company's Asia division. He had a reputation as a strong, decisive leader and an instinct for the next hot development opportunity, but was beginning to show his temper too often and had no problem verbally abusing staff in front of others. His boss, the man who had hired David out of college, had recently retired, but still served as chairman of the board of directors. Taking over the company as president would be the founder's son, Jack Thompson, a young man just as smart, confident, assertive, and challenging as David could be. The chairman's son currently held the position that David lusted after. Once Jack took over for his retired father, David expected to be tapped for Asia. Quarterly board meetings had been the only occasions to see Jack Thompson in the past. Now David planned on getting to know the younger man personally. The first step would be an invitation to his home in Baltimore, then after assessing Jack's level of interest in socializing outside of business, David would show him the world of Las Vegas and all that it offered a wealthy man.

But over the last year, David had started becoming sloppy in his work while riding on his reputation in the company. He had begun lying about why he needed to spend so much time in Vegas. Oblivious to the turning tide, for the third time in half an hour David tilted back his head and pinched his nostrils after snorting the pure white powder.

Hank looked at his watch. Althea was visiting her sisters with the baby for the night and there were no other deliveries to make. He surprised Shanti and David when he said, "Time to see what I've been missing. I have no other place to be tonight." Leaning down, he quickly snorted five lines.

David said, "It's about damn time." He welcomed the company, since Shanti didn't use drugs of any kind.

A few minutes later, uncurling her long legs that had been tucked up on the couch, Shanti caught Hank casting a leering look. He'd paid little attention to her in the past and a shiver ran up her spine. She was suddenly uncomfortable in the sheer black robe. It wasn't a good feeling, more like a sense of foreboding.

While David had his head down on another line, Hank let his eyes flow slowly over the beautiful woman. "Try it, Shanti."

David's head snapped up. He cast an eye in Shanti's direction and waited to hear what the answer would be. They had never offered coke to her before and she wasn't interested

"No, thank you. I have my martini. That's all I want."

"Come on, baby. Join the party for a change," Hank demanded.

"No."

David was still watching Shanti, and said, "Hank, leave her alone. She'll just go if you give her a hard time. She doesn't want to try it."

Hank stuck to his challenge. "As a professional, you get paid plenty for makin' this a party—for makin' your man happy."

Shanti stood up. "No. David, are you in town tomorrow?"

David jumped up and grabbed her wrist. "It's okay, Shanti. Hank is leaving, not you."

Hank and Shanti were surprised that David rose to her defense. But Hank was too high to be rational and jumped up too. He grabbed Shanti's other wrist.

Shanti's voice was starting to rise when she demanded, "What is this? I'm leaving."

The game had begun. David and Hank kept their hold while Shanti began to struggle.

"What the hell are you doing, David? Hank isn't above this type of behavior but you!"

Hank twisted her arm backward and pulled her against him. He was clearly aroused. David was getting interested too. Shanti's demand to stop heightened the men's excitement. Each was ready to push her down and hold her for the other.

Shanti refused to scream or fight. Instead she went limp, forcing Hank and David to either hold up her dead weight or let her fall to the floor. They let her fall.

Hank was unfastening his belt while David stood over Shanti watching in a daze, suddenly not understanding what was going on. Everybody was squirming and the room was swirling. Voices blended into an indefinable noise.

In the moment that Hank kneeled down to rip off her flimsy thong, Shanti reared up and scratched at his eyes and kicked him in the crotch. Hank doubled over. David took a step backward, away from the two on the floor; he fell over the glass coffee table, cracking it and hitting his head when he landed. By the time Hank was able to breathe again, Shanti had jumped up, grabbed David's sports jacket, and run to the door. She raced barefoot down the hall to the elevators.

David was unconscious. Hank couldn't stand. Shanti punched the elevator button several times while pulling on the jacket. She composed herself in the elevator on the way down. Knowing she would, Shanti found David's wallet in the inside pocket and went straight into one of the hotel dress shops. This was Las Vegas. The shop girls had seen stranger things than this barefooted woman wearing little more than a man's jacket come into their store. Shanti quickly selected the items she needed, dressed and was out hotel's revolving front door just as Hank caught up to her.

"You killed David!" he whispered.

She was shocked, but didn't quite believe him. "He's been dead ever since you showed up! It wasn't my problem that he couldn't handle that shit you brought tonight."

"No, you the evil bitch he couldn't satisfy. He always tol' me what a frigid bitch you are." Hank lied. Lapsing into his childhood grammar, "You was always pushing him to prove himself."

Shanti stopped walking. "If David is dead, which I don't believe, it's your fault. If he isn't dead, he will be with your help and that makes you a murderer," she spat. "You're nuts. If you don't kill yourself too, you'll never be anything more than a crazy bastard drug dealer."

Hank was fighting the urge to laugh when he said, "What? Just 'cuz you pretty, you think you're not a stupid slut? You think you're not usin' David?" People walking past them thought they were a couple having a nasty argument. No one realized that Shanti was being held against her will. They made a good looking pair, except Hank's words were venomous as they stood face to face on the busy sidewalk.

Hank's spewing bounced off her calm glare. The fact that she wouldn't further engage in the fight fueled the rage that was backed by several beers and several lines of coke. Hank was out of control. His grip became a vise, cutting off the circulation in her arm. Shaking now in the cooling night air, Hank hauled her down the street to his car. He never parked close to a client's delivery site, so his car was several blocks away on a side street. He shoved her in through the driver's side.

"Get over!" Hank pushed her until she moved over the gear shift. Hank jumped in fast behind her and locked the doors. "Stay put!"

Fear taking over, Shanti finally spoke up. "Where do you think you're taking me? Home for a quick fuck? I'll be surprised if you can. In fact, that's probably why you have to take down others. You making up for something that's missing in your life, Hank? Can't you do *it*?"

"Shut up, you stupid bitch."

Hank pulled away and drove to his second apartment. One that he'd intended to give up now that he and Althea had their own place. Clearly Hank made a good living at what he did. Shanti noted the nice car. "You must supply most of Vegas with coke, crack, meth, whatever. That must make you an important man. Clever, charging someone, then helping them use it after becoming their pal. That's a good way to stay high for free and make a lot of money at the same time. Risky, though," Shanti added.

Hank looked over wondering why he had taken her with him, but decided to show her what she didn't think he could do when they got to his place.

Dragging her into the building and avoiding the elevator, they went up the stairs to the third floor. Hank pushed Shanti inside and threw down his keys. Finally registering that she was fully dressed after leaving David's apartment in nothing but lacy underwear, he grabbed her by the waist and lifted her to the counter. Shanti fought back and threatened to kick him again, but this time Hank avoided the viciously pointed toes of her shoes. After shoving up her dress, Hank found his mark and let her have it. He was so worked up that it only took a minute before he jerked to a halt and threw her to the floor.

"Get out of here!" he shouted with the last of his energy. Hank was crashing and suddenly exhausted.

"You will regret this." Shanti said. "By taking me, I promise you will lose everything you have." And with that, Shanti left, closing the door quietly behind her.

"Not gonna happen, bitch." Hank said under his breath when the front door closed, then went to answer the ringing phone.

It was David. "What the hell happened? What did we take? Where's Shanti?"

"Never mind man. I found a new supplier who promised the best stuff. Must have been laced. Wild, huh?"

"Yeah. One minute we're talking like everything was polite and nice then you and Shanti go off on each other. What happened?"

"Shanti was flirting with me right in front of you. Didn't you notice?"

"She's never done that. She's a classy woman, committed to me. Especially considering what I pay her."

"Oh, right. Well, maybe she had too much to drink and couldn't help herself while looking at me across the table. I didn't do anything to provoke her. In fact, you know me, David, I never even look at her. She's yours. Even when she's walking around half-naked, I keep my mind and body on the business at hand."

"Uh-huh. Okay. I'll give her a call later."

"How's your head? You passed out. What do you remember?"

"I've got a raging headache and don't remember much. Was I on the floor when you left? Did I break the table?"

"I don't know what happened except Shanti was coming on to me. When I said I was leaving, you stood up suddenly and fell over. I put you on the couch. You must have rolled off, but Shanti was still there when I left."

"I'll call her. Don't bring that shit back though. It's too much for me. I'll call you next month."

"Yeah, sure man. I'm not feeling so good either. I broke a rule not to use on the job. Talk to you later." After talking to David, Hank decided to call Jimmie about the bad batch of coke. He was worried about Shanti's parting threat, and mentioned that to his boss, too.

∾∾∾

Shanti found a taxi after walking nearly twenty minutes away from Hank's apartment building. She called David's number from her cell phone in the cab and hung up when he answered. She only wanted to confirm that he wasn't dead.

Once home, she stripped off her new but rumpled clothes and ran hot water for a bath. Slipping down into the bubbling Jacuzzi she replayed the scene in her mind. *They were too high and lost it*, she thought, *but that's no excuse. Especially for David, who was about to participate in the rape Hank started. It's over with David now—it was great while it lasted. I'll have to get his wallet back to him, but it's over. David's wife is probably really nice and he should see his kids, treat them better. I should bust Hank, but the police will ask me what I do for a living. I don't need that.*

Shanti started to drift off after the bath and a glass of wine. She was in bed with the volume on the TV down low when the phone rang.

Thinking it was David, Shanti answered with a sleepy, "Hello?"

"Is this Shanti? A friend gave me your number."

"What *friend*?" Shanti asked.

"David. David Hendricks."

Surprised that David would pass out her name but not enough to think about it twice, Shanti asked, "What is this about?"

"Is this Shanti? The most beautiful, sexy woman in Vegas?"

"There are a lot of women who fit that description in this city."

"Assuming you are the woman I want to meet, I want to make a date as soon as possible."

"Tell me about yourself." Shanti asked everyone this, knowing they would probably lie. But she knew enough about David after spending the year with him to probably pick up some clues of truth.

"I'm a colleague of David's—from Canada. I work with him. He's told me that his marriage has been a nightmare for years and that since he met you he's never been happier. My name is Jack. What do you want to know?"

Shanti remembered David mentioning his new boss named Jack. She also vaguely remembered something about Jack being affiliated with Asia, not Canada, but thought she had probably got it wrong. David could go on and on about his business and never realize she wasn't really listening.

"What's your name and what do you want?"

"I told you. My name is Jack and I want a date."

"Last name?"

There was a pause. "Thomas. I need a date for a dinner party. It's formal and David said you'd be perfect: smart and classy, capable of carrying on a conversation without sounding like a call girl."

"What do you think a call girl sounds like? Just because I don't have a degree doesn't mean I'm stupid."

Backing down and putting on the charm, the caller got specific. "The dinner is tomorrow night. Would you please consider meeting me in the morning for coffee? Then we can discuss your terms and take it from there."

"That sounds reasonable. What time and where?" asked Shanti.

"I'll be the guy at a table for two at Le Louvre Café at The Paris with a white rose. Don't worry. I'll know you when I see you from David's description."

Shanti agreed to meet him at ten o'clock the next morning.

Hanging up, the caller turned around and asked the man standing over him, "How was that?"

↩↩↩

After agreeing to meet "Jack," Shanti hung up without noticing that the wrong last name was given. The caller should have said Thompson, not Thomas. But had it registered, she would have shrugged it off as a protection of identity for "Jack Thompson slash Thomas." *One more call, then I'm done*, she thought. It was three o'clock in the afternoon in New Delhi. Shanti called her mother once a week at a prearranged time so that her mother could be at the house of a neighbor with a phone.

Every conversation would begin with news of the town and Shanti's five younger siblings. Shanti would tell her mother how much money she was wiring and that she missed her more than she could say, while reassuring the worried woman that she was safe, happy, and healthy.

"I promise to come home soon, Mom. I'll call you next week. I love you."

❧❧❧

The following morning Shanti called David again. After getting no answer and leaving no message, she hung up and left to keep the meeting with Jack.

Jack Thomas did not look like anyone she would expect David to work with. He was huge, rugged, and looked uncomfortable in the suit he was wearing. As promised, he had a white rose with him and handed it to her as she sat down at the small table.

Jack explained that he had learned of David's extracurricular activities in Las Vegas. He didn't talk about the company or David, and pushed her to attend the party that night with him.

Half an hour later, against her better judgment, Shanti agreed to the date, thinking that she was doing David a favor. She was far too forgiving of David's behavior on the previous night, but she attributed it to an unusual and bad high. She had a harder time forgiving Hank, though he'd always been a gentleman in the past.

After the meeting with Jack, Shanti returned home and tried one more time to reach David. *Maybe he's left town. God, I hope he's okay*, she thought. She was getting worried, but lay down for a nap.

Jack had insisted on sending a car that would take her to the house where he would meet her, saying it was too far for her to drive alone and he himself would be out there all day with no time to come and get her.

56

Shanti woke two hours before she was to be picked up in front of her apartment building. She had just enough time to get ready. It was head-to-toe work to prepare for a formal dinner. Shanti started with a hot, fragrant bath to relax and meditate and ended with professional-precision make-up, pedicure, manicure, and hair styling, before selecting the gown and accessories. Shanti was a stunning woman without trying. When dressed up, she defined mystery, beauty, and grace. Her wavy, thick black hair gleamed, shiny in a swept-up pile on her head. Tendrils fell in perfect place down her graceful neck. Treating herself before pawning it, Shanti decided to wear a Turkish gold choker with a three-carat diamond. Her shoulders were bare in a fitted strapless beige gown shot with pink and gold thread. No stockings, just high, thin heels with two straps holding the shoes in place on her elegant feet.

Shanti was ready on time. Stepping out of the lobby elevator with a pale pink silk wrap on her arm, she looked out the glass door for a waiting car. It was there.

The building doorman was not around, but the driver nearly ran to escort her to the car.

Before closing the limo door, the driver said with a leering smile, "You look beautiful, Miss." Shanti ignored the compliment. She wasn't happy about the situation and again wished she could have reached David.

"How long will it take to get there?" Shanti asked.

"Not long. It will be about forty minutes. Just sit back. There's music and a stocked bar."

Shanti resisted alcohol on a first "date" until she got a feel for who she was with. It was imperative in her profession to stay clear-headed.

CHAPTER 7
HANK

Having slept off the residual effects of cocaine and beer, Hank was fully ashamed of what he'd done. In spite of his background, he had never been a violent man. He also knew that he shouldn't have called Jimmie to complain about the dope and at the same time explained what had happened with Shanti.

He called Jimmie again.

"It's Hank. I don't want you guys to get involved with my mistake. I'll take care of it."

Jimmie wasn't around, but his right-hand man said, "We're gonna be sure Shanti won't bust our parade. The situation is under control."

Hank told the man not to hurt her, but the goon answered, "Don't worry man. It's all set. Pretty soon none of us will be worried about what she might say."

After a few minutes of trying, Hank couldn't get the plan for Shanti out of the guy and gave up. Dialing David's cell number, he got the sick, hung-over man on the line and told him that he thought Shanti was in danger.

Holding his head, trying not to move, David asked, "Why? Why is she in danger, Hank?"

"Just give me her address, damn it!"

"What's going on?"

"I'll tell you everything later. Just help me the fuck to find her!"

It took Hank a full minute to extract the address from David. Hank hung up on David as soon as it was out of the man's mouth.

Now she probably really is in trouble, thanks to me. What a fuck-up. I can't think straight," David berated himself

Taking three more aspirin, he tried to sit up and think through what could be going on. He lost the battle. His system was still saturated with tequila and cocaine. Lying back down, David fell into another deep, exhausted sleep. He didn't hear the maid knock, enter, and gasp when she saw the mess, the cracked table, and David passed out on the couch.

ِوِو*ِو

Hank sped down the main roads, running every yellow and red light, hitting his steering wheel and saying "Fuck!" every time he had a close call at an intersection. He risked getting a speeding ticket, but knew he had to stop Jimmie's men from picking up Shanti.

Hank arrived only minutes after the limo carried Shanti away. Checking the address, he generously tipped the doorman to take care of his double-parked car and hurried upstairs. *Oh, shit! Come on, answer the door, Shanti*, Hank's thoughts screamed. He pounded on the door, ignoring the possibility of disturbing the neighbors. *Fuck it if someone sees me*, he thought. A minute later, there was still no answer at Shanti's door. Hank pulled out his phone. He called the man in charge of the situation and threatened to kill him if he didn't tell him where they had taken Shanti.

This time Hank spoke to Jimmie, who said, "You got something for the lady? Regrets? Second thoughts about going down with the cops if she talks? It's your choice. But you're a dead man if we get popped by a prostitute."

When Hank heard where Shanti was headed, he told Jimmie to get her back.

"Get her back now, Goddammit! I was wrong. She won't say anything. Don't hurt her!"

Hank fled down the hallway. Punching the elevator button repeatedly, he couldn't wait the eternity it seemed to take to reach the seventh floor. He shot down the stairs and out the front door with no word to the doorman in charge of his car.

There was one road to Shanti's destination. Jimmie had told Hank how to find it and hung up laughing.

It was a cool, black night in a remote area outside of Las Vegas. Hank was about twenty minutes behind the car he was after. He found the unmarked turn-off. Risking damage to his low-clearance sports car, Hank sped down the pot-holed, dusty road used for transporting ATVs into the desert. Fifteen minutes later, headlights of an oncoming car caught Hank's car in their glare. Hank slowed and pulled over, waiting for the car to reach him. He was shaking. The driver of the other car slowed down, then floored it, rushing past Hank, spitting up rocks and dust to obscure his vision.

Hank couldn't tell if Shanti was still in the car but guessed that she wasn't. He slammed his Boxster into gear and drove like a crazy man to the end of the road. Pulling up, leaving the headlights on, Hank nearly fell as he unfolded his long frame out of the small car. He was sure she was out here somewhere.

He had never intended for her to get hurt. Thinking if she was here, if the driver hadn't been called off by his boss in time, she was probably already dead, Hank yelled out, "Shanti! It's Hank! I won't hurt you. Where are you? Shanti?" After a couple of minutes running around the car in ever widening circles, Hank finally stopped to listen to the silence. He held his breath to hear any sound that might lead him to her.

"Shanti!" he called again.

Shanti emerged out of the black desert. She was holding her throat. Blood pasted the thin, elegant wrap to her slim form. It was a frightening sight. Her hair, styled for the evening, now trailed into the dark liquid oozing from her chest. Hank caught up to her, laid her down and cradled her head in his lap.

"I didn't want to hurt you. I was high, I was scared. Oh God, Shanti. I'm sorry, I'm so sorry."

Pulling her hand down from her throat, he saw a strange gash and signs of bruising from the necklace that had been yanked from around her neck. Taking her other hand, he saw she'd been trying to stem the increasing gush of blood pumping out of her body with every fading heartbeat. Her eyes were blinking in the car's glaring headlights, but Hank could see they were glazing over. Shanti managed to whisper, "Listen…listen…decide to…do something good…do something good…" Hank watched Shanti try to take a breath and finish what she wanted to say, but life ended as blood filled her lungs. Her heart stopped beating.

"I didn't mean to hurt you, Shanti. I didn't want you dead. Oh shit, oh God…" Hank sobbed, holding her close for several minutes, feeling the full weight of her body slumped in his arms.

Knowing he couldn't risk taking her with him, Hank left Shanti in the desert. He drove slowly back to the city, pulling over twice to vomit.

In town, Hank found a self-serve car wash. Exhausted by the surreal situation, he slowly scrubbed off the dust and checked for blood in the car. He wore a jacket that barely hid the red stain on his jeans. That got him through the lobby of his apartment building without being noticed. He bagged the incriminating clothes with the intention of burning them later, then took a long shower and replayed the scene over and over.

"I didn't mean to hurt you," he repeated, letting the scalding water punish him. His words echoed off the tiled walls. "I didn't mean to hurt you."

The last two days had spun so far out of control that Hank was unable to function for weeks. He called 911 on a pay phone to report a murder and where to find the body. Then he called Althea and made up a lie about a project he'd been working on and said that he'd come home soon. Since she didn't know about the second apartment, Hank told her he was staying in a hotel. He missed his baby boy and sent Althea money but wouldn't go home with the guilt and hopelessness burning in his heart.

He didn't call David, and though he had several requests for a supply of cocaine, Hank condemned himself to isolation.

He relived the scene over and over, Shanti coming toward him in the headlights of his car. The ghastly sight of the bloodied woman. He imagined the killer pulling her out of the car and showing her the blade he was about to use. Jimmie's guy must have wrapped his ugly hand around her long neck while cutting her open with a knife. Hank thought about the impossible fear and pain Shanti must have experienced and wondered at her last words, which were for him. He only guessed that she meant for him to get out of what he'd been doing. She wanted him to make it up to her, to make it up to her for…killing her. To do good.

He knew the business he was in was dangerous and that he could get sent to prison for the rest of his life. He'd always known the risks, but now Hank was spooked. He had never been so mad at anyone before. He'd been high out of his mind that night: Shanti's last night on earth. Now she haunted him.

Her last words stayed with him. Hank asked himself, *How do I get out, what good can I do? Althea likes the money I make and I have no education. Who would pay me any kind of real money for a legitimate job*? Hank had no answers. He'd been dealing since he was sixteen. It was all he knew.

ৠৠৠ

Hank made a significant decision while holed up alone for weeks, caged by terror and shame. His first mistake had been to get high with David. No one in his business, if they were smart, used what they sold. Hank had always known he needed to stay sharp and careful. It was too dangerous otherwise.

Selling drugs to rich people made Hank rich, but what really mattered to him was his son. When his baby was born, Hank had experienced for the first time in his sad life what true love felt like. TJ had become Hank's purpose for living, and now Shanti's death woke Hank up to the chances he'd been taking for years, chances that finally scared him into becoming a very different person.

But it wouldn't happen overnight. Someone always wanted cocaine and as long as everyone kept their mouth shut and did their part, they all made a boat-load of money. Hank made thousands of dollars a week and that usually kept Althea happy. But she picked a fight when Hank returned from his self-imposed seclusion.

Cradling the baby in his arms, Hank tickled TJ under the chin.

Althea nagged, "Where have you been? TJ needs you to be here for him."

"Althea, he's a baby. He probably doesn't even know I exist."

"That's not the point. I'm stuck with him day in and day out. Can't you find work with normal hours? I'm sick of sleeping alone night after night and when you are here I have to tiptoe around trying not to wake you. Especially now with a kid, it's exhausting."

Althea started out this new demand calmly, but when her voice became screechy with the repeated complaints, Hank recognized

63

that what she wanted wasn't for TJ. It was for herself. Althea missed her friends and night life.

With that understanding, and admitting that he was missing important time with his son, Hank said, "Althea, I'll start looking around for another line of work." Though he had absolutely no idea what that would be or what kind of work would pay as much as he was used to making, he knew he would get out one day, not just because Shanti told him to, but because Hank was worried that his luck would run out and that he'd never see his son if he were to go to prison. Hank was ready to make a decision to change his life, but didn't know how to go about it.

CHAPTER 8
DAVID

David left Las Vegas two days after Shanti's murder without hearing about it. He called her cell phone several times but it wasn't long before he got a "not in service" message.

It had been two weeks since David was last home with Lindsey and the boys. His pattern while traveling was to check in every few days with the same old story about being so busy in Las Vegas trying to push the development plan through the city-imposed hoops. Lindsey didn't buy it anymore. She knew they were past trying to keep the family together or telling each other the truth. Her boys now enjoyed the funny man who was coming over for dinner more often these days and this time when David returned home, she surprised him by making him a drink. Handing it to him she said, "I quit."

David, rather obtusely, thought she was telling him that she had given up on some little project she had going.

"What are you quitting, Lindsey?"

"You idiot. I'm quitting you. We've never had a life together and these last two years have been hell. You're impossible to talk to. You're always angry. I'm not even sure you love your own kids. I'm filing for a divorce. In fact, I will be accepting a marriage proposal from someone I met last year."

David didn't try to talk her out of it. She was right about their relationship, but wrong about not loving his boys. He honestly did. Though his career always came first, it still did, and David wasn't ready to give up his fun in Vegas.

The same week Lindsey announced her intention to divorce him, David's new boss, Jack Thompson, called him in for a lunch meeting. It was to be a briefing on where he was on his projects. HGD had broken ground that year in Montreal and Calgary, and a new contract had just been signed in Mexico.

They were in New York City at a favorite financial district restaurant, where you could smell money mingling with the chicken parmesan. Barely saying hello, Jack began his agenda. "You've been researching the residential and spa concept in Vegas. What's the latest?"

"I've been stonewalled by the City Planning Commission. It's taken longer than usual to get our design through the first pass." David continued to lie by complaining about the assholes enamored with Disneyesque themes and the outrageous fees required for moving plans and applications from one desk to another.

"It's been how long now that you've been working on this?" Jack prodded.

"Just over two years. You know Las Vegas is a different animal in this country. It's all about the payoffs and knowing exactly who can be bribed or not. It's a slippery situation and one that I want to play straight and narrow as always, which means that I'm not playing by their rules."

"Maybe it's time to cut it loose. Back off for awhile. We've got other ideas to pursue. In fact," Jack continued, "there's one here in New York I'm considering. Closer to home. Should be interesting for you."

David's reaction was obvious. He had hoped this meeting would open the door for a promotion to take over Jack's old position in charge of development in Asia. Talking about New York certainly meant Asia was not what Jack had in mind for David.

David explained he was interested in Asia.

"Not a chance, Dave. I need an experienced man for North America. I have someone lined up to take my old job. He's stepping in already while transitioning out of his current responsibilities."

For an hour and a half David listened to his new boss's ideas about how to handle Las Vegas and quickly ramp up in New York. David knew exactly what was expected of him from this man five years younger than himself. David's first thought was, maybe it's time to say thanks and no thanks and walk out on lunch and the job. But he managed to keep the conversation going and pretended to be enthusiastic about the scenario Jack laid out for him.

A month later he went back to Las Vegas to tidy up what little business he had started there. He also called Hank.

"I'm moving to New York. My wife is divorcing me and my boss wants to stop things here."

"Probably best," was all Hank had to say. "I've got a few changes going on, too."

After another minute, David asked Hank if he'd seen Shanti. He couldn't believe the woman was dead. Hank only told David what had been reported in the news. Not much.

Choked up, David voiced what he was thinking. "Strange about the timing. That she disappeared after that last night we were all together and things got wild."

"Yeah," answered Hank, "I kinda thought the same thing."

Before signing off, David suggested, "Come to New York sometime, Hank. We can have some good times there, too." They hung up after exchanging promises to keep in touch. It had become an odd friendship.

New York only proved to be another playground for David. He moved out of the house that Lindsey got in the divorce, and set himself up in a small condo on Manhattan's Upper East Side. This time, David did get some work done, but the time spent on work and play quickly went out of balance. David made his choices and created a life of song, dance, women, and cocaine, which were no longer choices but addictions.

CHAPTER 9
HANK

Hank was trying to change his life, though it was nearly impossible to disengage from the significant money he made for his family. Card dealing in a small casino was nowhere near as lucrative as dealing drugs, and it still kept him out at night, while Althea began complaining about needing a new, larger place to live.

Althea's a bitch, Hank thought suddenly one day. *It's all about her. I'm just a bank and sometimes a good lay.*

This turn about in his feelings for his wife had been festering for two years. Ever since Shanti's death, he realized. Althea must have known something was wrong but never bothered to ask him if everything was okay. Not that he would have told her, but sometimes it would be nice if someone—anyone—cared enough to be there for him. Hank thought about this a lot. Remembering Shanti's last words, burned into his heart and mind—"do something good"—*it's up to me*, Hank knew. *No one else. It's all up to me.*

With money, Althea expected to climb the social ladder, and she harassed Hank non-stop about not meeting her needs. She was leaving TJ with her mother more often while Hank went off to deal cards or drugs, whichever it happened to be that night. Hank didn't really know what Althea did during the day beyond finding ways to spend money until he saw her walk into the Gold Dust Hotel. For a few seconds of serendipitous timing, Hank was stopped at a red light and glanced over in time to see his wife pull open the gold-tinted glass door of the gaudy hotel. She was dressed up. Short black skirt, high heels, black halter top. Her waist was cinched tight by a wide gold belt. The one she had bought the week before and showed him how it matched her new shoes and purse. Althea was attractively plump and didn't seem to mind the few pounds that had never come off after giving birth to TJ.

When she got home, he was waiting for her.

"Oh! What's up?" she asked, without considering he might have come home from work because he was sick or something.

"Sit down. I have one question for you and I want a straight up answer."

"I always talk straight. What's with you?"

"Are you sleeping with someone?" Hank asked gently, in case his instinct was wrong and she had only met a girlfriend for lunch or shopping. Although it was an odd costume to wear shopping.

"What do you mean, baby? What's wrong with you? Why are you home?" Althea's voice was a little tight, high-pitched.

"Nothing's wrong if you can give me the truth," Hank answered, remaining calm. "And where's TJ?"

"He's at Momma's. I came home to change before going to pick him up."

"Yeah. I guess your momma would wonder why you're dressed like that, too."

"It's hot. I wanted to wear my new belt and this is all I had to wear it with." Althea thought fast, but Hank knew instantly that it was a lie. Lies were what he heard growing up and his senses were tuned to knowing one when he heard one.

"Cut it out, Althea. Just answer the question."

The argument escalated as Hank's temper began to fray. Althea stubbornly denied her affair until Hank finally asked her where she had been that afternoon.

"I had lunch with Terry and Samantha."

"Where?"

"Our usual place."

"And that is?"

"The Bellagio's Grill. You know I love that hotel and seeing the displays in the lobby. They have the summer theme up and it's unbelievable."

Hank erupted. "It's always *unbelievable* and you told me you saw it over a week ago. You bitch! You can't even get a story straight. I'm done feeding, clothing, and housing a selfish, lying, and CHEATING bitch."

Hank got scary when he got that mad. He would start out baiting his victim quietly and rationally, then explode and threaten. Althea cowered in the corner of the living room behind a chair. Hank had never hit her, but that night he looked like he was about to when his mother-in-law walked in with TJ.

Hank turned to see his son quivering next to his grandmother, holding onto her leg. Althea immediately began abusing Hank in front of the scared little boy. Seeing his son's face, Hank's temper lost all momentum.

Retreating, Hank said to his mother-in law in a low voice so TJ couldn't hear, "Your lovely daughter is a cheating, lying whore."

Hank left the apartment and drove around for a while. After half an hour he found himself on the highway heading toward the old dirt road he hadn't had the guts to go near for years.

Finding the spot where Shanti died in his arms, Hank sat in his convertible listening to the night approach across the forsaken desert. He closed his eyes and imagined what life would be like without Althea and away from Las Vegas. Where would he go? Would he have to give up TJ? Giving up TJ was not possible. He felt his breath catch and chest tighten at the thought. *TJ is my heart and soul.*

Three months later, Hank called David and told him he was coming to New York for a visit.

CHAPTER 10
CARRIE

Twenty years earlier, the Board of Directors of Kendall Innovations scoffed, joked, and generally refused to believe that the child who inherited her grandfather's company would ever be back to run it. While Carrie was growing up, the board members changed and the company profits ebbed and flowed during high and low economic pressures. The company was nearing its sixty-three-year anniversary. Justice Kendall had run it for forty-three years, and a succession of leaders after his death had kept it going. The fourth of those successors was young and brilliant. He knew the technology industry, had created a few innovations of his own that somewhat changed the computer industry, and was courted by the hiring committee of board members to take the newly named Kendall Technology into the next millennium. His name was Charles Baker.

Baker held a law degree, but had practiced for only a few years before pitching his computer concepts and program designs to a company capable of developing them. They paid Baker for his ideas, which only confirmed Baker's talent. He gave up law and went to work at the company that had bought his ideas. A few years later, Kendall Tech got wind of him. They made him an offer that he accepted. Baker was hired as president three months before Carrie's first day on the job.

No one from human resources or the interview panel had mentioned to Charles that the company founder's granddaughter might emerge out of nowhere for a five-year internship before taking over. The Chairman of the Board told him on the day Carrie arrived. Baker was outraged.

"That's a breach of trust. No one mentioned anything about my job being handed over to this woman in five years! Why wasn't that in the contract? Now I understand why there have been so many short-timers in this position. They knew they'd be ousted when this girl showed up."

The chairman tried to calm him down, and brought in the VP of Human Resources to help explain the situation. "Your contract is for five years. At which time, your performance will be assessed by the board of directors," the HR honcho said, reminding him of the terms of his contract.

"I *KNOW* the contract says five years, but you knew someone was in line for the job when that time came, and that I'd get booted. That's not exactly the same as implying performance review in five years."

Threatening legal action, Baker left the two alone and took the elevator from his executive suite at the top of the twenty-story building to the first floor to find his way to the mailroom.

The chairman asked, "The contract is in order right? It's tight? After all, Charles was a lawyer before turning tech." He was assured that nothing could be done legally against Kendall Technologies, Inc. Though the VP added, "He should have been told."

Baker had to ask the receptionist how to get to the mailroom and found it a few minutes later. Carrie was there. She was sorting envelopes and packages while discussing a few ideas for change with her supervisor, who was standing next to her. He noticed how tall and thin, skinny really, she was. Her hair was pulled straight back, tucked behind her ears, and fell to chin level. She wasn't striking, but looked sexy from the back in her slim black skirt and flat shoes. She definitely had long legs. He liked long legs.

Baker walked up to her and stuck out his hand. "I'm Charles Baker, president of your grandfather's company." Carrie stepped away from her pile and looked at him for a second before smiling and accepting his handshake. "I'm pleased to meet you Charles. I'm Caroline Kendall."

Carrie had never used her grandfather's last name before. She had always gone by Carrie Jeffries. But the spontaneous decision was made and she committed to it in that moment.

Noticing that she called him Charles instead of Mr. Baker was his first clue that she was already positioning herself as someone in charge.

"I'm here to learn as much and as quickly as possible, Charles. Perhaps you'll help me." It was a statement not a question. Looking her over impolitely, Charles decided that in spite of her long legs, he didn't like her and would make every effort to make her look inept. While thinking this, Charles smiled and said, "Of course. Who's directing your internship? I'll talk with him to transfer that privilege to me."

"Suzanne Waterton," Carrie replied, ignoring Baker's assumption of a male supervisor. "She's documenting my time spent in each department for the lawyer's review in order to satisfy the stipulation in my grandfather's will. I'll know when it's time to move on to the next department and for how long. What I need from you, Charles, is a briefing on how the company is doing, a copy of the business plan and a list of board members. I'll be attending every board meeting, as a fly on the wall, of course. I'm sure you understand. When is the next meeting?"

Charles took a small step backward and looked at his watch. He was going to be late for his lunch meeting with the Chairman. Refraining from inviting Carrie to join him, he said, "I'll have my assistant let you know."

As he turned to leave, Carrie stuck out her hand, forcing him to shake it again. She looked at him straight and hard. "Don't screw with me Charles. I intend to take over in one thousand, eight hundred, and twenty-five days—five years from now. I will work with you cooperatively if you work with me. It's your choice."

Letting go of his hand, Carrie turned away and went back to sorting the mail. During her exchange with the company president, the mailroom staff had watched the two while going about their business. No one had left the room, though some had duties elsewhere in the building.

Charles had made his first mistake with Carrie. He should have welcomed her in his office, instead of showing an uncharacteristically antagonizing attitude with witnesses in the mailroom, who were the primary source of gossip throughout the building.

Carrie's plan was to learn something about every job in the company. Her grandfather had done the same thing. He had made it a point to stay in touch with his company's greatest assets, each and every hard working employee who stuck with him in the best and worst of times. Carrie followed her instincts. She befriended anyone who wasn't too intimidated to speak with her. She ate lunch with janitors, computer programmers, and department heads. She didn't discriminate and quickly became someone the employees went to for advice or with suggestions for improving some aspect of the company.

❧❧❧

Carrie, Charles Baker, and each member of the board sat in high-backed leather chairs around the glossy oval mahogany table. Carrie recognized her grandfather's taste in art on the interior wall—original, modern paintings by various artists. A view of San

Francisco's financial district could be seen out the opposite wall of windows. A large custom-carved cabinet filled one end of the room. At the head of the table, Carrie sat to the left of the board chairman, Charles on his right. Thirty minutes into the meeting, Carrie broke her promise to be a silent observer and derailed the agenda.

"What is lacking here is vision. With the exception of Baker, you're all over fifty. New technology is readily embraced by "Millennials." Seeing that the older people in the room didn't understand what that meant, Carrie explained.

"Millennials are people born in the eighties. They have a particular generational culture, just like baby boomers and Gen X-ers. Millennials were born in a high-tech world and have an appetite for it—for the newest toy or program—whether it will make their life easier or not. This group of twenty-somethings is going to work for corporations that want to reinvent their industries. That's why people right out of college are getting snapped up. Find where they're looking for the latest technology solutions to their business problems and interests and you'll find gold."

Carried stopped to assess how she was doing, based on the expressions of fifteen faces, and then continued. "I realize I have a lot to learn about the mechanics of what we do here and how you've been running the show, but I will be watching, learning, and participating, so please don't expect to wait five years to hear from me."

And so, while getting to know the employees on a friendly basis, it didn't take Carrie long to make enemies on the board and of Charles Baker. That first remark, though a basic principle in business, demonstrated her over-confident, challenging nature.

She spent ten days in the mailroom, quickly learning the layout of the building and the people in it. She sat next to the receptionist for four hours one day, then moved on to research and development. She expected to be there for several months. R&D was the brain matter of the company, and Carrie immediately identified the brightest light in the department of twenty: Padma Singh, a meek young woman from India with a master's degree in aeronautical engineering and a second master's in computer science. After their first conversation, each recognized that they had complementary social skills. Carrie could be brash. Padma was sensitive and quiet, but very knowledgeable and secure. As they got to know each other during the time Carrie spent with the R&D team, they often sought each other out for company at lunch.

One day, over a bowl of minestrone and a tossed green salad, Carrie asked, "What's your vision, Padma? Where do you see my company going?"

The woman hesitated. She was a cautious person and wasn't sure if it was a trick question. They were in the employee lunchroom, away from the local restaurants frequented by the senior executives. As she gazed past Carrie at the turbulent city scene outside, they sat surrounded by hundreds of employees scrambling for food at the steam tables. The air was rich in all sorts of aromas rising from pungent marinara over pasta, herbed chicken, and fresh breads. It was high noon and every table was occupied. Padma and Carrie huddled at a small table for two in a corner.

"I will return to India, to my family and friends, and open my own international research and development company," Padma responded. Then realizing that Carrie had asked about her company, Kendall Technology, Inc., she flushed with embarrassment. Recovering somewhat, but still blushing, she added, "That's my personal dream. What I believe should happen for Kendall is a focus on something that will revolutionize the transportation industry. Specifically air travel. It's archaic."

Waiting for some response and getting none, Padma added again, "Of course that's my area of special interest, but I think

Kendall has too many projects going on in too many different areas. We should pull back resources to generate and develop one or two truly new ideas. I would review the current projects and re-evaluate a couple that haven't advanced for a year or two and pull the plug."

Still waiting for Carrie to say something, Padma stopped talking and moved her salad around on her plate. She was beginning to think that what she had said was off base, when Carrie finally spoke. "What projects that you're aware of would you pull?"

She couldn't shake the feeling of being set up, but answered anyway. Cautiously Padma named two projects. She spoke in a low voice to make sure no one passing by their table would overhear. Not low enough: three key words fell on the wrong ears.

Benita was the executive assistant to Charles Baker. He had asked her to keep an eye on Carrie whenever possible without being obvious. It wasn't easy to find reasons to be in the vicinity throughout four floors of 40,000 square feet, but she did her best, and happened to be hovering close enough that day to hear Padma say, "Baker's pet project."

Reporting back to Baker later that afternoon, Benita was thanked and dismissed to her desk. Her area was immediately outside the tall carved oak doors to his lavish office of wood paneling, leather, and glass. The sitting area boasted cushioned furniture. The entrance doors and décor were similar to the private home office of Justice Kendall that Carrie remembered. The view, however, was very different from the expansive gardens at the Kendall mansion. Baker's office window revealed the city streets below.

After closing the door behind his assistant, Charles returned to his desk and called the VP of research and development. "Do you have a few minutes tomorrow? Good. Let's make it ten. My office."

The VP didn't get much sleep that night. Benita always scheduled meetings with Baker's executive team, so something was up. Arriving promptly at ten o'clock, Benton Swank walked into his boss's office and sat down. Taking an upbeat tack, he said, "Good morning, Charles. What's up?"

For an hour Charles pumped him for information about all the projects currently in any stage of progress in R&D.

"There are five." Benton answered Baker's questions, going into detail about each one. "Padma is working on your project. Dave has started researching new connections for wireless ignitions, and Anwar, Gupti, and Shawn are in phase three development of the A/R, A/P system. That's nearing completion; then they'll move on to cross-platform function testing. I'm hearing about other ideas our competitors are working on through our usual contacts, and expect to know more in a few weeks."

Without giving Benton any idea of why he was asking, Baker stood up from behind his desk and thanked him. Leading him to the door, Baker casually mentioned that it was a strong team—and asked if he agreed. It was a bait and switch question.

Benton thought for a heartbeat, then spoke in a tone that hinted something or someone wasn't measuring up. "Actually, we'll be reviewing a new selection of students about to graduate and call for applicants. I could use another youngster in the group with new ideas."

Hiding his smile, Baker replied, "Keep me posted on that, Benton. I'm watching the budget, of course, and yours is a cost center. If you find new talent, you'll probably have to replace someone."

Left alone, standing behind his desk, Baker faced the picture window. Watching the company logo on the flags flying from poles angled over the front doors below, he noticed how hard they were slapping in the rising wind that promised to carry in the fog bank lying just off the coast.

CHAPTER 11

Carrie's apartment was located on Nob Hill. She loved San Francisco and loved living in the middle of it. She could get nearly anywhere in the city within twenty minutes if traffic was normal, but she preferred to walk most of the time. Getting to the office wasn't difficult. The nearest Bay Area Rapid Transit station was four blocks from her condominium. After a short ride, she would stride through the impressive double-wide glass doors of *her* company. Work was her life. She had studied hard at Wharton and was now learning the practical application of what they taught.

Breathing in the salty air on an unusually warm Sunday afternoon, Carrie walked for miles to the Embarcadero. Tour boats and ferries slipped in and out, picking up and offloading hundreds of tourists. She wore shorts, white sneakers, and a white T-shirt. Her hair blew about her face in the warm gusts. Her hands were free to swing without the burden of a purse. What she needed—her ID, a little cash, and a comb—fit in her pocket. In fact, Carrie had everything she needed except a friend. There had been a couple of short-term romances, but never anything serious. Women were usually too silly for Carrie, and men could never be just friends unless they were gay, and then the gays Carrie had met fit into the silly-woman category. It was a no-win and Carrie would usually ignore her loneliness.

However, on this day Carrie indulged in a certain train of thought while dodging the tourists at the Wharf. *There must be something very wrong with me. Gina was my only friend and I've completely lost touch with her.* Passing table after table of jewelry, paintings and photographs, and crafts being hawked on the sidewalk by the artisans, Carrie was reaching the business neighborhood of advertising and public relations agencies. The famous clock tower on the Ferry Building at Pier 20 said noon. The Ferry Building was a popular place for enjoying fresh produce, international flavors, and specialty wares.

Coffee, Carrie thought, and entered the charming, renovated building. She dodged those in her way to find her favorite stopping place for sitting and watching the goofy-looking human race pass by. Carrie was hyper-critical. She made it a game to watch people and pick out their worst feature—big nose, bad skin, floppy chins, beady eyes—the list went on and on as humanity proved itself to be the least beautiful species on the planet. Carrie watched the variety of shapes and sizes on two legs lumber by, wasting away a gorgeous Sunday afternoon in a spectacular city.

∞∞∞

The following morning, Padma entered the Kendall building at the same time Carrie arrived. Saying good morning to each other in the lobby, they split off to their respective areas. Padma always arrived at eight o'clock and rarely left before six o'clock. She loved her job, and though she had a vision for her future, she didn't expect to leave the company any time soon.

Turning on her computer in her cubicle, she went to fill her extra-large mug with coffee. She also grabbed a donut from the box that someone in R&D usually brought in on Mondays. Back at the computer, Padma settled into mining a plan for the project that had Charles Baker's full attention. It was Baker's idea that fusing two sources of natural energy, such as light and wind, should lead to a landslide profit for the company in years to come.

Benton stepped into Padma's cubical as she logged on. He had just watched her type the password before she felt someone standing behind her. While he could have simply asked the company's IT service for access to Padma's computer files, he didn't want anyone to know he was reviewing her work.

"How's it going? I need a daily report for Baker starting today."

Noticing her boss's tight voice and no mention of good morning, she responded in kind. "I'm expecting to finish the competitive investigation today, Benton. So far there's nothing remotely similar being done anywhere. I'm cautiously optimistic that I'll be able to report the same news at the end of today."

Surprising her with an unusually terse tone, Benton said, "Make it by noon. We can't wait for your slow caution this time."

Bad night, fight with the wife, whatever, thought Padma. *It's not me that he's mad at.*

By noon she gave Benton the same information she had that morning.

"After four hours, you didn't find anything new?"

"No sir." Padma had never called him "'sir.'" They had always gotten along very well and shared a mutual respect.

"You better be certain. We'll forward the report to Baker, but this is your baby and it has to be accurate."

This kind of treatment and the implication that they thought she wasn't doing a good enough job was not something Padma was used to. *Why the turn-about*, she wondered. Twirling her short cropped black hair and adjusting her glasses, she decided not to worry, but true to her usual reserve, also decided to step lightly and cautiously.

The next day she described to Carrie a modified version of what had transpired with Benton. "The deadlines have been shifted on the project I was given to lead. What's the big deal?" Padma asked rhetorically. "We were given six months to investigate competitive environments. Now the entire project needs to be completed in two months. That's impossible."

Carrie knew she was using Padma for information and now realized she wasn't the only one manipulating the woman. *They want her out of here for some reason. It's a set up for failure. They're beginning to manage her out.* Carrie didn't voice this speculation, but to her instincts the thought rang true.

Padma was fired two months later. The case was built against her that she couldn't move fast enough on Baker's project. Benton Swank had found a student to take the lead on the investigation phase that Padma had nearly completed for a significantly lower salary and equally less experience.

When Carrie heard the news, she stormed at Benton. "I want Padma Singh back! She was methodical and thorough. That's what you need for the project phase she was in the middle of. It was ludicrous to let her go."

"Leave it, Caroline. Charles wasn't satisfied with her work. She was leading the project and we didn't have anyone else to help her with it. She was too slow. The new kid is going to be fine. He's picking up quickly on what needs to be done. He'll finish the phase in two weeks. That's the kind of progress we need right now. The longer we take, the more likely the competition will hear about what we're working on. The risk is too great."

"Nonsense!" was all Carrie had left to say to the man in charge of R&D. *It's not worth my time to debate with an idiot,* she thought, turning on her flat-heeled shoe and bolting for the executive offices.

When Carrie called Padma from home that evening, the woman didn't know what to say.

"I'm confused, Carrie. They know how critical it is to thoroughly investigate and research the competitive market. There's a world of knowledge to be gathered that could give Kendall a significant advantage—a head start on that project if the right people put the right pieces together. That's the part I was looking forward to after the investigation. Why did they want to rush it all of a sudden? We were on track according to the original timeline. Why didn't they give me a chance?"

Sighing heavily, Padma then reminded Carrie of her desire to start up her own company in India and market her investigation/research services worldwide. "I was with Kendall Tech for five years. After dreaming about leaving for the last two years, I guess the choice was made for me. It's okay. I am all right, though I had expected to leave on my own terms, when I felt completely ready. I guess I was imagining my own business so often that now I need to decide to make it happen."

The words caused a little shiver to run up Carrie's neck and her scalp felt tingly.

"That's similar to something my grandfather told me before he died. I was six years old. When he said it, he implied a deeper meaning and promised to explain. He died before telling me anything more. After a few months of wondering and trying to figure out what he wanted me to understand, I gave up and forgot all about it. This is the first time in twenty years that I've thought about his message. He said, "Whatever you can imagine can come true—that his company was built on imagination—and something like, you have the power inside you."

"I would ponder his words again. It seems your grandfather has found a way to remind you of something important," Padma said.

Ready to hang up, Carrie said, "I will. I'm glad we talked. Feel free to call me if you like, Padma. Take care."

Having expected a very different conversation, Carrie plopped down on her couch and considered the mystery in Padma saying that her grandfather had found a way to remind her of what he'd said so long ago.

Carrie curled up and hugged a soft sofa pillow to her chest. She had wanted more information about Baker's project, but Padma had gotten onto the other thing. Staring straight ahead, she stopped seeing the picture and bookshelf on the wall while reliving those last few minutes with her grandfather, which then morphed into reminiscing about her old friend Gina.

A few minutes later Carrie went to the refrigerator and pulled out a bottle of Sauvignon Blanc. Taking a full glass back to the couch, the introspective stream of consciousness continued. She came up with, *our decisions today create our tomorrow.* Why does that sound so profound? Of course our decisions will affect what we do next. That's basic. I wish grandfather were here to explain the power of the imagination. *The secret is to help others, Caroline.* It was a whispered memory on a lonely night.

An hour and three glasses of wine later, Carrie stood and stretched. She was slightly drunk when it occurred to her to go online and try to find some information on Gina or her parents, Antonella and Tom Severns. Last known residence, Seattle.

She remembered to check the listings for architects in Seattle. That's where she found a number for Gina's father. *He evidently has his own firm now,* she thought. After writing down the number, Carrie went to refill her wine glass again before making the call. It was ten o'clock on a Friday evening. Thinking that no one would be at the office, she felt better about just leaving a message.

"Hello, I'm calling for Tom Severns. This is Carrie Jeffries, an old friend of his daughter, Gina..." Carrie left her number and hung up. There were no other listings or leads she could find for Gina on the Internet. *That's gonna have to do it,* she thought with some trepidation. Carrie didn't really know what she would say if anyone from Gina's family, let alone Gina, called. Maybe something like, "Hello. Remember me? I'm the girl who corrupted your daughter when she was ten and you wouldn't let her ever speak to me again. Well, I'm back."

Basking in a rare case of self-pity, sadness took over for her usual sarcasm, and loneliness replaced the emotional anesthesia that usually protected Carrie from her feelings. Having nothing else to do, once again on a Friday night, she went to bed early.

CHAPTER 12
GINA

Robert Cummings was fifteen years older than Gina. Not *that* much older, considering several girls Gina knew had dated men who were in their fifties and older. Robert had grown up in Los Angeles and knew everyone in the fashion industry. He was the classic womanizer and he had Gina on a string. Robert was smooth, handsome, charming, smart, and rich. Everything a shallow young girl could hope for. It was Robert who got Gina into Armani for a photo session with George Clooney. She was one of three girls being considered when Robert made a call. Four months later Gina saw herself on the cover of VOGUE as the mystery woman standing inches behind Clooney, who was in the designer tux he would wear to the Oscars.

Robert married Gina in a small ceremony in a magnificent Beverly Hills mansion. It was the home of one of his movie producer friends, someone Gina had not met before. Gina's parents and brothers flew in for the ceremony. Girlfriends from the agency and a few of Robert's buddies attended, too. Antonella, Gina's mother, was the matron of honor, and Robert's only brother stood up with him. Gina's engagement ring was a three-carat, square-cut diamond. The wedding band was a simple ring of diamond chips that showed off the hero stone. It was gaudy and gorgeous. Armani favored Gina with a form-fitting, off-the-shoulder gown of snow-white, pleated satin. It was a classic, stunning dress that suited Gina beautifully. Her hair was longer than it had been in years. She'd let it grow since there was more demand for models with plenty of hair to work with and be blown about by fans. It fell loose and soft around her perfectly made-up face.

Everyone from out of town stayed at the Beverly Wilshire Hotel. The small wedding party took over a private room for dinner and stuck together for an evening on the town. Robert's stamina was equal to Gina's on the dance floor. Sitting out only a few songs for drinks, they were enjoying every minute of their first day as husband and wife. Excusing herself, Gina set off to find the ladies' room, leaving Robert with his friends and her parents for a few minutes. Finding it down a long, low lit hallway, Gina entered a formally elegant room lined with mirrors.

As one woman was leaving, she stopped and said, "Congratulations, honey. Love the dress."

Another woman turned from the mirror to check out the dress on the woman being congratulated.

"Stunning," she said. "Where did you get married?"

"A friend's home," Gina answered modestly. "It was a beautiful ceremony."

"Must have been some house to match that dress." Obviously not from Los Angeles, the woman added, "If I ever decide to marry, I'll go home and get married there."

Gina continued the conversation. "What if the man of your dreams wants to get married here? Would you let him have his way?" Gina was fishing for support, even from a stranger, since it bothered her that she had given in to Robert's choice of wedding venue and honeymoon location.

"I have a feeling that problem won't come up for me. I've been here for nearly two years and haven't found anyone. But I'll end up back in my hometown. That's my intuition talking." Smiling, the women left the ladies' room, leaving Gina alone to touch up her lipstick.

✌✌✌

The next day, Robert and Gina took a town car to Los Angeles International Airport. Fiji had been Robert's idea. Gina had suggested Venice, but Robert described their perfect honeymoon on his terms. Everything was booked first class. After a twelve-hour flight, they landed on one of the 332 Fijian Islands and transferred to a prop plane headed for the small town of Savusavu. Bumping along the short airstrip, they came to a final stop. Gina led the way down the stairway that had been rolled up to the plane door, grateful to finally be breathing the pure warm air and no longer confined to a seat. They were greeted by a young woman.

"Bula," the Fijian beauty welcomed them in her native language. She wished them a happy stay after kissing Gina and Robert on each cheek and placing a sweetly fragrant flower lei over their heads. The woman grinned at Gina and cast her eyes shyly down and away from Robert, an extremely handsome American.

It was a short drive to the resort on a dirt road about half an hour beyond the quaint village. Reaching the five-star accommodations, they were again welcomed in the traditional island manner and assured that their stay would be perfect. The resort was on a seventeen-acre coconut plantation with twenty-five bungalows, or bures, built of local lumber with traditional thatched roofing overlooking the peaceful waters of Savusavu Bay.

"Gina," Robert explained, sounding like a kid at Disneyland, "you're going to love this place, honey. It's called the Soft Coral Capital of the World. Scuba divers come here from all over to dive."

Their first magical days as a married couple were spent shopping, swimming, eating, and making love. They watched divers take flight off cliffs and explored the hillsides. They wandered through the nearby town and watched farmers selling a colorful array of fruits and vegetables. Saturday morning was the best day for going to the farmer's market to see local produce and what would go into the preparation of the Lovo, or Fijian feast.

Gina drifted for the first few days, letting Robert lead her around to see his favorite sites, snorkeling at his preferred lagoons and reefs, and accepting his insistence that she learn to scuba dive. The thought of diving scared her to death but, wanting to please her new husband, she began lessons in the Olympic-size swimming pool. Everything about the sport scared her. Holding her breath instead of mastering the unnatural act of breathing under water had her coming up to the surface sputtering and coughing. Flunking out the first day, Gina began again the next day in a new class.

During a romantic breakfast for two on the ironwood deck of their bure overlooking an eternity of brilliant blue-green water melting into cloudless azure sky, Gina brought up her feelings about the diving lessons scheduled for that afternoon. "I'll never become certified for diving, Robert. Why don't you just do it without me?"

"I want you to share with me everything I love, Gina. You'll get it. Keep trying."

"Uh huh," Gina agreed, but she wasn't confident that she'd succeed.

"That's not the spirit, Gina. You need to get over your ridiculous fear. Nothing is going to happen to you. Just stick the tube in your mouth and take a breath. Breathe in and for fun watch the bubbles as you breathe out. Do it once. Do it again, and do it again after that. You have a mindset that's making it more difficult than it really is."

"O-*kay*, Robert. I said I'd try it again. Maybe taking it breath by breath as you just said, I'll get the hang of it." Gina was trying something that in her heart she truly didn't want to do. But it was

Robert saying something about a mindset that reminded Gina of what the woman in the ladies' room in Los Angeles had said about intuition. *If that's true*, Gina wondered, *I may be dead by tomorrow*.

The resort was renowned for its scuba diving concession run by an instructor who had worked with Jean-Michel Cousteau.

Gina joined a group of people in the pool who had already overcome the first day's challenge for diving. They remained underwater for thirty minutes, learning to read the air gauge, practicing with their partners on exchanging mouth pieces underwater, and taking off and putting on their tanks. Gina, on the other hand, was just beginning to take regular though short breaths underwater, pushing each breath out to watch the bubbles as Robert had suggested. She continued taking gasps of air from her tank, but was at risk of hyperventilating if she kept it up. Gina frustrated even the most dedicated and patient instructor. The man said everything he could think of to get her to relax and breathe normally.

"I'm still not getting it, Robert." Gina told him at dinner. "I guess I'm not a mermaid. Now if you want to see me on the slopes, that's a different matter. I'll bet I could ski circles around you down a black diamond run."

"Doubt it, honey," Robert answered. "I was president of the ski club in college and have skied nearly every tortuous mountain in North America and Europe."

"Well, let's go skiing this winter! I grew up skiing and love it. I'm just not sure I'll ever be comfortable diving, no matter how enticing the views are from the deep." Gina shuddered as she spoke the words *views from the deep*.

Robert continued insisting, "Try it again tomorrow, sweetheart. I'll go with you this time. We'll take the lesson together."

At the end of the third day, Gina was still very uncomfortable with the whole thing but had finally managed to stay under water in the pool for the required thirty minutes before being released to dive the outer reefs of Vanu Levu Island. Though she had hung on to the side of the pool, it was thirty minutes of pure hell for Gina and frustrating for Robert. He was convinced that she would overcome her fear if she would just stick with it. He knew that she had never stayed with anything uncomfortable long enough to get through it.

The big day arrived. Gina had her certification. Wearing a new blue bikini that contrasted with her darkly tanned skin, she slowly walked up the gangway to the boat that would take them five miles offshore for a day of adventure. "I'm ready," Gina whispered to herself. She shivered even though the air temperature was over eighty degrees. They were on the boat with three other couples, all experienced divers happy to be spending the bright blue-sky day in one of the world's most magnificent diving areas. Wet suits were not necessary for the tepid crystal-clear water. Except Gina, everyone was ready to have the experience they'd come for.

Being the last to jump into the calm, transparent, aquamarine water, Gina felt light-headed with fear. She couldn't see land from her low vantage point on the water's surface. Robert was next to her. The others had already moved away and disappeared below them. Gina fought her rising panic. She was trying to show Robert that she could do this. Putting the mouthpiece in for her and taking her hand, Robert pulled her down. Gina's brain took over. She couldn't control her breathing for the first minute and struggled against Robert. She fought every ounce of instinct to swim back up for air. Robert was determined to make her realize how incredible, how silent and amazing the underwater world was. He was sure that if he could help her through the first few minutes that Gina would soon forget her fear and watch for the underwater wonders they'd come to see.

Gina held onto Robert like a lifeline. Robert felt as though he was dragging an anchor. She weighed him back as he pointed toward a formation of rocks covered with purple and orange sea anemones. Magenta coral provided a backdrop for a large school of brilliant yellow and blue striped fish averaging three inches long that created a cloud of sparkling color around them. At that point, thinking she was distracted by the soft, tickling touch of the fish brushing against her, Robert pried Gina's hand off his arm and swam away to explore.

The warm South Pacific buoyed his body and spirit. Free and without a thought except for the moment at hand, Robert slowly followed a stingray as it flapped and glided along its course. They were about forty feet below the surface. The sun's rays cast slanted columns of gold light just above. Though a key rule of diving is to keep your partner in view, Robert had lost sight of Gina when he rounded a rock formation. It had been for just a minute or two and he was only a few feet away, but she didn't know that.

Gina was suddenly aware of being alone. Spinning around, churning up the darting and circling mass of fish, her breathing caught, her heart pounded, and unbridled fear set in. Scrambling for the surface, arms flailing, legs pumping, Gina became disoriented and moved away from reef shelf. She was getting dizzy from the short gasps of air, the light from above disappeared, and a black hole with no up or down swallowed her. Fear turned to panic. Gina was hyperventilating. Completely confused, not knowing which way to go, every bit of instruction and even common sense about watching the direction of air bubbles failed her. All Gina knew was that she was alone in a dark, watery grave, scared out of her mind. Minutes later, the dizziness overtook her. She lost consciousness and Gina's now fully relaxed body began to sink.

Only seconds had passed when flashlight signals brought the group of nearby divers together. They fanned out and dove further away from the boat's mooring rope. Going deeper and deeper,

Robert couldn't believe her stupidity. *I was right there behind the rocks. She saw where I went*, he thought.

He headed out beyond the point on the shelf where he'd left her, where it was dark and deep. Movement directly below him caught his eye. It could be a very large fish or Gina. He took his chances and plunged straight down. Gina's loosened hair spread away from her head like jellyfish tentacles, her arms and legs splayed out from her torso like a star fish, together confirming to Robert that the sinking, dark shape was human. Kicking hard, he reached her inert body. Robert grabbed a wrist and ankle first, then maneuvered Gina around so that he could wrap an arm around her waist. He replaced the mouthpiece and turned up the air flow. All the while, he was kicking furiously to take her toward the surface light. Another woman in their diving party saw them and signaled the others for help. The men took turns pushing Gina to the surface. Robert's legs had turned to rubber. Two other women had gone to the boat to alert the crew. All Robert could think of was that it was her fault if she died. His way of thinking took no responsibility for forcing her into the situation. He was scared and angry while pushing her limp body upward.

Breaking the surface of the shimmering, flat sea, the men yanked off Gina's diving gear and positioned her to be pulled up and onto the boat.

The crew was ready. This type of emergency rarely happened, but they were well trained in all manner of resuscitation. The hospital had been alerted and an ambulance was dispatched to meet them at the closest beach. By the time Gina was gently placed onto the deck, she had been unconscious for at least ten minutes and without oxygen for possibly as long as five minutes. Working with every skill, it seemed forever before the crew had water spewing out of Gina's lungs. Choking and spitting, she tried to open her eyes against the sun's glare. She couldn't see the faces circling above her. Her chest heaved painfully with every breath. *I'm alive*, was her first thought, before tears began streaming toward her ears and into her hair.

It was one of the women who tenderly brought Gina up to a sitting position and held her tight.

Robert was sitting on a bench behind Gina with his head in his heads trying to recover on his own.

Turning her head to look for him, she lay back down and allowed herself to be moved to a stretcher and covered with a light blanket. She felt awful. Her chest hurt and she was exhausted.

"Robert," Gina said, when he finally moved to her side just before the boat reached the dock where the ambulance was waiting. "Where did you go? You left me."

Taking her hand and kissing her fingers, Robert was shaking to keep his anger under control. "I was only a few feet away Gina, just behind the rocks. I thought you saw me following the ray."

"No, I didn't know where you were. You pushed me away." Gina was clearly uncomfortable trying to talk. One of the crew recommended that she lie still and stay quiet.

Another crewman spoke quickly to Robert, "We don't know how long she was without oxygen, but clearly you saved her life. They'll take a good look and run a few tests at the hospital before releasing her. But my guess is that she'll be able to leave in a few hours or in the morning, latest."

Gina was released the next day. They had X-rayed her lungs and found more water, which could lead to infection.

"She'll have a cough for awhile and won't feel like doing much," the doctor told Robert. "Keep her quiet. It will be several days before we know if she'll need a different prescription for antibiotics to ward off a lung infection."

Upon returning to their bure, Gina slept for eighteen hours. The accident was big news at the quiet resort and reached the ears of residents in neighboring towns. Several people who'd met Gina during their stay sent flowers and fresh local fruit with their wishes for a speedy recovery.

Robert moped around while Gina lay curled up in bed, sleeping a deep dreamless sleep. He was heading out for a run on the beach when he was stopped by one of the men who had helped rescue Gina. He invited Robert to join a dinner party in the main dining room that evening. Two couples who had also been diving with Robert and Gina were at the table and filled the others in on what happened. Robert noted that during the retelling, blame was not placed on him, but they prodded him to provide a reason why or how it happened.

With his new sweet wife sleeping off trauma-based exhaustion, Robert tried to be true and protective of her, but simply couldn't come up with an answer. "Frankly she'd gotten herself in over her head. Literally!" He laughed.

The others laughed, too, but the women who had been there that day and witnessed Gina's apprehension before entering the water didn't find it funny. They'd seen the half-dead woman lying on the boat deck. They had prayed for a miracle while watching the crew taking turns pounding on Gina's chest and giving mouth-to-mouth. Everyone except Robert had been screaming, "Gina! Please God! Come on Gina!"

Robert bought a few rounds of after-dinner drinks for the group in the bar. Then the party really got going when they moved to the beach and a few local musicians joined them. The natives had a large bowl of dirty-looking water with them, which they set down in the sand. As people sat in a circle around the bowl, one musician began dipping coconut shell halves into what was called kava. They taught everyone how to drink the musty fermented root liquid that made them giggle and their lips go numb.

It was two in the morning when Robert finally got up from the circle of partiers to work his way back to his room. A light was on in the bure, which helped him see his way along the path to his front door.

"Hello," Gina said after Robert closed the door.

"Gina! You're finally awake!"

"I woke up about an hour ago, took a shower and came back to bed to wait for you. I didn't know where you were." When she said it, Gina realized those were the words she kept repeating after coming to on the boat.

"How are you feeling?" Robert went to sit next to her.

He smelled funny. Gina wrinkled her nose. "What have you been doing? You stink."

"Well, that's not a very friendly welcome from a new wife." Robert traced her cheek and pushed a rope of damp hair away from her neck. He zeroed in to bite her there, in the tender place just below her earlobe. Gina wriggled her shoulder and gave him a gentle push away, saying, "No, Robert, you smell really bad. Can't you take a shower first?"

"Well, sure, Gina. I can do that. Is there anything else you'd like me to do for her highness?" Robert's lips were still slightly numb, and while he could always hold his liquor, the kava had made a strong impression on the muscles of his mouth. He slurred the words before slobbering a kiss on Gina's lips.

"Yes," she said pretending to herself that he was kidding. "You can bring me my magic wand and I will turn you into the frog that you smell like."

Robert pushed himself off the bed and went to the bathroom. It was a massive room. A room the honeymooners had enjoyed two nights ago, with its jetted bathtub and aromatic candles and soaps. There was also a separate shower with six shower heads. Fatigue caught up with Robert and he opted for a quick shower. He spent about ten minutes thinking about what had happened while lathering his firm, well-muscled body and thick dark hair.

Toweling off, Robert then climbed into bed. He kept his back to Gina and pulled the light-weight down comforter over his shoulders.

Her bedside lamp was on when he got to bed, but Gina turned it off when she saw that he was going to sleep instead of cuddle and love her. She listened to the waves flow back and forth in the same rhythm as her breathing. Why couldn't I just remember that rhythm while diving? The curling crash met the beach at the same moment Gina expelled a long breath. She practiced a couple of rounds, breathing in and breathing out in time with the ocean only yards away. It was a peaceful exercise for a few minutes, but then the nightmare returned.

She couldn't help but relive her panic in the deep water as she lay next to her husband in the pitch-dark room. She remembered hearing her gasping breath pound in her ears and what it felt like being surrounded by nothingness when the dizziness took over and unconsciousness replaced the panic. She would never, ever forget how close she had come to death. She would also never forget how disgusted Robert had seemed to be when the crisis was over and he sat with her at the hospital.

That was when Gina made her first adult decision. She needed to make some changes in her life. Fun, parties, men, and now an insensitive husband had been her priorities. Life was all about fun, doing whatever she felt like, when she felt like it. Now she thought she had nothing to offer anyone—that it wouldn't have mattered if she had died. Then she remembered the words on that card she was handed years ago in San Francisco: *I gave my life to become the person I am right now. Was it worth it?*

Gina fell asleep just as dawn presented another day.

Five days sooner than planned, Robert and Gina went home. During the long flight, both were quiet, rarely speaking unless necessary. When not deep in thought, Gina slept and watched movies. Robert slept, read, and slept some more.

❧❧❧

They'd known each other for three years and had been living together in Robert's Santa Monica apartment before getting married, which would continue to be their primary residence. Robert also conducted business in New York City and had told her he'd like to find a place there, too. Two weeks earlier on the way to Fiji they had talked non-stop about their future together. Gina couldn't wait to help Robert find their second home on the East coast. Now, on the return flight home, neither brought it up. Something was very wrong, and Gina was very aware of the mistake she had made by marrying Robert. Her chest still hurt from all that pressure on her lungs and the pounding to get her heart going. She had wanted to prove herself to Robert in spite of the terror she felt when jumping into the ocean. Berating herself, her thoughts wandered through the course of her life. She thought about her friendship with Carrie. Always doing whatever Carrie said just to be her friend, and now doing whatever her husband wanted. *I need counseling*, Gina thought, finally realizing she had a serious self-esteem issue.

Gina gave it another year with Robert. She tried at various times to defend herself and what she wanted to do, but in most cases, Robert would become impatient and imply that she was just another beautiful, but stupid, woman.

The last straw came on a Friday. She woke early to get to a photo shoot at the beach with her old friend (and secret fantasy)

Jake, and finish the work day at the gym. The plan was to meet Robert for an early dinner at Topper's Grill, their favorite restaurant in Venice. The reservation was for six-thirty. Cutting her workout short to allow time to shower and fix her makeup, she was entering the restaurant parking lot as her watch clicked over to the appointed time and her cell phone chirped.

It was Robert. "Hey, Sweetie. Guess where I am." His voice was light. He sounded giddy with happiness.

"I hope you're nearly here. Just pulled in and I'm starving."

"Nope! I'm not coming. I'm on the tarmac at LAX waiting to take off for Chicago."

"What! Are you kidding?" Waiting for more information, she let Robert continue.

"Sophie Rogers called this morning. The realtor, remember? She has a condo to show me and knows it won't be on the market for long. The owner's wife is gravely ill. He's desperate so it's priced to sell immediately. It's on Wacker Drive with a lake view and only blocks away from the fashion house." He waited for Gina to respond.

After a few seconds absorbing what he had just told her, she finally asked, "Since when are *we* looking for a condo in Chicago?"

"I've been thinking about it for a while, but didn't mention it since we've been looking in New York."

The conversation escalated into a screaming match. Gina was sitting in her car in the parking lot on a beautiful summer evening while Robert was on the real estate agency's private jet waiting for clearance to take off for Chicago.

"The point is not about what a great deal this is that we can't pass up, Robert. This is about you standing me up for dinner at the last minute and not even apologizing, let alone now filling me in that you've been thinking about a place in Chicago." Gina had never raised her voice to Robert before, but this was beyond rude. It was mean. Mean and selfish. Gina's eyes were wide open now. The reality of his lack of consideration for her and their marriage was pounded home.

"Done! I'm done! We have no marriage if you're going to make these decisions without me." Hanging up on him, Gina sobbed, tightly gripping the steering wheel of her new BMW.

❧❧❧

Three days later, a devastated Gina was curled up on the couch at her parent's home in Seattle holding a hot cup of coffee and watching the afternoon sun break through the clouds over the Sound. Her mother was in the kitchen. Happy to have her daughter home for awhile, all her mothering instincts had come to the forefront. It had been years since one of her children had been home for an extended stay. Ever since Gina had met and married Robert, she hadn't spent any time at home, not even for Christmas, when the entire family, even Antonella's family from Peru, would traditionally gather. Antonella wasn't surprised about the news when Gina called to announce she was leaving Robert. Antonella had never said it, but she didn't like Robert.

That night Gina's father arrived home from work with a message for Gina. "Carrie Jeffries called the office over the weekend and hopes you'll call her."

"That's amazing! I've been thinking about Carrie lately." Taking the slip of paper from her father that provided Carrie's number, Gina left the kitchen where she'd been helping her mother prepare dinner.

CHAPTER 13
GINA AND CARRIE

Gina dialed the number Carrie had left on her father's answering machine. It rang four times.

"This is Caroline Kendall. Please leave your number and a brief message. I will call you back as soon as possible."

Gina thought, *she's using her mother's maiden name*, then realized that Carrie wouldn't think of 'Kendall' so much as her mother's maiden name as it was her grandfather's last name. Continuing to speculate about what Carrie had been doing during the years they hadn't been in contact, Gina thought, *she must be running the company by now, that's why she's going by 'Kendall.'*

The message Gina left told Carrie how happy she was that she'd found her. That she was at her parents' house for a few days and left the number. She also left her cell phone number and signed off saying, "I hope we can connect soon, Carrie. Please call again."

That evening Gina's cell phone went off. She had kept it in the pocket of her cargo pants all evening.

Looking at the digital display, Gina recognized the caller's number. It was Robert. He had called a couple of times since she'd left their condo in Santa Monica but she hadn't called him back. His messages were the same. Robert didn't take rejection well. It was an insult to his massive ego—no one had ever dumped him, let alone a wife. All he could muster was, "Gina, we've got to discuss this like adults. Call me back." There was no apology or promise to change, and certainly nothing about loving and missing her.

"I think he just wants to discuss terms for divorce," Gina told her father. "What do you think, Dad?"

Like his wife, Tom Severns wasn't a fan of his son-in-law, but he wouldn't encourage his daughter to call a lawyer and get the divorce proceedings started. If Gina and Robert made up then he'd be remembered for having advised her to divorce, making it awkward whenever they all got together. After letting that thought ramble around his head for a few minutes, he decided the hell with it. So Tom told his beautiful daughter who was still so young and inexperienced to "dump the bastard. He's arrogant and rude to you and I don't like him. You shouldn't live in his shadow, always jumping when he says jump. That's not a marriage of love. He doesn't respect you. If he did you wouldn't have nearly died on your honeymoon."

"Oh Dad, let's forget the honeymoon trauma. That was my fault."

Whenever Gina blamed herself for nearly drowning in the middle of the South Pacific, Tom would go ballistic. Only Antonella could calm him down and lead him away from the subject. It rankled every part of his being and he would remind his wife that their daughter had always been afraid of deep water and yet her husband had forced her into a situation that nearly killed her.

"Dad," Gina tried again. "I don't know what to do. I love him, and isn't marriage supposed to be forever, like you and Mom?"

"Your mom and I are unfortunately the rare exception these days. We were blessed with a true, unconditional love for each other from the day we met. That just doesn't happen to people normally, and sadly, you are one of those unlucky people. Robert does not have your best interest in his heart, Gina, and you know it."

"Your dad's right," Antonella said, coming into the room carrying a tray of dessert. The pink hues of light from the setting sun bounced off the Olympic Mountains. The great room was darkening while they talked. Tom got up to light a fire to cozy-up the ambiance.

Setting the tray down on the thick rough-hewn plank of teak-wood that served as their coffee table, Antonella then turned on one lamp after another until they could see Gina's sad face. She continued. "We're not the norm, Gina. Everyone should experience the depth of our love, but you must be careful about choosing a husband. Robert was your first serious romance. He can be charming and is very handsome."

"But divorce!" Gina whined.

"Of course, it's up to you and Robert. But I can assure you, he won't change, and you may be in for a long life of sadness before you realize your mistake in marrying him."

"I do realize I made a mistake, that's why I left him. But what about our vows? I took them seriously."

"Search your heart, Gina. Don't make one mistake a bigger one by toughing it out. I hate to say it, but if you go back to him, I think that Robert will lose any remaining respect he may still have for you."

That was a stunning statement for Antonella to make and it sent Gina to her room in tears just like a little girl who's been chastised for some wrong-doing. While lying on her bed, noticing for the tenth time that her room hadn't changed since she first left home for college, her cell phone rang again. This time she didn't recognized the caller's number and answered with a tearful, "Hello?"

"Gina? Is that you? It's Carrie."

"Oh, Carrie! What perfect timing! I need a friend!" Gina gushed.

"What's wrong?"

The nine years since they'd last spoken fell away in the joy of finding a long-lost friend. The emotion nearly overwhelmed them both. After a few minutes of expressing how glad each was to be talking again, Carrie prodded Gina about why she had been crying when she answered the phone.

Gina caught Carrie up on what she'd been doing since college, then turned it over to Carrie to share what she'd been doing. When they hung up after a long talk, Gina left her room, found the chocolate cream puffs her mother had returned to the refrigerator, and went into the great room. Her mother and father were sitting side by side on the couch as usual, shoulders touching. She was reading. He was watching a football game.

When they saw their daughter smiling again, they smiled back at her and waited until she told them what was up.

"I'm going to San Francisco! Carrie called and we were on the phone for almost two hours. I'm going to visit with her for a few days and decide what to do about Robert."

Exchanging glances, Antonella and Tom appeared relieved. They were praying that Gina wouldn't go back to Robert, and hoped that maybe Carrie's objectivity would help Gina see the light.

When Gina left the room to do a load of laundry before packing, Tom voiced what he was thinking. "Carrie might just be the best thing for Gina right now."

Antonella nodded in agreement. Still smiling, she resumed reading and Tom turned the volume back up on the game.

CHAPTER 14

Carrie walked at her usual purposeful speed through the hallways of Kendall Tech and nearly collided with the person who had replaced Padma Singh on Baker's special project. Carrie stopped just in time as the boy rounded the corner. He kept going, darting around her at the last minute.

"Hey!" Carrie called.

He was already several yards away before turning down another hallway. Carrie had to shout, "Excuse me! Come back here."

Finally realizing that someone was calling after him, he walked back to an infuriated Carrie. He had no idea who she was, and certainly no clue that they had narrowly missed each other. Both had been in a hurry. He thought that was normal in the intense corporate environment. He had been hired right out of college and loved being on a cutting edge project that he wasn't supposed to talk about with anyone but his boss, Benton Swank, and company President Charles Baker. In fact, Baker had stopped by his work station three times since he started working there.

Carrie looked the young man over, judging him to be no older than twenty-two. He was pimply and had missed a couple of spots on his chin during that morning's attempt to shave the black fuzz sprouting in patches along his jaw line.

"What's your name?" Carrie demanded.

"I'm John Higgins, ma'am."

Oh geez, I'm not old enough to be called ma'am, Carrie thought, but she knew she looked older than twenty-seven. She intentionally dressed in dowdy, conservative suits and comported herself seriously.

"My name is Caroline Kendall. Does that name mean anything to you?"

It was noon and almost everyone was in the employee cafeteria, so they had the hallway to themselves.

"Are you related to the Kendall who owns the place?"

Carrie smiled at the squirmy little fellow. She wasn't much older than him, but towered over him. She used her height and attitude to her advantage.

"I *am* the Kendall who owns this place," Carrie answered.

"Wow! Sorry, ma'am! I thought Mr. Baker was the boss."

"Come with me, John. I want to talk with you." Carrie redirected him back to his cubicle. Checking again to see who was lingering in the area and seeing no one, she sat down in the extra chair jammed into the corner of the tight space while John took his seat at the computer station.

"How do you like it here? You just joined Kendall Technologies about eight weeks ago. Is that right?" she asked quietly.

"Yeah, it's great. I love my job and it will be seven weeks next Monday," John replied while scratching his palm. He was nervous talking with this intimidating woman. He was also hungry and needed to pee.

Carrie continued testing him to see how brainwashed he was about not talking to anyone about the project he was working on.

"So." Carrie amped up her smile and charm. "What are you working on?"

"I can't explain it, ma'am. You'll have to ask Mr. Swank."

"I own this company. You can tell me."

John was quiet, then said, "I'd be more comfortable if you would ask Mr. Swank or Mr. Baker about it."

"Well, you're a gutsy guy, John. Standing up to someone who could pull you off the project or worse, fire you."

"I was told that you might be asking, ma'am, and to let you know that Mr. Swank or Mr. Baker would be happy to explain it to you."

"Choose your friends carefully, John." Carrie sounded more threatening than she intended to, but continued, "This is the big-time now, and as a favor I'll warn you not to trust everyone so easily. I, on the other hand, can be trusted. I'm not going anywhere, but everyone else is expendable. Especially you." Carrie left John with his sweaty palms and now rapid heartbeat. She heard him murmur "Oh shit," after she stepped out of his cubicle.

The following week John found Carrie in her small, window-less office on the second floor of the building.

"Ms. Kendall?" John stepped in uninvited as Carrie looked up from what she had been writing in longhand. She rarely used her computer, knowing that nearly anyone working there could tap into her files. It was like locking a car before entrusting it to car thieves: pointless.

"Ms. Kendall, I'd like to fill you in on where I am so far on that project you were asking about."

"Close the door and sit down, John."

A few minutes later Carrie knew everything John knew, which disappointingly wasn't much. One week later Benton Swank fired the young man.

Word spread fast throughout the company that Carrie was poisonous to one's career at the company. The rumor was that anyone she befriended was fired—though in reality it had been only two people, Padma and John, who had coincidentally been working on the "special Baker project." But many of the employees didn't know that and avoided speaking with Carrie. That made Carrie's internship nearly impossible. No one volunteered information. Carrie had to think of every possible question to ask as she worked in each department. She could only hope that she had gained enough understanding about each job function before moving on. It was an awful feeling that fed her loneliness.

Baker had gotten the upper hand by having those she got close to fired. He relished the idea of discrediting her. He had effectively turned the entire company against her. Everyone was afraid they would be fired if they spoke privately with her. Even several of the board members were beginning to hear about some new problems at Kendall Tech, and Baker did what he could to encourage them to think that it was Carrie at the root of those problems.

It didn't really matter that Carrie was curious about the energy project that Padma and John had been working on. Charles would have told her all about it if the circumstances were different. But it was that curiosity that supported his plan for making a fool out of Carrie while protecting his position as president. At the same time, he was building up the energy project as secretive; an extraordinary idea—his idea—that would make huge amounts of money. Shareholders will not want Charles Baker to step aside for a young woman with no experience in running an international corporation. Carrie may fulfill her obligation according to her grandfather's will, but the board will need to agree on installing her as president.

When Carrie figured out that Baker was sabotaging her, she knew she had to do something to stop him. No one was going to keep her from her rightful place as president and CEO of her grandfather's company.

෴෴෴

At Carrie's invitation, Gina left her parent's home in Seattle to visit her friend in San Francisco. She was to stay in the guest suite of Carrie's Nob Hill condo. The last time the women had laid eyes on each other was before Gina ran away from home when she was sixteen. Carrie had been eighteen. To celebrate their reunion, Carrie treated Gina to dinner at the "Top of the Mark." They got dressed up and upon entering the elegant dining room with a fabulous view of the city, were immediately escorted to their table. It was obvious to Gina that Carrie was known here. She was greeted formally by name and a slight bow. Her favorite drink was placed in front of her while the waiter took Gina's order for a celebratory flute of champagne.

They reminisced and laughed over their childhood antics, then turned to Gina's current situation. After hearing the details of Gina's near-death trauma in Fiji and about Robert, Carrie made Gina's decision for her.

"Dump him," Carrie said. "You're too wonderful to be treated like that any time he doesn't agree with you. Chalk it up to a false start in the relationship department and relax. You'll have some fun finding some other hunk who will sweep you away. But next time be sure you're his priority in tough times, not just when you're having fun."

"Carrie, have you ever been in love?" Though Gina suspected she knew the answer, she asked it to gauge Carrie's interest in the possibility.

"No, I haven't. There have been a few guys, but no one that's come close to being someone to spend the rest of my life with, which is nearly unimaginable to me. I've spent my entire life focused on living up to my grandfather's legend and last wishes for me to take over Kendall Tech. That's what he wanted for me and I want it, too." It unnerved Carrie to think about not having someone in her life who loved her, and she quickly said, "Let's get back to you."

Understanding that discussing love in Carrie's life was an uncomfortable subject, Gina ventured to describe Jake and how they had first met in Beverly Hills.

"He was with Anne Hartford."

Carrie raised her eyebrows, "The actress?"

"Yeah. He was with her when we followed Anne into a shop on Rodeo Drive. He invited my college roommates and me to a party and that's where I first met Robert. Jake and Robert both had a hand in launching my career as a model. Now I'm busier than I'd like to be, though the jobs I'm getting are taking me all over the world and I love it."

"Since I left Robert, Jake has called three times to see how I'm doing and asked when I'll be back in Los Angeles. He knows everything about Robert and me, but he never said a word about his relationship with Anne. I guess that's fair. They did a good job avoiding the paparazzi. He's a great guy. A good friend."

It was obvious to anyone listening that Gina's feelings for Jake ran deep when she added, "He's dating someone else now." Gina trailed off.

"Does he know you're in love with him?" Carrie finally asked.

"Who? Robert?"

"Don't be dense," Carrie snapped, reminiscent of the way she sometimes spoke to Gina when they were kids. "You're in love with Jake. Does he know?"

"I fell for him at first sight but, no, Carrie. He's always been a good friend. That's all he'll ever be." Gina trailed off, saying more to herself than to Carrie, "Since he's not available, what's the use of dreaming?"

Carried countered, "Where's the fight in you, Gina? You always let something or someone direct your life. Isn't it time you took control and went after what you want?"

Gina, without realizing how wrong she was, defended herself by attacking Carrie. "Well, you were born with your life's path all laid out for you. You've never had to fight for anything."

Letting it drop for the moment, Carrie changed the subject. Their entrees were delivered by two formally dressed waiters. With exact precision, Carrie's filet mignon with béarnaise and wild mushrooms was placed in front of her as Gina received an equally beautiful presentation of steamed salmon and baby asparagus with no sauce or butter.

Carrie silently cut a small piece of steak and left it speared on the fork. The savory morsel lingering inches from her mouth, Carrie spoke. "Gina, first, you're wrong about my not having to fight for something. Second, I have a very special favor to ask of you."

Waiting for a response, Carrie took her first bite.

Gina's expression registered surprise, masking the suspicion she felt. As kids, Carrie could always get her to do anything, and it usually led to trouble. The silence hung between them while Gina sampled a small bite of her low-cal dinner befitting an in-demand model.

"Yeah?" was all Gina answered, and she waited for Carrie to explain.

"I need your help at Kendall Technologies. It's complicated, but you would be perfect. It shouldn't take too long."

"Well, you know I have a career that keeps me busy." Gina wasn't going to let Carrie talk her into anything that would compromise her current position at the La Vie Modeling Agency. Curious, though, Gina gave Carrie the reins for explaining by asking, "What's it all about?"

"I have about three years to go before taking over the company, if everything goes well. My problem is the current president, Charles Baker. As much as I hate to admit it, he's beginning to succeed in turning the board members and most of the employees against me."

"What good will that do him? Why doesn't he just play nice and maybe you'll make him VP of something?"

"He was threatened by me from my first day," Carrie continued. "And finally found a way to sabotage my credibility. That company is my life. It has been my life since I was six years old and it means everything to me. I've worked hard. I've been focused on nothing but meeting the requirements for my inheritance. It's my dream and an insignificant, insecure bore isn't going to ruin my life by turning everyone against me."

Carrie had Gina hooked. "What's he done and how could *I* possibly help?"

The waiters had checked on them twice since serving dinner to make sure everything was in order. Carrie waited until the dinner dishes were cleared, then ordered a sweet aperitif for dessert before going into detail about the years since her first day as an intern.

Gina sipped a Perrier with lemon. She asked, "What do you have in mind that would involve my help?"

Carrie smiled and said, "I want you to set up Baker. Integrity and moral dignity at Kendall are part of my grandfather's legacy. The board, to its credit, has upheld the professional and personal standards set more than sixty years ago. It's the foundation of the company. That and having vision and taking calculated risks. I want to take Baker out by maneuvering him into showing how low his moral standards are, and his lack of respect for the position he holds. I want to undermine him as he's done me in the eyes of the board. They have the authority to overrule my grandfather's will if they don't think I'm capable of handling the responsibility. I can't let that happen based on one idiot's insecurities.

"Baker will go for you, Gina. All you have to do is get him in, shall we say, an awkward situation at work. I'll hire you as my assistant, which means you won't have to do anything but show up and get him to try something with you—preferably in his office. His assistant Benita always knows what's going on."

"What do you think I am, Carrie? Why don't you hire an actress or a hooker?" Gina whispered vehemently.

"I thought it might be fun to play a role as seductress, Gina. If I remember correctly, you can be a great flirt. You're my only hope and I trust you. Plus, I haven't come up with any other way to discredit him. He's actually very good at what he does, but he started this nonsense."

"This is childish, Carrie. Why don't you go to the board chairman and explain what's going on?" Gina was insulted. Apparently Carrie still thought Gina would agree to be her patsy.

A final pass on offers of coffee concluded the meal. Attendants pulled out their chairs and helped the tight-lipped women on with their coats. Leaving the restaurant, at least thirty pairs of eyes followed Gina as she and Carrie wended their way around tables of well-dressed diners. Carrie overheard someone say, "That's an unbelievably beautiful woman." Knowing the comment wasn't about her, an old feeling of resentment that had been buried for years returned with a lump in her throat. Tears threatened before they reached the front door. Gina sensed Carrie's sadness before turning to see the grey eyes watering. The last thing her old friend would allow herself to do was cry in public.

Returning to Carrie's austere, spacious condo in one of the most expensive districts in San Francisco, Gina took over. Carrie hadn't said a word during the cab ride and continued her silence while hanging up her coat, kicking off her shoes, and flopping down on the contemporary white couch. Clutching a large striped pillow, one of ten judiciously placed around the room, Gina noticed the protective body language and dash of manipulation Carrie was exhibiting. Gina sat next to her friend and succumbed to Carrie's unconscious tactic to get her to do it.

"Look, Carrie, I could do it, I guess," Gina offered against her better judgment. "But I need to straighten out my own life as soon as possible. Let me get the paperwork going on the divorce, then I'll come back and help you out. But I want to think this through from all angles before meeting Mr. Baker."

Carrie indulged in another minute of pouting before accepting Gina's initial terms for taking down Charles Baker.

"While I'm in Los Angeles, though, please think about another way. I still don't think this is a good idea and it could backfire if anyone finds out you were behind the set-up. Then you'd really be out on your ass and what would you do then? Think about this carefully, Carrie."

"That company is my life, Gina. I have all the money I'll ever need, but I didn't earn it and I have nothing to show for it except a fancy degree and an expensive apartment. I want to prove that grandfather entrusted his company to the right person. He loved me. He's the only one in this world who did. I have no good friends except you. Frankly," Carrie confessed, "I've never admitted this to anyone before, but I can't shake this lonely feeling. That's what triggered my calling you this week. You were the only friend I had as a kid and I hope you'll be my friend now. I don't want to jeopardize that by dragging you into my problems at work. So if you reconsider, I'll understand."

The lump returned to Carrie's throat and this time the tears flowed freely. Gina was touched and took Carrie's hand. "I'm here, Carrie. I'm your friend and will help you through this. It must be terribly stressful to have to prove your worthiness to strangers even though on paper you own the company. It's an unusual situation."

Carrie managed a grin. Looking at Gina sitting so close made it difficult to ignore those damn blue eyes. She had always been jealous of Gina's great beauty compared to her own average appearance. Gina's compassion ran deep, making her a sucker for anyone in trouble. "Thanks, Gina. I don't mean to try to take advantage of your generous nature and I'm sorry for insulting you at dinner. I just didn't think it through. When it comes to business, that's my forte, looking at every angle, but this is personal. Baker is playing dirty. He wants me out and will do anything to keep his job."

Gina felt better now and secure in her friendship with Carrie. She said, "Let's think about what we need to do, but right now I would love a glass of wine and to watch a chick flick. Do you have any DVDs?"

Since she spent so much time alone on the weekends, Carrie had a full library of movies for Gina to choose from. She'd seen them all a couple of times and let Gina take her pick. Two hours later, slightly buzzed from the wine and happy that Meg Ryan had found true love with Tom Hanks in Seattle, the ladies said goodnight and went to bed.

Gina decided to leave the next day rather than stay a few days as originally planned. She was now eager to find a divorce lawyer and wriggle out of her bookings scheduled for the next three months. Her booking secretary at the agency wasn't happy, but acceded to Gina's pleading to clear her calendar without pissing off their clients.

CHAPTER 15
HANK AND DAVID

"Come on Dad!" TJ turned four years old today.

Hank was letting his boy beat him across the finish line identified by a stick ten yards from where the race started. It was a cool autumn day in Las Vegas. The grassy park was packed, with almost everyone from the neighborhood enjoying the great outdoors in the city after four months of hellish heat.

Althea was back at the house, exhausted from the work required to pull off, according to TJ at the end of the day, "The best birthday!"

However, their days together were numbered. Hank had told them he had business in New York and that he would be leaving the day after TJ's birthday. Spending every minute with his son until taking a cab to McCarran was crucial for Hank. He would miss his little boy, but the decision was made and arrangements were confirmed to visit David and see what opportunities New York would hold. He didn't want to back out. It had been a dangerous situation sitting in front of Jimmie, the little man in charge of Hank's drug supply chain with the numbers one and two "elves" sitting behind him, telling them he'd be out of town for a few days. Hank didn't know which one of the two had killed Shanti, but either would kill him in a minute if their boss snapped his fingers.

The plan was set. David told Hank to take a cab from LaGuardia to the Marriott in Times Square and that he'd meet him in the lobby for dinner at eight o'clock. "It will be good to see you, man. I have some fun scheduled."

"That's great, David." Hank had never told David that he was married and had a son. After Shanti's death, they hadn't spoken much before David was told to pack up the Las Vegas project and focus on the New York City plan. David left Las Vegas, Lindsey and his sons in the course of a month, and set up house in a leased apartment on the Upper East Side, known for its prestigious proximity to Central Park

Finding each other in the crowded lobby, the men shook hands and agreed to walk the few blocks to Maggiano's for beer and pizza.

"It's not Bellagio room service, but it's damn good," said David as they entered the low lit room with booths positioned in a semi-circle around a stage.

"Good what?" asked Hank, noting the dance poles and cages positioned on a riser behind them. "Pizza?"

"I wanted you to feel right at home on your first night in a new city. This is your first time out of Las Vegas, right?"

"Yeah, actually, it is. It's tough leaving town in my line of work."

"I'll bet," David answered. "Did you bring anything with you?"

"Sure. I'm that foolish," Hank replied sarcastically. "What did you think I'd do with it? Stuff it in my shoe? No, I asked around for a phone number in Manhattan. I'll call tonight."

"Call it now. So we can keep things interesting later on with the ladies."

"Ladies?" Hank asked. "What's the plan?"

"Two beauties who you'll meet after their show. You can pick the one you want. I happen to know that both are very talented and you'll be happy either way." David was leering as the tall slender waitress in a black body suit walked up to take their order.

Hank tried to explain his attempt at turning his life around. "I'm trying to settle down a little, David. You know, after Shanti got killed I don't have the appetite for hookers, and that last night on coke was my last night on coke, if you know what I mean."

"First, though paid, Shanti was not a hooker. Let's keep that straight. Second, I miss her. Guess I loved her and I'll probably never know what happened, but I hope whoever killed her gets what they deserve. Third, life goes on. You can't let our last night in Vegas change your whole life."

"Yeah, I can, and it did. I'm trying to change, though it's nearly impossible. It's been the hard way all my life and I have to find a way out."

"So are you telling me you're not gonna set me up tonight to reciprocate what I've got lined up for you? A little tat-for-tit?" David laughed at his crude humor, then smiled up at the girl putting down an extra-large loaded pizza and two more beers.

The dining room was full of men. Slinky young women flowed out of the kitchen doors nearly non-stop, carrying platters of food and bottles of beer. The music changed and the lights dimmed: the signal for the show to begin. The beat was slow at first, while David and Hank kept their eyes glued on the stage and a long satin-finished leg was presented from behind the curtain on each side of the stage followed by the rest of two voluptuous bodies. Hank succumbed to their charming features and watched, trying to decide which of them he would have for the night. Courtesy of David.

An hour later, now a foursome, the group left Maggiano's and walked toward Times Square to find somewhere to dance. They were huddled together over drinks when David raised his eyebrows at Hank. Hank knew the signal and excused himself.

Finding it quieter for making a phone call outside the bar on the busy sidewalk, Hank called the number he'd been given in Las Vegas. A few minutes later they were set and would expect a package to be delivered to Hank at the Marriott at midnight. It was the same routine Hank knew so well. Different faces, different city, same deal.

For five days David met Hank for dinner after the day's meetings and political standoffs with city planners. But David was good at what he did, and made a show of keeping things moving at work while getting only a few hours of sleep each night. He was single and free and making the most of Hank's visit.

During the day, while David worked, Hank saw the city sights with Beverly, the blonde of choice who turned out to be an intelligent companion. A native New Yorker, she showed Hank every worthwhile nook and cranny of her home city. By eight o'clock each evening, they would meet David and his lady friend, who was usually Beverly's dance partner, for dinner and discuss what to do for entertainment.

Two days before Hank was due to leave, David began pressuring him for the supplier's number. It was forbidden, a policy among "professionals" to never share connection information with a customer. Hank fought David about it.

"Giving you that number could get me killed!" Hank spewed. "Don't you get it? This isn't a game. We make a lot of money doing what we do and protecting our sources is part of why the system works. I can't do it."

"You're leaving in two days, Hank. The guy I knew got busted. How am I going to keep up my lifestyle? It's been keeping me going at work and chasing the blues away about Lindsey and the kids."

"Since when are you broken up about your family, David? I never heard you say the names of the boys. It's always, 'the kids.' Do you ever see them? How old are they?"

Hank pushed David to consider his absenteeism as a father. He missed TJ and didn't understand how David could be so cavalier about losing his sons. That subject would shut David down and keep him from badgering Hank for a phone number.

But, as much as Hank had talked about changing, his resolve slipped on his last night in New York. David, Hank, Beverly, and this time her friend, Sharon, were up all night jumping from one dance club to the next. Cocaine kept them invigorated and whisky shots made them sappy and maudlin about their lives. It was a long night of loud laughter and insensitive digs at the strangers seated at nearby tables. The boisterous group got kicked out of two bars that night. Around four a.m., they collapsed in Hank's room. Three on the king bed, while David lay on the floor with two pillows, oblivious to any physical discomfort.

By eleven that morning, the girls had left and Hank was trying to rouse David. He would miss his flight home if he didn't leave soon.

David was still out. Snoring loudly, stinking of whisky and sweat from dancing. Hank kicked him awake. "Wake up, man! Housekeeping is going to find you where I leave you if you don't move."

David rolled over on his back and painfully opened his eyes. He managed a few words. "Shit. What time is it?"

"It's eleven o'clock. I've been trying to wake you up for ten minutes. I gotta go." Hank was packed and dressed. His suitcase was at the door.

"Shit," David said again. "Where's the phone? I missed a meeting."

Disgusted, Hank said, "David, get up and find your phone. I've got to go. I'll call you next week."

David slowly pushed himself up and tried to grab the bed covers for help. Falling back to the floor, the blankets billowed down on top of him. He instantly fell asleep again until the maid slammed the door closed after calling security to make sure the guy on the floor wasn't dead.

CHAPTER 16

Hank saw it all again in his mind while staring out the window 35,000 feet above the flat fields of harvested corn or hay or whatever it was that created hundreds of geometric patterns across thousands of acres below. He relived that night in Las Vegas nearly two years ago. The last night with David and Shanti. His fight with Shanti. David falling over the glass coffee table. Him abducting and raping Shanti. Then, catching a terrified Shanti as she fell. Her blood-soaked body finding peace in his arms. The vivid nightmare caused Hank's own body to react. His heart began a rapid beating and his palms and forehead got sweaty. Hank didn't realize the person next to him, stuck in the middle seat with nowhere to go, had noticed his discomfort.

"Are you nervous about flying?" she asked softly.

"No. No, ma'am. Thanks for asking," Hank replied, then turned to face the window again, shutting off further conversation.

Back in his reverie, Hank also relived the night TJ was born. Seeing his son for the first time had caused an instant and absolute love. A sensation so pure and completely happy. An unconditional love that Hank had never experienced. His love initially for Althea had been great and he had been committed to her. But over the years, she had proved repeatedly that money was her first love. He was simply the means for living a comfortable life without having to work for it herself. It made Hank incredibly sad when he first realized that his wife didn't love him. Until TJ came along, he hadn't had anything to compare his feelings to. He'd thought he was in love with Althea when he first met her way back in high school. He was glad when he met up with her again years later and happy that she had proposed to him. But those feelings for Althea were nothing compared to what his heart held for his little son. His TJ. His ray of sun and hope and dreams for a good life. A life that would take him away from a dangerous business. That business, though, had helped Hank keep his vow to provide for his family, and if that meant living with Althea's selfishness, then so be it. She was cheating on him and for the first time, he'd just cheated on her in New York.

We can figure this out, Hank thought optimistically. *If it means taking two or three legitimate jobs and giving up the drug deals, then I will.*

During the four-hour flight home, Hank's introspection renewed his promise to his son and wife. He would change and for the first time he could imagine a happy, productive, normal life raising a son and loving his wife. Hank couldn't wait to see them again.

Waiting to exit his row on the plane, Hank finally smiled at the woman who had sat quietly next to him for so long. "I'm going to see my family," he told her as she moved into the aisle and pulled her carry-on from the overhead bin.

Smiling back, she said, "That's wonderful! Are they meeting you?"

"Yeah! I missed them more than I thought. I guess I'm excited." Hank drew a few "aaawws" and "that's so great" from others on the plane also waiting to exit who had overheard the tall, handsome, well-dressed man proclaim his love for his family.

One young woman even asked half-jokingly, "Do you have a brother?" Then she whispered to her friend, "What a catch! Why haven't we met someone like him?"

Hank found his suitcase on the carousel and looked around for Althea and TJ just outside of baggage claim. But Althea wasn't there.

Twenty minutes later he got through to her on her cell phone.

An exasperated Althea told him, "I left you a message, Hank. I guess your phone was turned off."

"Well, of course it was turned off, Althea. That's the law when flying. All cell phones must be turned off. Where are you?"

"I can't pick you up. Why didn't you just jump in a cab like I suggested in my message?"

Noting that no explanation was offered, Hank pursued the challenge. All the excitement and good feelings from his contemplation and renewed commitment to creating happiness for his family disappeared.

"Why aren't you here? What's more important than picking me up?"

"Never mind. I can't control the world and you should learn that, too. I'm just leaving my appointment now. We were running late."

While walking over to join the eternal line of people waiting for a cab, Hank asked, "Where's TJ? I can't wait to see him and I have presents for you both."

"Oh! Presents? That's so sweet!" Althea now gushed. "I'll pick him up on my way home. I'll see you there in about two hours."

"Two hours!"

Althea had hung up. Hank looked at the phone in his hand with disbelief. Shouldering his overnight bag and dragging his suitcase, he moved up in line another two feet. It was going to be a long wait for a taxi, but somehow he knew he would beat Althea home.

He was right. Two and a half hours later Althea walked through the front door behind a boy supercharged and running full tilt toward his father's outstretched arms.

"Daddy!"

"Hey champ! How's my best buddy?"

TJ launched into a detailed account of what happened every day while Hank had been gone. He explained what he did all week from morning to bedtime while Hank couldn't take his eyes off the young version of himself. *He looks like me*, Hank thought. *He's going to grow up looking a lot like me.* While the chatter continued, Hank took his hand and led TJ to the suitcase he'd been unpacking in the master bedroom. Pulling out a bag, Hank also fished out a small blue box and handed it to Althea. Then he handed the bag to TJ. "I brought you something. 'Cuz I missed you so much and am sorry I was gone so long."

TJ gave his father a look of love and wrapped his arms around the broad shoulders. "I love you, Daddy. Don't ever go away again. Okay?"

That about did Hank in. Hank held TJ tight. "Not if I can ever help it, buddy. I love you, too."

Althea shooed TJ off to wash his hands before dinner, then opened the light blue box from Tiffany's. Lifting out the 24-carat gold charm bracelet with a diamond dangling from every other link she smiled up at him and gave him a quick kiss.

Rubbing the trace of dark red lipstick off Hank's cheek, she said, "Thanks, Hank. Are you hungry?"

Hank had no idea if she liked it or not. It wasn't fair to compare TJ's exuberant reaction to the transformer toy that turned the Empire State building into a gorilla, to a more reserved appreciation for a very expensive gift. Yet, he had hoped for a little more excitement over the bracelet. *Maybe it's karmic payback since Beverly had helped pick it out*, he thought.

"I'll go wash up and see how TJ likes his toy. Call us when it's time to eat."

"PULEESE," Althea said, standing with both hands on her hips. "You can at least say 'p*lease* call me when it's time to eat'. I'm not the maid."

Hank repeated the word 'please' and even called her 'honey,' then left the room to find TJ.

He thought getting along with Althea would be easier if he could just get past the fact that she took him for granted. They'd been married for eight years and she still hadn't asked him about his work or appeared worried that it could be dangerous. *As long as the money keeps coming in, I guess that's what makes her happy*, Hank realized for the hundredth time.

That night they ate dinner together for the first time in years. Sitting between them, TJ took Hank's right hand and Althea's left hand in his own and made them hold hands like a three-way shake.

"Let's promise to play all day tomorrow!" TJ said emphatically. Meaning he wanted Hank and Althea to be happy too.

"I'll be here, TJ. How about the water park?"

"I won't be," Althea interrupted. She'd been quiet during dinner while TJ and Hank laughed and discussed their favorite cartoon characters.

Hank turned to Althea and asked, "What's going on tomorrow?"

Althea was silent while Hank and TJ ganged up on her to cancel her plans so they could all be together.

Althea went along for the ride the following day, but didn't engage in the activities. She sat on the grass watching the boys play catch and chase. She read, sent text messages, and made phone calls. After waiting for them to return from a short bike ride, TJ said he was ready to eat at his favorite buffet.

After lunch, Hank dropped off a tired boy and tense wife at home, then left to meet with his supplier, followed by a five-hour shift at the casino. He dealt cards until two a.m. and climbed into bed at three o'clock. He made love to Althea, but it felt different—empty and mechanical.

Althea woke Hank up at seven o'clock the next morning.

Hank groaned awake. "I could have used a couple hours sleep, Althea."

Ignoring the complaint, Althea sat on the bed and handed him a cup of coffee. "Hank, I have to go. I have a hair cut scheduled, then a massage. Then…"

TJ bounded in and jumped on the bed, upsetting the coffee in Hank's cup.

"Watch it, stupid!" Althea screamed. "Those are expensive sheets. Coffee stains don't come out. Can't you—?"

"Don't talk to him that way!" Hank thundered, now fully awake.

"TJ. Go back to your room. I want to talk to Hank alone. Go on!"

TJ quickly did as he was told—willingly, to avoid getting hit.

Althea was standing in the middle of the room now, watching her son run down the hall to the safety of his own bedroom. Hank put his coffee cup down on the nightstand and swung his legs off the bed. He was head and shoulders taller than Althea and looked down at her with new eyes.

"What's wrong with you? Don't you ever call TJ 'stupid' again," he said.

Althea looked Hank up and down, mentally registering the strong, finely-toned physique and said, "Put some clothes on. I have something to say."

"Althea," Hank tried to call her back. She left him wondering what the hell had just happened. He was stunned that Althea could treat their little boy like that and now wondered whether worse things had happened when he was gone.

Coming out of the bedroom, Hank found Althea in the kitchen slamming a cupboard door.

"We're out of Goddamn sugar!" Althea ranted. "I can't drink this crap without it."

"Where's TJ? Do you want me to take him to school?" Hank asked, cutting her off before she could continue bitching as if it were his fault about the coffee and being out of sugar.

"He's in his room. I told him to stay there."

"What's going on, Althea? Why are you so pissed off? He's just a kid. A great kid, in fact."

"It's not him. It's you, Hank. I need something more and you ain't it."

"What the hell are you talking about? I give you everything I can without going bankrupt!"

"I'm going now, Hank. I've got things to do." Althea replied.

"What? Another facial? Manicure? More clothes? What is it that you're not getting?'

"Yeah, well unfortunately, you are not the man I thought you were."

"And what's that? You thought I was, how did you put it when I came back to you with an engagement ring worth ten times our monthly rent, oh yeah…'momma, I'm gonna marry a rich man.' I let that slide b'cuz I've always loved you, Althea. And you've given me the greatest thing anyone could, a son. Our beautiful kid." Hank tried to continue, not wanting to hear what he feared Althea was about to say, but Althea stopped him.

"I have plans, Hank. I met someone. Someone with normal working hours."

What Althea didn't say was that her lover was a wealthy casino owner with guaranteed front row seat tickets for any show in town, unlimited cash flow, and a staff at his house that cleaned up after every lustful afternoon and wild party Althea had managed to sneak off to.

The news didn't surprise Hank and he didn't try to stop her, but it tore at his soul to see his son's face when she said goodbye a few minutes later. Before leaving, she told TJ that it was his daddy's turn to take care of him now, and that she was going to live somewhere else. She was walking out on her little boy. It was heartless and gut-wrenching.

They watched Althea walk out of their ground-floor apartment pulling her large Louis Vuitton suitcase over the threshold. She punctuated her departure by firmly slamming the front door behind her. Holding TJ's tense little body tight, all Hank could say was, "It will be okay buddy. You'll see. I know it hurts now, but it will be okay." Sitting side by side on the couch, they silently listened to the sound of Althea's car start up, roll out of the garage, back out into the street, and fade away down the block.

TJ's tears were dammed by grim determination. That worried Hank. *He should be crying*, Hank thought. But he recognized the resolve on his son's face not to cry, not to scream or react in any way, but to hold the pain inside, just as he himself had done all his life.

"TJ, I don't know why your mother did this, but I do know that she loves you very much. It's just that she stopped loving me, I guess, and found someone else to take care of her."

"How could she not love you, dad?"

Hank was impressed that his son would think of him first rather than indulge in his own confusion and sadness. "You are amazing, TJ. Don't ever let this take you down. I mean it, buddy. This has nothing to do with you."

"No, daddy! I made her mad and she left!"

Hank wasn't good at this and tried to come up with something that would assuage his heartbroken baby. TJ was taking all the responsibility for Althea's departure.

"Oh no, TJ. You're a smart fellow, but this time you are wrong. You did not make this happen." Hank was firm but kept his voice low. He didn't want TJ to think he was mad at him too. "But it's up to us to make the best of this situation. We decide what to do next. We can decide to love her anyway."

"I think she's gonna be gone forever," TJ whispered.

"You'll see her soon, when she realizes how much she misses you." Hank realized he was lying. Something he didn't want to do, but was at a loss for words. He had no idea how to comfort TJ.

TJ was staring straight ahead, kicking the edge of the couch with the heels of his black and white high-tops.

"So it's you and me. I'm taking the night off and we'll do anything you want today."

"I want to do nothin'."

Letting TJ take some time alone to absorb the shock, Hank went to the bedroom and called Althea's mother.

"Did you know this was going to happen? Did you know she planned to leave us?" Hank demanded of his mother-in-law.

"No! I didn't. Honest! How's TJ?" June answered.

"How do you think TJ is? His mother just walked out on him without looking back. No kiss goodbye. Nothing. She told him it was my turn to take care of him now, as if I haven't been around at all. As if he was a burden. I've been here as much as possible while trying to make enough money to keep her happy. She'll never be happy. There will never be enough money for her. It's all she cares about."

"I know she likes the money, Hank. Who doesn't? But I didn't think she'd leave TJ."

"I'm going to need some help, Junie. Can you stay with him while I'm working?"

Junie, as Hank always called his mother-in-law, told him she would gladly be with her grandson any time. She loved him too, and was angry with her daughter. Hanging up, Hank went to TJ's room, where the boy was sitting on his bed bending the new trans-former toy from New York into unreasonable positions, nearly breaking it. Anger was very close to the surface and Hank felt it. Not knowing what to do or how to deal with the emotions—his own and TJ's—he considered calling a child psychologist.

The week after Althea's sudden departure was rough for everyone as they settled in to a different set of circumstances. No one heard from Althea. Not her mother, sisters, friends, Hank, or even TJ. She had simply vanished. After a month of running back and forth between homes, Hank suggested to his mother-in-law that she move in with them.

"You're wonderful, Junie. TJ loves you and I can certainly keep up the pace of working and caring for TJ in the afternoons but…"

"It's okay, Hank. I'll do it. No need to go on and on asking. I'll do it because I love my grandson and feel some responsibility for my low-life daughter. I wish I could get my hands on her to give her a whupping."

June rented her condo and did everything she could to make a good home for TJ while Hank worked every night of the week. He had quit the casino job to make more money than usual dealing drugs during the summer following Althea's disappear-ance. Everyone kept their hopes up that she would at least call her mother or sisters one day.

CHAPTER 17

One morning while sitting at Althea's desk, Hank looked through old bills, their checkbook, and credit card statements. It appeared that Althea knew exactly what he did for a living and what he had done in New York. There was a summary report dated June 10, 2009, from a private investigator that included his whereabouts and who he was with every night during his week with David. *Not good*, Hank thought, when he opened the envelope. *Althea wanted me to find this. She knew I'd been cheating on her and never said a word. That's why she left.*

Hank called the only friend he felt he had and confessed the circumstances. "…except that she was cheating on me *before* I went to New York."

"I wonder if that made it okay in her mind to leave you, or if your sordid ways caused her to find her own fun. Take it from me," David added, "Ya just never know with women."

"It was the only time, David. I've always been faithful to Althea." Hank couldn't believe he'd just said that as images of raping Shanti cut through his words. But he continued, "I think now, we were doomed from the beginning. I knew she just wanted to be with a rich man, but I have to take responsibility for this."

"Hank, what mother would leave her son like that? Don't take on the guilt. She wanted freedom not just from you, but total freedom to run off with the first millionaire that looked at her. She made a choice and now has to live with it. Was she good-looking enough to be a rich man's trophy wife? Sorry man, that's rude, but it might be when this guy gets tired of her she'll be back on your doorstep begging forgiveness and asking for her son back.

My advice is that you call a lawyer and do whatever it takes to get full custody."

"That's not a good idea. She had a PI trail me, us, in New York. What we did could come to light."

"And the case against her is called abandonment," David reasoned.

Nothing came of David's advice. Hank wouldn't risk anyone else knowing about how he made most of his money. He still thought about getting out of the business, but considered himself completely stuck in the world of dangerous drug deals. He had tried the straight and narrow route by working double shifts at the casino but it just didn't pay enough. The lure of making thousands of dollars a week was too great and kept Althea quiet.

But she's gone now. How much do I really need? Hank thought. *We could move somewhere, maybe California. Maybe it's not just Althea who has her freedom now. I can do whatever I want as long as I have TJ with me. But what kind of work could a guy raised on the streets of Las Vegas do*?

Finding a photo in another drawer of Althea's desk, Hank recognized the man standing next to his wife among a group of others posing together at a party. *Could that be the guy*? Hank wondered.

It didn't matter. It was Dan Ramsey. Hank knew him as a greasy multi-millionaire with a drug problem and a string of hotels and casinos all over the world. Hank had a lucrative connection at his hotel on the strip and he suspected the bulk of the business came from the hotel owner himself. *If that's who Althea ran off with, it will be a short-lived affair*, Hank thought.

࿇ ࿇ ࿇

Hank devoted every possible daytime hour to TJ and half the night to making money. When finding a rare minute to think about his next move, Hank would pray. He didn't know how or when the choice to turn to God for help came about, but making a better life for his son was the goal. Extricating himself from the drug world was what held him back. He took greater risks to make more money, to save up for a significant change. The first decision was to move to California. Preferably to a small, friendly town where TJ could make new friends at a good school.

It was going on eight months and there was still no word from Althea. Hank told Junie his plan and that it would take about a year to save up enough to move them into a comfortable home in the more expensive state.

"I'm taking TJ for a short trip to California and will start scouting around. Come with us, Junie. I'd like your opinion." Though he had no intention of letting her decide where they would live, Hank dangled the compliment in hopes that it would persuade her to go with them. The apartment in Las Vegas was two thousand square feet with three bedroom suites and a common pool area. It was nice. He wasn't sure that he could replicate it wherever they moved, but Hank knew he'd never break away from the lifetime of memories and dangerous nightlife if he didn't get out soon. He had no friends, wisely keeping his on-the-job acquaintances at a distance. David was the only one Hank had finally told about TJ and being married. He hoped no one in Las Vegas paid any attention to his personal life.

When TJ was told he was going on a trip, he ran to his room and pulled out his favorite T-shirt, his best sneakers, a pair of jeans, shorts, and two pairs of socks and underwear. After shoving his clothes and toothbrush into a plastic shopping bag, he was ready to go. Five days later, Junie dropped Hank and TJ off at the airport and they flew to Los Angeles. The warm sunny day was unusually clear. Hank rented a red two-seater convertible. He threw their bags in the tiny trunk and headed north. They drove until Hank couldn't drive any longer, logging about three hours. They found a motel in Santa Barbara and slept off the excitement of the first day on the road.

"I like it here," TJ managed to mumble the next morning between bites of IHOP pancakes smothered in sticky strawberry syrup and whipped cream. "I like the ocean. Can we go swimming? I brought shorts."

"Whatever you say, TJ. We have about two weeks to do everything we want and see as much as possible. We can go back to the motel when you're finished pigging out, pack up, and find a beach on our way out of town." Hank hadn't seen TJ smile in months. He had missed his son's froggy-voiced giggle since Althea left. *Whatever comes out of this trip, it was a good idea to bring TJ along,* thought Hank. *I guess this time, I didn't screw up.*

❧❧❧

Back in Las Vegas, things weren't going as well. The headline news was all about a major drug bust at the Gold Dust Hotel involving Daniel James Ramsey. Ramsey lost his temper one night when a high roller began winning far too much. When he was accused of cheating, the gambler called for the man in charge. Upon seeing Ramsey, he returned the accusation of cheating and called the hotel a drug pit for junkies. Ramsey had just snorted so much coke that his eyes rolled around as he tried to focus on his hotel guest. Finally making a lunge at the gambler, he tripped over the leg of a chair at a crowded blackjack table. Easily dodging the advances, the customer started laughing at how ridiculous his attacker was. Camera flashes started going off while security tried to get their boss under control. The police responded to a 911 call, and ten minutes later both men were escorted to Ramsey's office, where a residue of white powder dusted the cherry wood coffee table.

Ramsey was booked that night. The hotel's manager comped the guest's room and meals for the week he'd been with them, and issued a public apology. A close-up photo of Ramsey uselessly swinging a fist at the man who had originally been accused of counting cards took up half the front page of the next day's newspaper. It also captured the man laughing at Ramsey in ridicule.

Her boyfriend's public altercation flushed Althea out of hiding from her family. She called her mother the next morning and begged to know where to find Hank.

"You made your bed, missy. You left your husband and son for a slimy man as selfish as yourself. You deserve whatever comes your way. Now leave Hank and TJ alone. I hate to say this to my own daughter, but they're better off without you."

A half hour later, Althea showed up at Hank's apartment. Her mother opened the front door. "How long have you been living here, Mom? What's going on?"

"It's none of your business. I'm helping Hank out while he's working, that's all. It's easier to live under the same roof instead of driving back and forth to my condo. But I don't owe you an explanation. Just leave! I can barely stand the sight of you. You look awful, by the way. Are you a druggie, too?"

"I have no money of my own. Dan paid for everything I charged to his credit cards. His accounts have been frozen since he made bail, but he don't want to see me anymore. He told me last week that he was done with me. I just persuaded him to let me stay at the hotel until I could figure out what to do."

Althea wormed her way back into her mother's heart, but not completely. June didn't tell her that Hank was planning to move to California with TJ.

"Call your sisters. Maybe one of them will take you in. Though you don't deserve any kindness after dumping us all for almost a year. I was worried sick about you."

"I'm sorry, Momma. I couldn't take the chance that Hank would come after me and ruin what I thought I had with Dan. He was so good to me at first. But then he started seeing a waitress in one of the bars and I found out. We fought all the time after that. But I was sure if Hank showed up that Dan would get really angry. I thought I was protecting Hank. Besides, Hank was no angel. Did you know he was cheating on me?"

"That's not my concern. I won't discuss it. Hank is a good dad and he's taking good care of my grandson. No thanks to you. Go call your sisters. Maybe they'll give you pity. Get out of here."

After Althea left, June sat down and cried until she was too exhausted to move. It was the hardest thing she'd ever done, talking to her firstborn like that. She thought about what to do next, then picked up the phone and dialed Hank's cell number.

∾∾∾

Hank and TJ had found a ranch just north of Monterey Bay. It was a bed and breakfast with hiking trails through the redwoods.

"This is the best day of my life!" TJ said over and over as they waded across a shallow stream and up a little hill. They broke out of the woods into the warm, cloudless day to stand on a grassy knoll. Miles away, but with a clear view, they gazed at the glorious blue Monterey Bay National Marine Sanctuary rimmed by white sand beaches. Hank picked TJ up and kissed his curly head. They could see tiny sailboats carving their way through the sprinkling of whitecaps. The breeze on the hill ruffled the tall grass and all they could hear was a quiet shushing sound.

TJ's fingers found Hank's ear and he tugged on the lobe.

"I love you, daddy."

Hank held his son in both arms for a big hug. He couldn't say a word.

Back in their room after the hike, TJ ran around shouting, "Daddy, stop! Stop! I—" TJ was laughing so hard he nearly peed his pants and ran into the bathroom for quick relief.

As TJ closed the bathroom door, Hank's phone rang. Calling out to his son Hank yelled, "You better rest up in there for a rematch…hello?"

"Hank, it's June. Althea's back."

Closing his phone seconds before TJ returned, Hank's expression was very different and TJ noticed.

"What's wrong?" the perceptive little boy asked. He sat down on the bed next to his father.

"Nothing son. It's not important right now, but I promise I'll tell you later."

TJ took up his father's hand and pressed it to his soft little cheek and said again, "This is the best day of my life."

"I love you, buddy. And guess what! This is the best day of my life, too."

CHAPTER 18

"David, let's meet for lunch today at noon. I want to catch up on the next steps for the condos on Thirty-fourth." Jack Thompson, David's boss, had been out of the country for two months, checking up on the Hong Kong office and taking some time off to vacation in Macau. Word had gotten back to him, however, that David had missed an important meeting with the owner of a building Heritage Global Development had been trying to buy for over a year. Negotiations had finally opened up again and it was to have been the first meeting between the owner, David, and HGD's legal team. Everyone was optimistic that the time had come to move forward. Timing was crucial, as interest rates were fluctuating and the lawyers wanted to lock up the terms. They all needed to convince the owner that it was the right time to sell, as well. But David was not at the meeting that day. He was expected to lead the negotiation. The owner waited for thirty minutes, while David's colleagues tried to reach him. They even called his ex-wife. They were desperate.

David knew he had blown an important deal and wondered why Jack hadn't discussed it with him. Though he'd made every effort to make amends with the building owner, his calls were never returned. It was a dead deal. His excuse to his boss was ready and David had waited and hoped that his mistake had been buried. There were other projects everyone was involved in, and David assumed they were too busy to take one mistake seriously.

A day later it hit the fan.

"David, thanks for joining me on short notice. I know you have a lot of irons in the fire." Jack was a gracious man, but shrewd.

It was a known fact throughout the company not to take him at face value. David was nervous and dying for a whiskey over ice with a lemon twist but thought better of it and ordered iced tea with his smoked salmon panini. His hand shook slightly when he lifted his glass, making the ice rattle, which caught Jack's eye.

"Relax, David." Jack began playing with his prey. "Let's just talk about how things are going in New York. I want to make sure we exceed our numbers this year. Shutting down the Las Vegas project last year helped, but the condos on Thirty-fourth Street will be our salvation. What do you think? Will we lease every unit within a year after the renovations are complete? I'm very excited about the potential. If it goes according to projection, you can be sure we'll discuss involving you on something in Asia."

It was David's dream Jack was talking about. Moving into the Asian market. He had wanted that since he joined HGD just over eight years ago.

"David? So tell me. What's going on?"

Something about the way Jack smiled when he posed the question made David realize that Jack knew exactly what was going on. And that the answer was "nothing."

Stammering slightly, David was trying to remember his excuse for missing the meeting when two men walked up to their table. "Hey Jack. You're back in town! How was Macau?"

While Jack answered their questions and made a golf date when they would all be in Palm Springs the following week, David tried to think of something to say. He was given a five-minute reprieve from answering Jack's question, but wasted it, thinking, *Surely, I can think of something other than how much I need a drink.*

Jack introduced David as an afterthought, and then said, "Ciao," to his golf buddies. Leaning back in his chair, pushing his empty plate aside, Jack waited to pounce, drumming his fingers on the white linen tablecloth, watching David closely. A full minute ticked by. Jack waited for an answer to his earlier question with a calculating expression on his angular young face. He clearly enjoyed his power and pretended to wait out David's silence.

When David broke the tension, he railed. "Oh cut the crap, Jack. You know I screwed up, so stop trying to corner me, pretending you didn't hear about the meeting with Schuster. I didn't show because I was too sick. I'd had a bad night and slept through the alarm. The maid woke me coming in to make up the room. I actually considered going to the hospital the night before, but—"

"Don't accuse *me* of pretense, David. You're lying. You have a problem with booze. Everyone knows it and rumors are that you're into coke too. It's obvious. You screwed up in Las Vegas and now you're screwing up in New York. We can't afford these problems. Out of loyalty to a long-time employee, I want you to check in to rehab and clean up before you kill yourself. If you can do that, I might think about keeping you on at HGD in some capacity. But starting today, you're no longer the VP of project development for North America. In fact, as of now, you're off the payroll."

Jack left a stunned David sitting at the table alone. He settled the check at the maitre d's desk and left the restaurant.

"How did I get so far off track?" David wondered. Signaling to the waiter, who thought the table would become available for a waiting couple, David ordered a double shot of whiskey neat. Hoping David would give up the table, the waiter offered, "The gentleman who left settled the bill, sir." But David didn't get it and answered rather loudly, "What do I look like? A bum? I can pay for it." David sneered and the waiter hustled back with the drink and an apology.

David had nowhere to go. He didn't dare go back to his office, since it was clear he was unemployed as of thirty minutes ago. As he downed his third whisky, the waiter began recommending that he leave. "Perhaps you've had enough to drink sir. We'll be happy to serve you a complimentary coffee in the lounge."

"Forget it. I'll leave now." Standing up suddenly, David caused his chair to topple backward and fall with a clatter on the hardwood floor. He tossed a twenty on the table and left, leaving the waiter short-changed by four dollars and no tip. He flagged a cab and nearly fell into the back seat. He gave his home address. Ten minutes later David was unlocking the door to his home with views of Central Park. *Time to call in a favor*, David thought, and picked up his phone.

"Hank, it's David."

"Hey, man. Whatcha doin?"

"I need that number, Hank. I've had a horrendous day and need to blow off some steam with a little blow, ya know?" While David was chuckling at his way with words, Hank recognized the tension and the slur in David's voice.

"What happened, David? What's so urgent? You sound drunk already. Go to bed. Get some sleep."

"Just give me that number. I swear no one will know where I got it."

"I can't. Sorry man. I'm not home and don't have it with me. You're out of luck."

Slamming down the phone on his only friend, David grabbed his overcoat and left the building. *Out of luck like hell*, David thought. *Well, fuck you, Hank! And fuck you, Jack Thompson, HGD's asshole golden boy*. He ignored the doorman's greeting and turned left toward the north end of the Park. That was his best bet for finding what he needed to forget the humiliation of losing his job.

He noticed the increasing incidence of litter on the tree-lined sidewalk. It took forty-five minutes to reach the neighborhood he had in mind. At seven o'clock in the evening it was too early for anyone to be loitering, hoping to make a sale. David found a door on the street with a small neon sign in the front window. "Smiley's, Come on in." That's what David did, and he stayed in the dark, snug little bar with loud jazz and a fat bartender for more than two hours.

David had a long talk with the man called Smiley about how much bullshit there was in the world. It was nothing Smiley didn't hear a hundred times a week. And yet, Smiley kept wrapping a big grin around the lower half of his face and flashing his two gold teeth. He watered down David's drinks after the first one, knowing his new customer wouldn't notice. He didn't get many white executives in his bar, and listened to most of what David was slurring. By nine o'clock, David waved Smiley over to his end of the bar again. With little remaining sense left for keeping the question quiet, he asked, "Hey. Where am I gonna get some white stuff around here?"

Smiley made a quick call and set David up. It wasn't a safe situation for a man in an expensive suit flashing around a lot of cash, but David had reached a careless point in his addiction. It was cold outside. He'd left his overcoat in the bar, but didn't want to miss his appointment with Smiley's contact and kept walking. After fifteen minutes, he found the billboard that signaled the meeting place behind an apartment building.

The transaction was completed with three little words: one hundred dollars. Minutes later David felt much better and wandered Harlem until he came to the edge of Central Park. Stumbling around whistling show tunes was no way to avoid trouble in this area. Two young men, Smiley's friends, trailed him through the park before making their move. He was oblivious to being followed when he tripped over an uneven section of paved trail and fell. While he was down, one boy plucked David's wallet from the inside breast pocket of the fine Italian-made, wool sport jacket, then took off at a casual pace. David had made the robbery easy. He never got up after finding the ground with his face, but crawled to the base of a tree and passed out.

ﻌﻌﻌ

The bright sun found David's closed eyelids and woke him at ten o'clock the following morning. He was in a remote part of the park, a vague dark shape under one of hundreds of trees and he drifted off again.

It was a dog that caused David to finally open his eyes. A pit bull sniffed his custom leather shoes and lifted a leg, letting go a long stream of urine over both feet. David welcomed the warmth for an instant, then clumsily swung a foot at the dog. Yelling at the brown-and-white-speckled mutt set his already throbbing head on fire and forced him to lie back down on the frosted grass. Satisfied that it had adequately marked its property, the dog trotted off.

David stayed there for an hour after the dog left and nursed the searing pain in his head, which worsened whenever he moved.

A patrolman on horseback from his high vantage point, noticed the body in the shadows. He tried to rouse the filthy, nearly overdosed man. "Come on mister. Rise and shine," the cop shouted from the top of his horse.

David ignored the man and tried to roll over.

"Get up and get out of here or I'll have to help you. And you don't want that. Trust me."

"Fuck you," David managed to say. "Just fuck you. I'll get up when I'm ready."

"You were warned." The policeman dismounted and reached David in three strides. He bent down to pull on David's jacket. Noticing David's wet pant legs, he said, "Man, you're lying in your own piss! Last time. Get up!"

David rolled over on his back and forced himself to look at the man who was trying to help him up. David kicked up one leg and jammed his foot against the cop's right knee cap forcing it to hyperextend backwards, saying, "*Last time*! FUCK YOU!"

Swallowing the pain, the cop said, "You just kicked out the knee of an officer, mister. I was gonna let you slide since you're obviously new to passing out in the park."

The handcuffs were tightly linked around David's wrists.

"Why the fuck didn't you just leave me alone? Huh? Why did you have to go and provoke me?" David whined as the reality of the situation sank in.

David was booked for assault on an officer, use of illegal substances, and being drunk in public. He spent three more nights away from his swank apartment with the king-size bed and 500-thread-count Egyptian cotton sheets, until his lawyer arranged for bail.

Two weeks later, it was his turn in front of the judge with his attorney by his side, and David pleaded guilty to the charges. He was sentenced to 160 hours of community service and six months in rehab. A punishment that heaped more humiliation and rejection into a life that only David himself had created.

CHAPTER 19
GINA AND CARRIE

"Okay, Carrie, I've got three months to help you out. What's the plan?" Gina was ready to temporarily leave her current life to help her friend. She'd met with a divorce lawyer in Los Angeles, and got her agent to extricate her from a full schedule of photo sessions.

Meanwhile, Carrie had found Gina an apartment at the west end of the city. The manager was willing to negotiate a short-term lease for a higher monthly rate. It was a rip-off, but Carrie wanted Gina to have a nice place to live. Gina moved into the furnished unit on the fourth floor. The apartment was small but it had a view of Golden Gate Park.

Sitting in the tiny kitchen having a cup of tea and splitting an apple crumb muffin, Gina and Carrie set out the rules.

"First and foremost, of course," said Carrie, "is that we don't know each other. We've never met."

"Second," added Gina, "is that I'll go through the usual hiring channel at Kendall. I can fake whatever credentials on a resume in this case and you'll have to put the pressure on Human Resources to immediately fill the new position as your assistant."

"No problem there. Suzanne Waterton is VP of Human Resources. I'll be working directly with her to find the perfect assistant. However, we need to manufacture a few references to go with that fake resume of yours. Suzanne isn't stupid."

Gina furrowed her forehead, creating two deep lines in her otherwise wrinkle-free, creamy complexion. "That will be the hard part. How will we do that?"

"I'm not sure. Don't you know anyone who can vouch for you in Los Angeles? Surely someone will play along with our scam. It's harmless enough."

"Harmless enough for everyone but Charles Baker," Gina surmised. She hated the thought of possibly ruining someone's career. It wasn't right. But she vowed to keep her promise to her vengeful friend.

"Maybe…" Gina volunteered after giving it some thought. "Maybe my agent would do it. She'll probably find it all very funny. I'll call her for yet another favor. She makes plenty of money off me and likes to keep me happy."

"Great! She'll need to write a letter and we'll offer references upon request. Next," Carrie continued, "you'll need some different clothes. No high-end designer labels. You're a working girl from L.A. who just moved to San Francisco on a shoestring budget, desperate for a job."

"Target, here I come," said Gina, who happened to be lounging in the kitchen with Carrie that day in a $600 sage green silk blouse with jade buttons, perfectly fitted black wool slacks, and soft, black leather ankle boots with spike heels that bumped up the cost for the entire outfit to $2,500. Ready to go all out for the part she would play, Gina added, "I'll also get my hair cut, though Jules, my agent, will have an absolute fit."

"Well, how about Macy's, anyway, for two or three business suits, skirts and blouses, maybe from Liz Claiborne or Jones of New York. No Chanel, Prada, or Armani. And you don't have to cut your hair. Just pull it back." Gina had her mother's raven hair now colored with dark auburn low lights that bounced throughout a thick and wavy mass that reached her lower back: perfect super-model hair.

"Men love long hair. Don't forget you're not really becoming my assistant; you're going to knock any sensibility out of Charles when he sees you. I'm sure he'll take any manner of risk to be with you."

The plan of attack developed.

✌✌✌

Three weeks later Gina was hired. She had sailed through her first interview with Kendall's head of Human Resources, who, after checking the phony references, introduced her to Carrie saying, "I'm sure Gina Juarez will be a good fit for you, Carrie. She's sharp, experienced, energetic, and hungry for a job. She can start right away."

When they were alone Carrie said, "Juarez? Your mother's maiden name, right?"

"Yeah, I've always heard that if you're going to lie, use as much truth as possible in your story."

After an hour of joking and further plotting sealed off in Carrie's office, Carrie looked at her watch. "Okay, I've spent a respectable amount of time interviewing an applicant. You're hired!" Carrie laughed, realizing it was the first time she had really enjoyed herself with anyone since her carefree days in Europe. Gina was having a good effect on her, even though she was worried about whether their ploy would work. She hoped she wasn't underestimating Charles.

Gina was setting up her new work station when Baker walked by for the first time. He ignored her and entered Carrie's office without knocking.

"Carrie, what are you doing? I've just heard that you hired an assistant. I won't tolerate being undermined while being held responsible for this company's bottom line. Why do you need an assistant? You're moving from one department to another every few months with no responsibilities."

It took Carrie a minute to think about this. She had forgotten about justifying the bogus job description she had drafted and given to Suzanne in Human Resources to complete.

"I'm ramping up, Charles. I have eighteen months to go before unseating you and I need help organizing meetings and travel. You continue to forget that I own the company. Don't worry about the bottom line in this case. We're not paying Gina all that much, anyway, and it's part-time. I think you'll like her." Carrie couldn't resist being the one to introduce Charles to Gina. She didn't want to wait for some coincidence of happenstance when Gina collided into him in a hallway or found a seat in his line of vision during the weekly staff meetings.

"Gina," Carrie called, "Please come into my office. Sit down if you like, Charles."

Gina entered Carrie's office. She was the perfect presentation of a professional executive assistant, but with a sexual edge. Her hair was pulled straight back into a low pony tail held with a broad silver clip. Her pale green tailored blouse tightly tucked into a dark green wool pants suit set off her brilliant blue eyes that sparkled at Charles and complemented her warm, sexy smile.

Extending her French manicured hand, she said in her naturally velvet voice, "I'm very pleased to meet you Mr. Baker. I'm excited about working here. Kendall Technologies is renowned for its vision and global solutions in a very competitive, unstable market. I hope to help you make a real difference in a tough industry."

Charles dropped her hand quickly after shaking it, while locked in a visual embrace with the stunning woman in front of him. He replied, "The pleasure is mine, Gina. Welcome to Kendall Technologies. I hope you'll be happy here."

A gracious comeback from someone who hadn't heard a word anyone said since Gina had entered the room. Carrie's mind raced, *This is going to work*!

After that first meeting, two frustrating weeks passed without seeing Charles again. Carrie finally discovered that he had left for Toronto the day after meeting Gina. Busy-work barely kept Gina active, so Carrie told her to just come in two days a week until Charles returned at the end of the month.

"I have a month and a half left to go before I need to go back to Los Angeles, Carrie. Can't we catch up with him on the road somewhere? Surely you can wrangle a reason for going to those meetings in Toronto and I'll tag along, you know, in case you need anything."

"He'll be back in a few days. Hang in there then we'll go after him like sharks to blood."

"You really *are* out for blood, aren't you? Well, let's give it everything we've got and if it doesn't work, you'll need a plan B."

Noticing that Gina didn't say, *"we* will need a plan B," Carrie felt that old lonely feeling creep up again. *I'm on my own. I always was and probably always will be*, she thought sadly.

That evening in her apartment, Carrie added cat food to fluffy-furred Louie's bowl and popped a prepared dinner from the nearby deli into the microwave. After zapping it for a minute, she spooned the contents onto a plate, a slab of meatloaf and a few spears of asparagus with cheese sauce. Sitting in her dining room with a book, Carrie had taken one sip of wine and two bites of the flavorless meat when the phone rang.

Her cell was next to her. Reaching for it, she knocked over the wine and it ran down the center of the long glossy-black dining room table. "Hold on!" She shouted only because the caller was shouting. She grabbed a kitchen towel and started mopping up the dark red liquid threatening the cushy, white carpet.

"Hello? Sorry! I just knocked over my glass. Who's calling?"

Plugging her ear now with one hand while pressing the phone hard against the other, Carrie could just hear Gina's voice out of a raucous background of music and laughter.

"It's Gina! You've got to meet me at O'Dulley's on Sanborn. I'm here with my friend Jake, he came up for a visit today and decided to stay one more day. Anyway, guess who's here!"

"Gina, are you kidding? Is Baker there?"

"Yes! He got here a few minutes ago, but I wasn't sure it was him at first, because he's acting so informal and is dressed kind of sexy. Nice shoulders, trim. He looks good away from the office. He hasn't seen me yet, but Jake keeps asking me to dance and Baker will see me for sure if I do."

Carrie thought fast. "Can you keep Jake ignorant of what you need to do while doing it?"

"What do you mean, Carrie? Flirt with Baker in front of Jake? No. I can't do that. I'm not jeopardizing any possibility with Jake even if he is just here on a job and didn't come up from L.A. to see me specifically. Do you want to meet us here or not?"

"I don't see any reason for me to come, Gina. But try to catch Baker's eye from the dance floor. That might shake things up a bit in the office on Monday."

"I'll try, but it's gonna be subtle since my attention is going to be on Jake."

"Okay, but it's important to make contact in some way. Remind him who you are. Not that he'll have forgotten, but it would be the polite thing to do. Call me tomorrow morning ASAP to let me know what happened, will you?"

"Yeah, sure. I'll do what I can." Gina flipped closed her phone and returned to the table where Jake was waiting for her.

"I don't get the sabbatical, Gina," Jake said. "You look a-a-a-mazing and seem to be none the worse for wear over divorcing Robert. What's up? Are you thinking about moving here?"

Not wanting to explain anything to this man friend she hoped one day would be her lover, Gina gave him one of her megawatt smiles and said, "Let's just dance, Jake. I haven't had any fun in a long time."

Carrie gave what was left of her dinner to Louie, who gobbled up the meatloaf and cheese sauce but left the asparagus. She refilled her wine glass and scanned the movie channels for something to watch that she hadn't already seen. *I want a husband*, Carrie thought suddenly. *I want to feel loved and to love someone. I want to have friends and go places with them. I'm sick and tired of being alone.*

An echoing voice challenged her thoughts. *So why didn't you go meet Gina at O'Dulley's?*

*Because **he** was there*, came the answer. *And because Gina was with Jake and that would make me the third wheel, as usual. What can I do to change my life?* Carrie continued having an inner dialogue with herself. *Ask Gina*, came the answer. *But Gina can't make friends for me or find someone who will love me.*

Moving off her favorite spot on the couch and into the bathroom, Carrie ran the hot water in the large jetted tub. After pouring in a couple of capfuls of jasmine scented bath oil, she lit the candles on the shelves above the tub and turned on some moody jazz. Then she stripped off her jeans and T-shirt and stepped into the waiting pool of fragrant warmth. It was her favorite thing to do whenever she singled herself out from all of humanity. Carrie allowed memories to wash over her. She wandered aimlessly through the halls of her beloved grandfather's mansion and watched the cars flow over the Golden Gate Bridge from her bedroom. Her thoughts turned to some frightening nights at her uncle's house, when he would enter her room and rub her body with his big rough hands. She had never told anyone about that except Gina. Gina was her confidante and here she was taking advantage of the only friend she'd ever known.

Carrie continued to berate herself for several more minutes before returning to the question of how to change her life, and the even bigger question, *What do I want in life?* She visualized herself as a child again, sitting at her grandfather's huge office desk fantasizing about being in charge of his company. *Well, that's going to come true in a few months, as long as Baker doesn't oust me first.*

Mentally she flipped back to her grandfather's last words, "You will grow up with everything you could ever want, Caroline." *True enough*, Carrie thought. "If you make other people happy, then you will be happy too. Use your imagination. You can make whatever you want happen."

Carrie made a wish while lingering in her bubble bath. *Will I ever have someone special at my side, through thick and thin?* Carrie wondered dreamily. She had a difficult time picturing herself married with kids. Everything about her life had been and still was about the business. *But maybe I can have both,*"she finally thought, and forced herself to imagine falling in love. Standing in the rain, laughing without care. Kissing her mystery man passionately and being held close and tight against the elements. The image shifted to her wedding, a gorgeous satin and lace gown and long, long veil trailing behind her, walking down the steps through her grandfather's garden—she would be married at her grandfather's house, of course—close friends and family gathered, smiling…

A creaking door startled Carrie out of her fantasy wedding. Louie entered with an inquisitive *meow*. "All right big boy, let's go to bed."

Carrie slept better that night than she had in years, not waking up once until after eight o'clock the next morning. It was Sunday. Usually she'd get up early and go for a walk, but this was going to be the first day of change.

The departure from her Sunday morning routine started by lounging in bed with a second cup of coffee and daydreaming. Then Carrie picked up the phone and punched a speed-dial number. "...what are you doing, Mom?" Carrie never called her mother. Usually her mother would call her every three or four months from wherever she happened to be. "Mom, are you going to be in San Francisco anytime this year? Or maybe I'll come see you in Seattle. What do you think?"

Gina called later that morning to report in. "I don't have anything to tell you, Carrie. I'm sorry. Jake and I danced for hours. I tried to get Baker's attention, but failed. The place was packed and he seemed absorbed in talking and drinking with some guys the whole time. He's not gay, is he?"

"I'm pretty sure he's not gay. But I don't know much about him," Carrie replied. "His being gay would certainly change our set-up strategy." Letting that idea drop, Carrie asked Gina for another favor.

This time, Gina gave an enthusiastic and resounding, "Yes! I would love to help you Carrie. What time do you want to meet?"

CHAPTER 20

Gina met Carrie at the Westin hotel on Union Square for lunch, wearing red *faux* snakeskin sliders, a skirt that skimmed over her slender hips and flat stomach before flaring out at the knee, and a fitted, long-sleeved cotton blouse that accentuated her bust line. Her long hair was pulled softly into a high ponytail, leaving tendrils around her oval face. Carrie wore comfortable loafers, beige Capri pants and a plain white tailored shirt cinched at the waist by a colorful, cloth belt. She hid her slender frame under a bulky cardigan the same color as the blue in the belt. Her fine hair was loose and hung straight to the top of her shoulders.

"We're going to have some fun today!" Gina exclaimed when she first saw Carrie. There was no judgment in her expression about how Carrie was dressed. All Gina saw was her friend coming toward her with a mixed expression of fear and excitement. "What's the budget?"

"No budget. I want to do this right."

"That's good. Do you know how hard it was to get a last minute appointment at Chez Feliz? And Feliz never works on Sunday—except for celebrities, and then he gets top dollar. That's our first stop. After your haircut, we'll go to Saks and the boutiques on Maiden Lane."

It was an exhausting day for both women and Carrie had never had so much fun. Gina was an expert in fashion and even made a few suggestions to Feliz about Carrie's hair and makeup. He balked at Gina's interfering suggestions a few times, but finally agreed Gina had a good feel for how to bring out Carrie's best features.

It was a new Carrie striding through the lobby of Kendall Technologies on Monday morning. She even got a few double-takes from the guys in sales when she stopped in to talk about their new client in London.

"Wow, Carrie! What happened to you?" Benton Swank was the first to voice his appreciation. Everyone else was professionally respectful of their future boss.

"Thanks, I think, Benton. I'll assume that's a positive reaction to my haircut."

"It's more than the haircut, Carrie. You look great and rested too. Must have been a good weekend."

"I decided that while some changes are needed here, that I should start with myself and that's all there is to it." Carrie wasn't going to discuss her personal makeover with anyone, especially with Benton, where the sabotage of her credibility had all begun.

"Good morning, Gina," Carrie said with a straight face while passing Gina's desk.

They were back to the charade.

Gina stood up from her bogus letters and followed Carrie. Closing the office door, Gina said, "You look fantastic!"

"I feel fantastic." Carrie let herself laugh. "I feel so good!"

"What's going on today? How are we going to get this thing moving with Baker?"

"I gave it a lot of thought last night. Would you check with Benita, Baker's assistant, about his schedule this week? See if she'll tell you where he'll be and when. The pretense is that I'll schedule myself to attend those meetings, but back out and send you instead. My excuse will be a family emergency. In fact, I will be flying to Seattle tomorrow, so being with family won't be a lie."

Knowing that a heart attack had killed Carrie's dad during her first year as an intern, Gina asked, "How is your mom?"

"Oh, she's okay. Everything's fine. I just want to spend a little time with her before things here really start taking up all of my time."

Gina attended every meeting that week, taking copious notes in Carrie's absence. She made a point of sitting directly across from the president any chance she got. Casting glances in his direction as often as possible without drawing attention to the fact that she was trying to catch his eye, Gina struck out. In a last-ditch effort on Friday while Carrie was still away, Gina worked up a plan of her own to put herself in a room alone with Charles Baker.

"Benita, I have to talk with Mr. Baker right away. Is he in?" Gina wore a borderline provocative dress. It appeared modest at first with long sleeves, conservative length and high turtle-neck style. But the light weight knit material clung to Gina's perfect figure, leaving no doubt that she had very little on underneath it.

"Gina, right?" Baker asked when she entered the extravagant office.

Gina stood directly in front of her victim, straight-backed, chest out as if at military attention. Baker averted his eyes and rested them on a piece of paper on his desk. "What do you need?"

"I, ah, I wanted to explain how much I love working here. I'd like to establish myself in a more active role here, and thought maybe you could give me some advice." Gina was unexpectedly nervous. She was prepared, but had assumed that her looks would do all the talking. As she babbled along, making it up as she went, Baker interrupted.

"Ms. Juarez, you should take this up with your manager, Carrie Kendall. I'm sure you're better at communicating with her than you are with me right now."

"I'm sorry, Mr. Baker. I'm nervous." Leaving an opening for the company president to take control and reassure her that it was fine and to relax, Gina gave him a seductive look forcing him to stare appreciatively at her. His gaze took her in from head to toe. But he didn't ask Gina to sit down to keep the conversation going. Instead, Baker remained all business and focused on his job. The job he was determined to keep at all costs.

"If Carrie isn't interested in helping you, then talk to Suzanne Waterton. Register your complaint against your boss, sounds like she's not paying attention to our greatest assets here, our people. Also explain to Suzanne your interest in a management program that we have here. That's the best advice I can offer." Baker stood up from behind his desk and walked Gina to the door: a full and abrupt dismissal.

Jerk! Gina thought, as she turned away and left the executive offices.

Benita watched her go, then went into the inner sanctum. "Mr. Baker, why do you suppose, Ms. Juarez would come to you? And why is she so interested in working here? She's a model. A rather successful one at that if you count the cover of *Vogue* with George Clooney a couple of years ago, among several other covers of the top fashion magazines. I think she was even one of those Victoria Secret angels."

"She's what? Why didn't you mention this before?" Baker nearly shouted. Then he calmed down, having connected two dots. "Carrie is trying to set me up."

Benita looked confused. "What do you mean?"

"Carrie is trying to set me up by catching me fraternizing with an employee. Maybe even getting secret photos of me and Gina that would compromise my integrity."

"That's a terrible thing to do!" Benita readily bought into Baker's theory, especially since she'd had a hand in undermining Carrie's reputation among the employees. "It makes sense somehow, since

Gina couldn't possibly be interested in the tech industry. She's a glamour girl from Los Angeles."

"Who knows, and I don't care. In any event, whatever Gina is up to, with or without Carrie's knowledge, her looks and come-on body language won't work on me." Charles was resolute. After Benita left his office, Baker thought to himself, *Gina could walk in here naked and I wouldn't budge.*

❧❧❧

When Carrie returned from Seattle, Gina filled her in on the visit to Baker's office.

"This isn't working, Carrie. I'm starting to make a fool of myself and I don't like the looks I'm getting from people. I think the rumors have started that I'm in love with Baker and doing everything possible to get his attention. It's getting embarrassing."

"I understand, Gina. I can see now this isn't going to work. Baker is going to continue sabotaging my credibility to keep his job. Even a gorgeous supermodel won't distract him," Carrie said sadly.

"I don't know about the gorgeous supermodel part, but I did what I could."

An instant later, Baker barged in without knocking.

"Ladies." Charles stopped short just inside the office door when he noticed Carrie. A new Carrie. A pretty Carrie with short layered golden-blond hair that framed her face and brought attention to her high cheekbones and lively grey eyes. She was wearing makeup, too. Something she'd never bothered with except for special occasions.

Carrie looks good. No, she looks great, Baker thought, but said nothing.

"Baker." Carrie remained seated but Gina stood, and just barely brushing past him, left the room.

Letting Gina go, Baker closed the door and sat down in front of Carrie's desk. "I understand you've been away. I hope your family is well."

Carrie was wondering where this was going. Baker never talked about personal matters or held polite chitchat with anyone, let alone her. She remained silent. Leaning back in her chair, she waited for him to get past his insincere attempt at being friendly.

Waiting half a beat, Baker changed the subject. "I know what Gina has been trying to do and I'm sick of it. Please tell her to start acting more professional or get rid of her."

Playing the innocent, Carrie asked, "What do you think Gina has been doing, Baker? You'll have to be more specific."

Outlining the obvious attempts to catch his eye during meetings and the overt disruption last Friday in his office, Charles put it all on Gina and was careful not to accuse Carrie of trying to set him up.

Tiring of the game, Carrie simply said, "I'll speak with her. Just don't fault me that you appeal to a beautiful woman. It doesn't sound like a problem for a man to have, but I'll do something about it if it bothers you."

A slight smile slipped across Charles's expression at the possibility that maybe Gina was attracted to him and that it wasn't a set-up.

"However," Carrie was still talking, "stop trying to undermine me with the employees and board members. They have no idea how hard I'm working and you continue to tell them that it will be a mistake to vote me into the position. I've been stomping out the fires you keep lighting against me with staff and it's ridiculous. In addition to that, I'm getting concerned about your misdirected attention focused on me and not the company. I'll take my rightful position as head of this company with or without you. And, it had better not have been run into the ground when that time comes or I'll take legal action against you for slander and intentional disruption of business. Then where will your precious career be?" Waiting for a response and hearing none, Carrie continued with a surprising suggestion and change in tone. "Baker, I've given this a lot of thought. If I have your support, then I'll propose we co-lead this company into the future. What do you say?"

Carrie had thought out her plan B quickly when Gina had alluded to the need for one. It was based on the old adage; keep your friends close and your enemies even closer. But it went way beyond that. Carrie instinctively knew that keeping Baker on to work with her at the top made a lot of sense and she hoped he would see that, too.

He's intelligent and knows the tech industry on a global basis. Unfortunately I could really use him, Carrie thought, while trying to read his expression.

Baker didn't expect this from Carrie—his enemy, his nemesis, as he'd come to think of her during the past three and a half years. "I don't like the threat, Carrie. You have no proof that I've intentionally discredited you with the staff and board. I think you've done a fine job of that yourself."

Fuming at the reaction to her generous proposal, Carrie stood up to tower over him and said, "You're a rude bastard and not as smart as I thought you were. You have twelve hours to get back to me with a go/no go deal to work this out professionally and as adults. I hope you make the right choice because I do have proof of your sabotage and I will seek revenge." Dropping her eyes to her computer screen Carrie sat down and began answering an e-mail.

Dismissed, Baker left the office with a sour feeling in his stomach. Passing Gina at her desk he attempted to test the suggestion that Gina really was interested in him. Without realizing that it was the exact right thing to do, Gina returned his smile, tossed a long curl of dark hair off her shoulder and gave him a wink, which the egotistical Charles interpreted as a come on. Charles returned to his own office confident that Gina was hot for him after all, and that there was no collusion between her and Carrie.

CHAPTER 21

"Twelve hours? Why did you give him so much time?" Gina challenged. "It's a no-brainer. Baker would be an idiot not to accept your suggestion."

They were in Carrie's apartment. Carrie had asked Gina for help in getting ready for a fundraiser dinner party at the San Francisco Museum of Modern Art. Kendall Technologies was a major sponsor. Carrie, the executive board members and their wives, and Charles Baker were going.

The bed was covered with gowns borrowed from local boutiques. Whatever Carrie chose to wear, she would be able to purchase at a discount simply for the free exposure it would receive at the elegant gala attended by San Francisco's wealthy philanthropists. Carrie's new cropped haircut exposed her long graceful neck and high cheekbones. Gina suggested a simple, straight cut, off-the-shoulder gown that showed off her friend's slender figure. The midnight blue of the gown contrasted with Carrie's golden hair and fair complexion. A subtle pattern of swirls in the fabric carried the same deep blue, sage green and gold threads around the waist and cascaded from one hip to Carrie's matching blue-and-rhinestone stilettos. The pattern reminded Carrie of the window-seat upholstery in her grandfather's home office. She remembered how she had once traced the gold threads with her fingers and told him she wanted a dress in the same colors. "Like a princess dress," she had said. "Then everyone will love me."

Carrie gazed at her reflection in the full-length mirror. Focusing on the similar pattern and colors, she relived the memory of being six and seeing her grandfather for the last time. Now she saw an elegant woman standing before her. Someone who had grown up confident and ready to take over a company that her grandfather had founded. "This is an important occasion for my career, Gina. Make me beautiful."

"Easy! You're already that. Let's just step it up a notch, shall we?" Gina was doing what she did best. Finishing Carrie's makeup, she fussed over and lightly sprayed the fluffy layers of bangs and the crown of golden highlights. When Gina finally let Carrie turn back to the mirror she said, "There! You're done. You're a perfectly gorgeous Cinderella."

Carrie did feel like a princess when she entered the museum's expansive reception room. It was filled with tuxedos and gowns; young and old, men and women, were already laughing, networking, backslapping, and gossiping. It looked like everyone knew everyone, the way the room hummed and buzzed over the twelve-piece orchestra. Tables set for eight glittered in white, silver, and crystal. Rose-colored floodlights cast rays from the twenty-foot ceiling, making everyone look their healthiest. Waiters wove through the crowd with drink orders and champagne. A stage was set up at one end of room.

Carrie didn't know anyone there other than the board members, and Charles, of course. She had never met the wives, and felt nervous standing to the side after leaving her wrap at the coat check counter. An observant waiter didn't let her linger long without a drink. Carrie took the proffered flute and scanned the room for a familiar face.

"Use your imagination and whatever you want will come true," whispered her grandfather in the back of her mind. *Is this what I want? I'm not sure now. Maybe. I do wish I had some friends here and at least an escort. Everyone seems to be paired up.* At that moment a light hand on her bare lower back made her spin around, sloshing a splash of champagne over the rim of her glass, just missing the tuxedoed sleeve belonging to Charles Baker.

"Carrie! I hardly recognized you. You look great!"

"That's gracious of you, Baker, if it was a compliment." Carrie sneered. "You seem comfortable enough in that suit. Is it yours or do you rent one on occasion?"

"Hey, I was being nice. Let's try this again."

This was a very different man from the one who'd left her office steaming just that afternoon. He was clearly making an effort, but now Carrie was reluctant to make it easy for him. Finally deciding how childish that was, she heeded her grandfather's advice about helping people and, *Clearly Baker needs help*, she thought. So she forced a smile and exclaimed a bit sarcastically, "Oh, Charles! I declare you look so handsome tonight!"

It was her best Scarlett O'Hara imitation and it was pretty good. Unmistakably Scarlett, flirting with her beloved but unattainable Ashley Wilkes in *Gone with the Wind*.

"Pretty good! I must say. Corny, but good," Baker responded.

"Corny! That movie is—" At that moment Baker took her elbow and interrupted Carrie's defense of her favorite classic.

"I have to talk with you. It can't wait until tomorrow."

"What's this about?" The truce she wanted wasn't easily drawn. "I'd like to have some fun tonight; even though I'll have to watch you eat and fawn over the members." Referring to the board members who hadn't surfaced yet, Carrie sighed and let Baker lead her to the bar.

Charles ordered a scotch on the rocks and took a bar stool. "Carrie. I want us to show solidarity tonight. I've been thinking all day about your suggestion to co-lead Kendall Technologies and I'd like to discuss that with you first thing in the morning. You deserve to understand my position on this, but I'd like to work with you."

"I'll have a scotch on the rocks, too, please," was Carrie's response, forcing Baker to act like a gentleman and relay her order to the bartender.

An hour later, Charles Baker and Carrie Kendall began enjoying themselves with the others at their table, and then Charles surprised everyone who knew them. Rising from his chair, he turned to Carrie and extended a hand. "Carrie, will you do me the honor of dancing with me?"

Lapsing into her fake southern drawl again in an attempt to cover her embarrassment at the attention, Carrie smiled up at him and extended her own hand for help out of her chair and said, "You are sincerely gracious, Mr. Baker."

On the dance floor, waltzing stiffly at arm's length, Baker said, "We'll make an incredible team, Carrie. I'm certain of it." He was still thinking about the company.

Carrie, on the other hand, after three drinks was on the verge of thinking romance.

CHAPTER 22
SARA, CARRIE, AND GINA

Sara advertised Dare to Dream under event planning services in the San Diego, Los Angeles, and San Francisco phone books. She lived in San Diego and felt she could handle new business in two other major cities. It was just Sara and an assistant sharing one room in a new office space on the ground floor of a retail and business mall. Karen was a young girl with experience in hotel catering. She was a perfect match for Sara's work style, energy, and ethics. Karen was always open and smiling. Callers could hear sincerity and warmth in her voice and most would comment on it to Sara. That's exactly what Sara had wanted as a first experience when someone contacted Dare to Dream. It was that friendly, welcoming voice that an executive assistant in San Francisco heard when she called to interview the company about the possibility of helping her with the installment dinner for the new president and CEO of Kendall Technologies, Caroline Kendall.

"Our new president is the granddaughter of the company's founder. She's completed five years of internship and is about to take over as president. Her grandfather left the company to her when she was six and now, after all these years, she's about to claim her inheritance."

"That's an amazing story!" Karen exclaimed. "Dare to Dream, would love to create an incredible, exciting event for her." After explaining how Dare to Dream worked with its clients, Karen buzzed Sara to take over the conversation and close the deal.

"I just read about Caroline Kendall," Sara told the caller. "Never met her, but she must be an inspiration to the company.

The story in *Forbes* said she's very young for the job but a brilliant, competitive force. It also said that toward the end of her five-year internship, she refocused the company and nearly single-handedly turned it into one of today's most profitable, niche-marketed corporations in aero science and technology. Very impressive."

"Oh yes. She's all of that, and there is a great team of people working alongside her, including a co-president. She refuses to take credit for the accolades. Now, about the event."

Clearly Carrie's new assistant had decided to hire Sara during their first conversation. Sara had exhibited a good understanding about the woman who would become president of Kendall Tech. They made a date to meet for lunch in San Francisco.

"I'll make a reservation at Greens restaurant at one o'clock. Is that all right with you?" Sara asked.

The assistant was amazed. "Well, it's one of my favorite restaurants in the city, but it can be difficult to get a reservation so quickly."

"Karen just slipped me a note suggesting Greens. You told her if it was up to you, you'd select salad and pasta primavera for the dinner menu. Sounds vegetarian to us."

The woman laughed and confirmed that she'd stopped eating meat years ago.

Sara replied. "The reservation will be under my name. We're looking forward to meeting you."

Three days later Sara and Karen flew to San Francisco to meet Carrie's representative for lunch and seal the business contract for Dare to Dream Events. The event was scheduled to be held in two months.

"There's never enough time between the first client meeting and the event," Sara reminded Karen on their flight back to San Diego. "We're going to pull out all our magic tricks for this one.

Caroline Kendall is already famous for being a perfectionist. If she's happy with what we do, we'll have more business than we can handle and I'll be hiring several full-time people."

❧❧❧

Caroline, "Carrie" as Sara was later asked to call her, lived up to her reputation. Carrie had very high standards and expectations for herself and others. That was obvious when Sara and Karen sat down for lunch in the executive dining room on the top floor of Kendall Technologies. It was a second meeting to discuss the installation event. The purpose was to formally announce Carrie's position as CEO and co-president with Charles Baker. But, Carrie insisted on incorporating her grandfather's memory into the celebration by adding a fundraising element for a new Justice Kendall Heart Research Foundation that would share research results and new knowledge with the California University system. During her speech, Carrie would announce the start-up amount available for the first research grant in her grandfather's name.

The private research center was a new idea that came about when Carrie visited her mother in Seattle while still at odds with Baker. It was a cathartic conversation for Carrie and her mother. A bond was finally formed between mother and daughter, and it was then that Carrie's mother explained what had happened to Carrie's grandfather.

"Certainly as a young child, you wouldn't have understood what happened. He died so suddenly," Carrie's mother began. "A heart attack took his life that day. I was devastated when he died, and the news that you had inherited his company compounded problems your father and I had been having. We were probably headed for divorce, but I realize now that he'd been 'toughing' it out with me, thinking I would become the majority stockholder of Kendall Technologies and appoint him president.

"We didn't realize how close you and my father had become over the years. The imperious Justice Kendall never paid much attention to me while I was growing up, and I always assumed your step grandmother would be the one to watch you when you stayed with them."

Without relaying personal details learned from her mother, Carrie explained to Sara and Karen over their salads and peach iced teas why she was creating the research foundation. To them, keeping Justice Kendall's memory alive in the magnitude Carrie was thinking about was astounding. But she was a rich woman and could readily afford the start-up cost for a new building and funding an initial research project. She already hired a director for the non-profit enterprise. Launching the center in her grandfather's name at the gala was more important to Carrie than the announcement that she had fulfilled the requirements stipulated in his will and had been unanimously approved by the board of directors for the positions of CEO and co-president of Kendall Technologies, Inc.

"While Karen and I will be reviewing every detail for the gala on a daily basis, I'll call you once a week, Carrie, for approvals and further ideas," Sara said. Sara liked the tall, skinny, golden-haired executive right off. She even thought they might become friends if their business relationship continued to be as much fun as it'd been so far.

"That's fine, Sara. I want to know every detail," Carrie replied.

৵৵৵

The gala was six weeks away. Carrie had chosen her grand-father's birthday for the event. The caterer was working up extraordinary ideas for a five-course dinner. Decorators were consulted and provided proposals. Carrie and Sara would jointly decide who would get the contracts. A handful of national business editors were personally invited and formal invitations were mailed to a dozen reporters, as well as about three hundred friends, former colleagues, and acquaintances of Justice Kendall. A general press release would go out immediately after the event about the new foundation. The event became one of the toughest invitations in town to get among notable corporate executives and socialites who made it their purpose in life to attend every important charitable fundraiser. Carrie's mother and grandmother were coming, and would be seated at the head table with Carrie, Charles Baker, and the Chairman of the Board at Kendall Tech. All Kendall employees were also invited, from the VPs to the mailroom staff. That alone added another three hundred to the guest list.

Sara was nervous and excited. This event would not only launch Carrie as the CEO and the new Research Foundation, but would achieve more press for Dare to Dream Events than she had ever *dared to dream*. After years of not giving up and staying focused on what she wanted her life to be, Sara was living her own fantasy for achieving success in a creative, exciting environment.

But something else was harbored in Sara's dreams. A guilty compassion would creep over her sense of well-being whenever she saw someone on the street pushing a shopping cart loaded with their worldly goods. She passed the homeless every day, and every day she wondered about the choices the individual had made that got him or her to such a sad point in life. Sara also wondered how she could help that person decide to change their circumstances.

CHAPTER 23

Three days before the big night, Carrie worked with a media trainer, practicing her speech until it was memorized and perfect. She had no idea that Charles Baker was practicing a few special words of his own.

Gina flew in from Los Angeles. Her mystery date, someone Carrie hadn't met before, had the use of La Vie Modeling agency's private jet. He was scheduled to arrive on the day of the event, in time to jump into a tux and meet Gina at Carrie's apartment.

Gina was in charge of getting Carrie ready, and had contacted a few designers to pull some things together from their latest collections for Carrie to choose from. For hours, Carrie and Gina dismissed gown after gown, finally agreeing on an amber form-fitted bodice with deep hip-to-heel-length folds that created a lovely swirl when Carrie walked. A gold-and-diamond choker and matching cuff bracelet bounced ambient lighting around Carrie's bedroom. Carrie's hair was still cut short and shaped around her face with long bangs just clearing her sculpted eyebrows. The golden blond layers reached around her small ears and showcased her almond-shaped eyes, which Gina accentuated with smoky shadows and liner. A pale pink lip stain completed the formal elegance befitting the new CEO of a major international company.

Sara had called Carrie earlier that afternoon and was invited over for a quick glass of wine before heading to the ballroom venue. She rang Carrie's doorbell and was greeted by the recognizable supermodel, Gina Severns. She'd only seen Gina in magazines, modeling nearly everything, and wasn't prepared for the real-life beauty opening the door and inviting her to enter. Gina's shimmering black hair was gathered at the middle of her back and held with a thin band of diamonds. The soft curls fell to her waist. The ice-blue gown matched Gina's eyes, and her figure was outlined in satin; the drape of clinging fabric fell to the floor from a sapphire nugget at the top of her right shoulder. Being used to the highest heels possible, Gina stood two inches taller than her natural five-foot-six.

"Wow! I'm Sara," Sara exploded as Gina opened Carrie's front door.

"Wow yourself! I'm Gina."

Both women laughed, which brought Carrie out of the bedroom to see what was going on.

Sara and Gina gave each other a quick smile as Carrie entered the room, and in unison said, "Wow!"

"This is going to be a fantastic evening," Carrie said, feeling an exuberance she'd never felt before. Not only had she accomplished everything she set out to do for the last ten years, she suddenly realized that she was now enjoying the friendship of two extraordinary women.

"We have about an hour before the car will arrive. How about a drink?"

Sara and Gina readily accepted the beverages to take the edge off their nervous excitement. It was easily to be the most important night in Carrie and Sara's lives, and Gina was along for the fun to see her best friend acknowledged for her tenacity and hard work.

"Amazing how things work out. You know, Carrie? I mean with Baker and all that undercutting each other for nothing," Gina said once they were settled.

Three beautiful women were seated on the couch around a large square glass coffee table. Candles filled the center of the table and their drinks sat on marble coasters. No one dared to make a sudden move in case a drop of liquid spilled. It was tempting to further fuss over a strand of hair, but each refrained from patting or smoothing anything down or fluffing anything up. They were picture-perfect. Princesses waiting for their Prince Charmings. Baker and Gina's date, Dmitri were to meet them at Carrie's apartment in a few minutes.

For Sara, it was a work night. She was to be ringmaster for the evening, making sure every detail in the plan was executed to perfection. Looking elegant in a dark green sheath that flattered her auburn curls and deep-set brown eyes, the evening ahead presented the opportunity to prove herself to herself and secure notable success for Dare to Dream Events. If everything went well tonight, Sara expected the phone to be ringing off the hook in no time. Turning back to the conversation, Sara heard Carrie's answer to Gina.

"Yeah, the best laid plans, or worst, as the case may be. And in this case, trying to set up Baker was a bad idea. I told Sara all about what we schemed. What you don't know, Gina, is that Baker thinks you were seriously flirting with him. I didn't correct his arrogant assumption because things would have turned out quite differently if he knew we had been conspiring against him."

"So what does Charles think about your friendship with Gina, who you weren't supposed to know before she pretended to be your assistant for three months?" Sara challenged. "Won't he think it's odd that Gina is here tonight when you know he thinks she was flirting with him?"

"That's going to be an interesting piece of the drama," Carrie replied. "They haven't seen each other since I 'fired' Gina at his request. But I think it will be fine. Gina will surely be busy with her date, who by the way, I can't wait to meet."

"It might be weird at first, but my attention will be on Dmitri, who's crazy about me," Gina bragged.

"And over a year has passed since our little plot. Fortunately, Carrie came up with a better plan, a generous compromise, I thought," Gina added.

"A lot has happened since then. Lately Baker and I have been obnoxiously inseparable. But tell me about Dmitri," Carrie prodded.

A moment later the door bell rang, interrupting Carrie's interest in Gina's new boyfriend.

"Ahh, so punctual," Gina exclaimed as she again went to the door. "It's a requirement for models to be on time or they become known for being unreliable," she explained to no one in particular.

"Hi, baby!" Gina ended up saying to Baker by mistake, who happened to be first in line to enter the apartment.

"Hey there, Gina! I heard you would be here. But I think this guy behind me is here for you." Baker gracefully handled the situation, knowing her welcome was for the man standing directly behind him. Walking quickly past Gina, Baker crossed the room to arrive at Carrie's side. "Carrie, you look incredible!"

That little scene diminished any potentially awkward feelings between Gina, Charles, and Carrie, Sara thought. *Apparently no worries there.*

Handing each man a short drink, Carrie explained that they should be getting a call from the doorman in a few minutes to let them know the limo had arrived.

For the first half of the evening, nothing went wrong as far as Carrie was concerned. Everyone who said they would come arrived and added to the excitement. Dressed in their finest, some of the wealthiest people in the city began participating in a spirited silent auction that ultimately added another $100,000 to the charitable foundation.

Sara's staff did their job. No cues were missed. The lighting and sound technicians were on top of their instructions for changing the mood throughout the evening; exciting cloud patterned magenta, orange, and yellow blended on the white ballroom walls during dinner; slightly brighter rose-filtered lights with no music during the speeches; a mixture of blues and greens for dancing later. The lighting was to mimic the setting sun over the course of a few hours. The room was filled with roses and maidenhair ferns. The huge room was even lightly fragrant from the rose-scented mist added to the ventilation system.

Love that aromatherapy, thought Sara, as she watched over her creation and saw hundreds of people mingling and laughing throughout the grand ballroom.

Seated at the head table were the Chairman of the Board, William McNamara and his wife, Carrie and Charles, Carrie's mother and her date, who happened to be a significant auction winner that evening, Carrie's grandmother, who came alone, and Gina and Dmitri. After the sumptuous dinner was over and the final spoonful of dark chocolate mousse with white, mint chocolate rose petals had vanished, Charles Baker wiped his mouth and announced to the table that it was "time." Carrie noticed, not for the first time that evening, how handsome he looked in the well-cut tuxedo as he bounded up the stairs to the podium. Her heart fluttered and her palms began to sweat.

Charles kept the opening speech to ten minutes. He welcomed the guests and expressed admiration for Justice Kendall, a man he'd never met, but he knew of the visionary imagination and strength of conviction the man had been famous for. To her pleasant surprise, Charles introduced the founder's widow, Carrie's grandmother, Roberta Kendall. A spotlight found the normally reserved old woman smiling broadly with no embarrassment. He lingered on what it must have taken to start a company of innovations sixty-eight years ago and highlighted the company's achievements over the years. Then Charles introduced Chairman McNamara.

Drawing out the anticipation among the attentive listeners, the Chairman shared a few anecdotal moments witnessed in his role as Chairman of the Board. He briefly recognized and thanked Charles Baker for his fine work and dedication to the company for the last five years.

Looking up from his notes, the tall man exhibited a talent for building out a moment just long enough before saying, "I would like you all to understand the magnitude of accomplishment this remarkable young woman has achieved. The woman we honor tonight never took her eye off the ball while dedicating her life to her grandfather's legacy and dream."

The Chairman noted Carrie's impressive educational record and tenacity while interning for five years according to her grandfather's wishes.

"She has earned her rightful place as a powerful leader in the world market. I am honored to represent the Board of Directors of Kendall Technologies and announce the unanimous vote to install Caroline Marie Kendall as Chief Executive Officer and Co-president of Kendall Technologies Incorporated."

It was an emotional moment for Carrie when the Chairman's booming, deep voice sounded her appointment. It had been twenty-five years since the reading of her grandfather's will. Carrie had grown up knowing that one day she would hold the reins of her grandfather's enterprise. At thirty-one, she was the youngest female CEO of a fortune 500 company, and she'd earned her dream. Carrie fought the lump in her throat.

Now it was her turn. Carrie suddenly wished she had had time to visit the ladies' room before taking the stage. As she listened to Chairman McNamara introducing her, the world began to turn slowly. Cameras appeared and flashed, as reporters and friends clicked off shot after shot. Everyone wanted to hear from the golden girl who had joined the "boys club" in a boardroom full of men. What they didn't know was how she had turned her enemies into champions during her internship. But those personal challenges were behind Carrie now. Walking in what felt like Jell-o, she reached the podium and accepted handshakes and kisses on the cheek from the Chairman and Charles Baker, who then stepped off the stage and returned to the dinner table.

The standing ovation continued while Carrie stood in front of the microphone somewhat in shock. While taking in the entire room, she thought, *I did it, Grandfather! You put all your faith in me. I never let go of that, and now my dream is coming true.*

Just as she had felt so many years ago on the day he died, Carrie could feel her grandfather's presence in her special moment in the spotlight. It was the same sensation that Carrie had felt while sitting in his office in that huge chair as a skinny little six-year-old, with her hands folded on the great desk. She even remembered what she had told the imaginary audience on that day so long ago.

Her grandfather had been with her then, and he was with her now, as she stood ramrod straight, looking out over the elegant crowd. As the applause subsided and the room became still, Carrie thought, *Thank you grandfather. I'll take great care of your company.*

Then, Caroline Marie Kendall spoke in a strong, energized voice and gratefully accepted her new position. She provoked thought in the vision that would carry on her grandfather's work and recognized the talent and expertise Charles Baker would continue to provide as her co-president. Then Carrie paused to change the subject.

"Now I have something very important to announce." Carrie waited a beat. "It is with great love for the man and his memory that we have created the Justice Kendall Heart Research Foundation, a center for heart science and research that will subsidize new work and continue the work in progress at university research labs.

"With your help tonight and the start-up capital of ten million dollars, we will take on heart disease with a vengeance." With that announcement, Carrie pulled at the white velvet cloth that had been covering a painting next to her to reveal a portrait of Justice Kendall.

Carrie left the podium to another standing ovation as the musicians struck up the first dance of the evening. Charles met Carrie before she could accept the numerous congratulations from those seated nearby while making her way back to the table. He took her hand and led her to the dance floor. Several couples followed them and soon the party reached a crescendo.

"You are magnificent, Carrie," Charles whispered. "That was perfect. Everyone, and I mean everyone, was spellbound. You captivated them, and me, for that matter."

"Thanks, Baker. You did a great job, too, and you look particularly handsome tonight."

Charles put both hands on her waist and pulled her in for a kiss. Several people surrounding the couple, including reporters, captured the intimate moment between the co-presidents of Kendall Tech with their cameras. *Oh great!* Carrie thought. *That wasn't supposed to happen.* Then said softly, "I hope this relationship doesn't get caught up in corporate politics as a conflict of interest. What will the shareholders think when they see that photo with tonight's message? I hope it doesn't overshadow the importance of launching Grandfather's new foundation."

"All this worry from a woman who makes her dreams come true!" Charles exclaimed. "We can handle it. We've been open with the board. They know we've been seeing each other. Stop worrying. In fact..."

Charles whirled Carrie around the entire dance floor twice before Carrie finally asked, "In fact, what?"

"In fact," Charles repeated and kissed her again right in front of a widely known reporter, "What do you say we get married?"

"Married! Are you crazy?" Carrie couldn't believe he had picked this night out of all nights to propose. "Isn't there enough going on tonight to celebrate without adding a marriage proposal to the mix?"

"Well, gee, that's not exactly the answer I'd hoped to hear." Charles took a step back, but led her to sway in time with the music. "In fact, I thought you'd see just how perfect the timing really is to offset any speculation of surreptitious doings in the office. It's intentional. No one can suggest that we're doing anything wrong. I thought it was a genius time to propose. And why are we talking about the timing of my question, instead of the importance of what it means for our future? *Our* future, Carrie. Not the future of Kendall Tech."

"My life is Kendall Tech, Charles. You know that." Carrie rarely called him by his first name. Recognizing that she needed a little more persuading, Charles stopped dancing. They were in the middle of the dance floor with people bobbing past them in a fast beat to the light blues-y sound. Carrie was standing directly under a spotlight that had been moving around the dance floor capturing one or two couples in its warm, rosy glow. Charles kneeled and pulled a little velvet black box out of the inside jacket pocket.

"Carrie." As the word left Charles lips, everyone stopped dancing and turned to watch what was happening between them. A few women gasped quietly, "Oh my God, he's going to propose."

The music conductor changed the music abruptly to something quietly romantic and Charles finished his sentence so that only Carrie could hear him. But there was no mistaking to the hundreds of guests and media representatives what the man down on one knee was doing in the middle of the spotlight on the dance floor.

"I love you, Carrie. Will you marry me?"

Carrie's first thought was, *this is a trap*. Followed by, *how can I say no and ruin this perfect night*? Looking down at the man who was looking up at her with a bright gleam of love and hope in his deep brown eyes, Carrie smiled and said, "Yes, Charles Baker. I will marry you."

Charles opened the box, stood up and slipped the magnificent diamond onto Carrie's finger. Then he picked her up and swung her around in his arms. The crowd erupted into applause and shouts.

Gina, dragging Dmitri with her, ran up to Carrie and gave her a huge squeeze. "Congrats you guys! What a night!"

Carrie smiled a bit tightly at first, then downed the champagne Gina had pressed into her hand. "Here, you need this, and I'll get another. You're going to look like a deer in headlights in the newspapers tomorrow morning."

Sara missed the drama. She had been backstage giving final instructions to the caterer and lighting guys when the proposal took place. She overheard what had just happened from a waitress. That explained the sudden change in music. *Bad timing, Charles Baker. Very bad timing*, Sara thought, but knew she wouldn't say so to Carrie or Gina unless they said it first.

CHAPTER 24

The following morning Gina had been right and Carrie's fears came true. The photographer caught Carrie's stunned, pop-eyed expression and Charles down on one knee. The proposal was the headline and leading paragraphs of the story. The announcement of Carrie's becoming CEO of Kendall Tech followed and the story ended with news about the Justice Kendall Research Foundation and ten million in capital funding. The story topped the society pages and not the business page that Carrie had hoped for.

"Shit, what a mess!" Carrie told Gina the next day on the phone. Charles had stayed overnight at Carrie's and had just left for a racquetball lesson, saying he'd be back after lunch.

"What a doofus!" Understanding what sold newspapers, Gina asked, "How could he not think a marriage proposal in the middle of the dance floor surrounded by all those society people wouldn't be the lead for your story?"

A new research foundation, no matter how great, was not going to out-headline the personal lives of two high-powered corporate celebrities. That's when the nickname, Doofus Baker, was born and stuck.

"Gorgeous ring, though. You have to admit he has great taste in jewelry." *A typical comment from Gina*, Carrie thought as she hung up.

Sara was the next to call Carrie to check in on how she thought it had all gone. Personally, Sara hoped the proposal hadn't ruined the entire event for Carrie. So much work and money had gone into making it spectacular.

"Sara, I was going to call you tomorrow." A very soft-spoken Carrie had answered the phone again. "The party was incredible. You did a fantastic job."

When silence hung on the line, Sara couldn't help but ask about the elephant in the room. "Of course, we've only just met, so I hope you don't think I'm being nosy...are you going to marry him?"

"Yeah. In some weird way I feel that I have to. But I love him, so it's not a bad thing. It's just that he blew off the purpose of the evening and one-upped me, so to speak."

"I certainly wish you all the best, Carrie. Of course I know you'll be tremendously busy, but I hope we can stay in touch. Maybe have lunch sometime when I'm back in San Francisco."

"Sara, you're not getting away from me that easily. I understand if you have to return to your other clients' needs, but I want to start planning the wedding with you soon."

Sara was flabbergasted. "Really? That's great Carrie! Have you set a date already?"

"We're going to talk about it tonight over dinner. I want to plan it out fairly quickly. Frankly, I want to get it over with so I can give Kendall Tech my full attention. Even so, I hate the idea of leaving on a honeymoon instead of sitting at grandfather's desk. Oh! Did I tell you? When my grandmother received her invitation to the gala, she had my grandfather's desk moved from the Marin house to my new office as a gift. It was a fantastic surprise.

"Wow! That was generous," Sara commented, without realizing how much the desk meant to Carrie. "I'll call you tomorrow to find out what you and Charles decided."

"Sara," Carrie stopped Sara from signing off. "Gina will be my maid of honor and I'd like you in the wedding party too. I think we've become good friends in this short period."

Sara was touched and happy about the request. "I think so, too, Carrie," she said warmly. "I would be honored. I'm so glad we met. I'll call you tomorrow."

Carrie had an hour to herself before Charles was expected back. Sitting in her usual spot on the overstuffed couch with Louie on her lap, Carrie said out loud, "Be careful what you imagine for the future Carrie Kendall—you got everything you've always dreamed of."

CHAPTER 25
HANK

"TJ, I have something to tell you, buddy." Three days after getting the call from June, Hank was getting around to letting TJ know that his mother had returned.

They were heading south on their way back to San Francisco after discovering two great towns they both could agree on as a place where they would like to live. Now, sitting in a booth at yet another IHOP, TJ was finishing his daily ration of bacon and pancakes. This time with boysenberry syrup.

Hank didn't know how to ease into the news. He took a swig of coffee and said, "Your mom came home and she wants to see you."

"HUH?" TJ's eyes got very big and round. His usually happy little face dropped and tears started to flow down his round cheeks. He had been holding in his sadness for nearly a year and now it erupted on the surface. Embarrassed since he was in a public place, TJ tried stemming the tears with the palms of little hands. Wiping hard at his eyes that wouldn't cooperate, the outpouring of tears continued. The waitress came up to offer Hank a refill on his coffee and quickly left after seeing the change in the darling little boy who had bounced into the restaurant just half an hour ago.

Moving to the other side of the booth to sit next to TJ, shielding him from other patrons' nosy glances, Hank took a napkin and gently mopped his son's face. "Let's go." Hank dropped some cash on the table and got his boy out of the restaurant with only a few heads turning to watch as they left. In the car TJ let loose a mixture of anger and confusion.

"I don't want to see her! I hate her!" Hank took his son's balled up fists into his large hands. "It's okay to be mad. What she did to us, to you, was terrible. But I guess she realized how much she loves you and wants to see you." Hank couldn't believe he was defending Althea's despicable actions and the pain she had caused her only child.

"Tell you what. We have to go back to Las Vegas, but we'll make a plan. You and me. It's time we got things together." TJ didn't understand the choice his father was giving him, but whatever it was, sounded like he'd be with his dad and that's what he wanted most.

June was waiting for them at the Las Vegas airport. TJ ran into her arms and she was barely able to scoop him up. "What have you been eating boy? You weigh a ton and you've only been gone for two weeks!"

"Pancakes, Gramma! Dad let me have pancakes and hot chocolate every day for breakfast!"

"Well, we'll see about your diet once we get you settled back home. But I am so glad to see you both. It's been pretty quiet for me, up until a couple of days ago, that is."

June and Hank couldn't talk freely in front of TJ on the ride home from McCarran Airport, but they shared worried looks as they noticed TJ getting quieter and quieter the closer they got to home. Finally, TJ asked, "Is Mom gonna be home?"

"No sweetie," June answered, "I don't think so." Hearing that, TJ shoulders relaxed, but he didn't say anything else.

Jumping out of the car when they got there, TJ ran straight to his room.

"What should I do, Junie?" Hank asked as he dumped their suitcases in the hallway. "I have no idea how to handle this."

"Let Althea take some responsibility here, Hank. She made the mess. She needs to clean it up and talk with the boy."

"But that's my heart and soul in there. I can't stand aside and let her take control of the situation."

At that moment the front door slammed open and Althea shouted, "Where's my baby?! TJ! It's Momma! I'm home!" Dropping three large shopping bags filled with boxes of toys, Althea swept past Hank with a glance and walked down the hall toward TJ's closed bedroom door.

"Where's my guy? TJ?"

TJ was not in his room. He was nowhere to be found in the apartment. They checked the pool area and apartment complex community room. They called up and down the street. TJ was gone.

"Oh my God!" Althea screamed. "What have you done with him? Where is he?" Althea turned on Hank and her mother. "You're both evil. You've taken my boy!"

Hank ignored her ranting after saying, "You're insane, Althea." He called the police, then grabbed his car keys and ran out the front door. Turning the key in the ignition, Hank whispered, "And thanks." Without knowing what she'd done, Althea had just helped Hank make another big decision.

Neighbors were called and everyone who knew TJ was out looking for him. *He couldn't have gone far in such a short time*, Hank thought. But TJ had snuck out the back door within a minute after getting home and had a fifteen-minute head start. He didn't want to see his mother. He was serious about that, and if his dad didn't do something about it, then he decided he had to leave.

Hank's heart was breaking and his mind was racing while driving through the neighborhood. *Where are you, Buddy? Don't do this to me!*

Five hours later, TJ still hadn't surfaced. Althea was sitting on the couch waiting for the phone to ring, while June, Hank and Althea's sisters and their husbands drove up and down every street and walked down every alley, shouting TJ's name. It was getting dark and Hank's panic was rising. Back home, he walked into the kitchen talking to himself, "I can't believe this. This is a nightmare. How could he leave me?" And for the first time in Hank's life, grief erupted and he cried inconsolably.

Hands shaking, Hank took a deep breath and reached for his phone. Punching in the most often used speed dial number on his cell phone, the call was immediately answered.

"It's Hank. I'm back and I need help."

It was a signal of urgency when one of their own asked for help. "What's up man?" The resonant voice asked.

"You don't know this but I have a son and he's my world. My heart...everything...he's run away...it's a long story...but he's run away and I can't find him. He's been gone all day and now it's dark and late. I need help finding him."

"You sure you want our help? This sounds like something for the cops."

"They're looking too. Everyone is looking. We need more help. I can't breathe without this kid."

"Okay. Okay. Calm down. What do you want us to do?"

"I'll meet you with a photo. Check the bus stations, the airport, and the hotels. On the normal rounds, just ask the bellmen. He doesn't have any money that I know of. He's just six and couldn't be too far, but he could be anywhere."

"Yeah, got it. I've got five guys here sitting on their asses. We'll take a look around for ya. No worries."

"I'll be there in ten minutes with a picture."

Hank had mixed feelings about bringing in more help from the men he'd known for so long. He knew they'd go after anyone who threatened them, but they wouldn't hurt a helpless kid, Hank told himself.

Looking at his watch, he saw that it was eight o'clock, TJ's bedtime; he'd been gone for eight hours.

Between Althea's family, Hank's network of associates, and the police, a web was cast over Las Vegas. Still, finding one small boy in the city bustle was nearly impossible. Hank couldn't stand the idea of TJ out there in the world without him. He knew all too well what could happen. As a youngster he'd seen firsthand just about everything while hiding behind dumpsters in alleyways or trailing people pretending he belonged to them as they walked down the glittering strip. The worst of it was not knowing if TJ was hurt or just wandering lost beyond his familiar neighborhood.

Althea walked into the living room and slumped onto the couch beside Hank.

"Get away from me, Althea."

Ever the peacemaker, June said, "Now you two, keep it together. I don't want to hear you fighting on top of what's happened."

"I'm just telling your daughter to stay away from me. This is her fault. She's finally taken everything I have away from me. No amount of money was ever enough. No house big or good enough, no car...nothing. She always wanted more. And now that she's back, my son has run away...why didn't you just stay away?"

Althea stood up and glared at Hank.

"You left us for money, Althea. You're a whore. No better than a lousy whore. You broke TJ's heart and after you'd been gone for a year, he didn't want to see you when he heard you'd come back. That's right, it's true. He told me that and I didn't really believe it. Well, I believe it now. He didn't want to see you, but I brought him home anyway, and then he ran off so he didn't have to look at his lousy whore mother. I can't sit here any longer. I'm going back out to look for him again."

As Hank stood to leave. Althea raged back at him, bringing up his infidelity in New York, but her words were lost. Hank was deaf to her. She didn't exist. "Junie, it would be wonderful if you could get her out of here before I come back. This is not Althea's home and I want her out of here. Please call if the cops or anyone calls with any news. Otherwise I won't be back until I find my son."

Hank grabbed two coats, one for himself and an extra heavy one for TJ. It was getting cold outside.

Driving around for another hour, Hank began reliving some of his hiding places as a kid on the street. Dumpsters were always some of the best for hiding, but filthy, vile places at the same time. The nearby school. Did we walk through the school? There's plenty of hiding places there if you can get in. Hank called Junie to call the cops again and get someone to open up the school. "He could have found a way in Junie. It's worth a shot."

Hanging up, Hank continued his mental checklist of places to look. Startled when his phone went off, he pulled over to get out of the traffic. "Yeah? Did they find him?"

"Hey man. It's me. You sure do sound upset."

"Did you find something? Did you find my son?"

"Well, we found someone, but it's not your kid. It's a woman. Not one of ours. She was beat up pretty badly and left dead in the park. Gyno left her there for the cops to find. We don't want to get into that kind of trouble."

"The park? Which park?" Hank nearly stuttered, hoping his son hadn't gotten picked up by the murderer or drug addict.

"The park near Rancho in that dumpy neighborhood near Joe's Bar."

Relief flooded Hank. TJ couldn't possibly be that far from home, but the idea of other parks hadn't occurred to him before. "Thanks for the call man. I really appreciate the news." Hank wasn't being sarcastic. He knew the caller was an idiot, but a new idea for where to look for TJ came out of the conversation. Hanging up and immediately calling Junie, Hank asked her to research all the parks within ten miles of their house. "We'll start with the closest and work our way out."

The search party reorganized and headed for every large and small public park in the vicinity. The police searched the school. Then someone decided to call the hospital. Maybe he got hurt and someone dropped him off. Any idea was a good idea, but no young boy had been dropped at the county or private hospitals.

Time rolled by and Hank had to gas up before trying to find another park in the area. After driving around all night, seven a.m. came slowly and Hank was numb. He couldn't drink any more coffee.

By noon Hank was ready to drop dead with exhaustion. TJ had vanished. He couldn't keep his eyes open and drove himself home. It was quiet there with June and Althea gone. He lay down on the couch with the intention of taking a short nap. Instead of getting a rest, Hank was tortured for three hours. Nightmare after nightmare of filthy men injecting heroine into his son's little arm then molesting his helpless body. Then a knife appeared across TJ's throat. TJ was screaming for his dad but Hank couldn't get to him. Althea came and went in each scene, but it was TJ's screams that were continuous.

Drawn and sick, Hank woke with a start and a new idea of where to look exclaiming out loud to no one, "I know where he is!"

Grabbing his car keys, Hank called the police. "Did you guys check the tube under the river bridge? I'm on my way there now."

The "tube" was a cement cylinder left over from a massive water main project. It had been placed under a roadway bridge three miles away from TJ's favorite park to keep teenagers from racing motorcycles down the dry, abandoned aquifer. But it also provided shelter for junkies and the homeless. TJ had asked Hank about it months ago when they were passing over the bridge.

Hank swerved around slower traffic and charged through intersections as lights turned red. He laid on his horn to get past trucks and nearly sideswiped a police car heading in the same direction. Hank honked at them to follow. The police siren immediately blared. Hank didn't know if they were after him because of his driving or they'd gotten the call to check under the bridge.

Hank parked, blocking one full lane of traffic, and hurled himself down the cement embankment. Stumbling from exhaustion, Hank ran full out to the immense concrete cylinder and stepped inside. Squinting after being in the brilliant afternoon sunlight, he tried to adjust to sudden darkness. The enclosure stank of urine; the crunch underfoot was probably old needles and broken bottle glass. Going further inside Hank shouted, "TJ?" Hank's hoarse shout reverberated in the damp, cold tunnel. "TJ!" Hank called again while making his way deeper inside. A small dark lump moved about ten feet away from where Hank was standing. He saw it move. Knowing it could be anything from someone sleeping off a bad trip to a wild animal, he listened for a moment. Then he heard a weak, high-pitched little voice, "Daddy?"

For the third time in Hank's life, tears flowed freely down his face. Hank scooped up his son and cradled him tightly.

"Not so tight, Daddy. My stomach hurts."

Hank's loud echoing sobs attracted the officers who had followed Hank to the scene. As they approached they had no idea whether the boy was found dead or alive but it was obvious from the racking sound coming out of Hank that TJ was no longer missing.

An hour later TJ was sitting up in bed holding a bowl of chocolate ice cream inches from his face. The doctor had checked him over and found a bruised rib, which was causing TJ's "stomach to hurt." It had been a long cold night under a bridge. TJ would remain in the hospital overnight for observation.

TJ had got the point across to his dad.

"I'll never let you down again, buddy. I promise." Hank said while sitting on the hospital bed as close to TJ as possible. "I should have known you meant what you said about not wanting to see your mom."

"That's okay, Dad. I guess I have to see her, but I won't kiss her."

Hank had done everything but tie Althea down to keep her from coming to the hospital. He calmly explained that TJ simply didn't want to see her right now and that she could begin making amends to him by respecting that. But of course her promise didn't last long and Althea waltzed into the hospital room with her big bag of toys, making smoochy baby-talk. TJ stared at the mother he hardly knew anymore and turned his head, refusing to let her touch him. The doctor happened to be in the room at the time and suggested she leave. Indignant, she took her bag of goodies and stomped out of the room.

TJ saw his mom in the company of his grandmother a few times after that, but he would never touch her and ran if she tried to reach out to him. It was a tacit agreement that all would be well as long as she kept her distance.

A few days later, recovering quickly but still sore and forced to stay physically quiet while his rib healed, TJ was ready to pick up where they'd left off. "What are we gonna do, dad?"

"I'm ready for a change. How about you?"

"Yeah!"

"I keep thinking about that little town just north of San Francisco. You liked the horses in the fields. Remember that? We could go hiking and fishing. When you're older, you could go to that neat-looking school in town. You could even ride the bus to get there."

"I remember. Are we gonna move there? What about Gramma...and Mom?"

"Yeah. We're getting out of Las Vegas. Gramma knows she can live with us anytime she wants. Or come visit whenever, but I don't know about your mom."

"Let's go...I just want to be with you."

"Same here. I've decided to make some big changes in our lives. It's gonna be great."

Hank's intention was to move fairly quickly. To find a house and make the transition from drug dealer to used car salesman or whatever it was that he'd be doing in California. He wanted to set up a new home for TJ and get himself out of the drug business as soon as possible.

He made the first of several calls to David, hoping for some advice about making a move. Then he called his boss.

CHAPTER 26

"Jimmie, it's me, Hank. I need to talk to you."

"Hey, Hank. It just so happens I'm available today." Jimmie was always available, but played the role of a busy boss. "Let's get lunch at Jose's at two o'clock."

Schedules for lunch and dinner were far from normal when one worked most of the night. Breakfast was a meal unknown to thousands who worked through the night in Las Vegas, usually sleeping until noon or later. It was like that for Hank and the appointed time worked for him. He could talk to Jimmie, then pick TJ up from school at 3:30.

Jose's was the usual meeting place with the main man, who was known for his slight stature but always talked about his "big stick." Jimmie liked the hot spicy Mexican food. He also liked the hostess, who put up with his advances.

Hank entered the noisy restaurant. Plastic red-and-white checked cloths covered the tables and sombreros were tacked to the walls. The horns of Mariachi band recordings blared. Jose's was always busy, so the chips were still warm in the basket when a new customer was seated by the lovely Juanita. "Thanks for meeting me, Jimmie." Hank began, while Jimmie eyeballed Junita's retreating rump. "I want to express my appreciation for your help with finding my son. That was the worst day of my life."

"S'okay, Hank. What are friends for, except you should have told me you had a kid sooner. I thought we were tight."

"Well...you actually do know me pretty well. I like to keep professional and personal separate. It's smarter that way."

"Sure. Sure. I know that. Ya never know when that kind of information could be useful to the wrong kind of person. You just got the one kid?" Jimmie was pretty good at small talk for about two minutes before losing interest and wanting to get on with business. Without answering, Hank said, "What's your favorite here, Jimmie? I'm buying...you know, just to say thanks."

"That's real nice, Hank. It's good to show appreciation for your friends."

Figuring the nice chat had about run out, Hank got to the point after the waitress had taken their orders and brought their beers. "Jimmie. I don't know if you have kids or not. I don't need to know. But you understand that sometimes luck can just run out and I'm thinking my time may be coming to get out of Las Vegas." Waiting a beat while Jimmie sat back to let the information sink in, Hank went on. "I want to start up something different from what I've been doing. I won't compete with you and the guys—in fact, I won't be in the business at all, and you know I'll never look back or remember anybody from these past eighteen years."

"So, you asking or telling me that you want out?" Jimmie had finished his first beer while Hank was talking. "You want another beer?"

"Yeah. I'll take another beer." Hank ordered another beer for each of them when the waitress returned with their steaming plates of rice and beans hiding under tamales and enchiladas. There was enough food on each man's plate to feed a family of four.

"I guess that's what I'm telling you, Jimmie. But you've been good to me and out of respect for your position, I'm telling you first while asking for your good wishes...or good riddance as the case may be." Hank added the last bit as a joke, with a smile while Jimmie began demolishing his lunch and downing his beer. For a little guy he sure could pack down the chow.

"So what do you think? I'd like to leave pretty soon, but of course I'll line up the hotel contacts with a new guy if you want."

"You're a masterful middleman, Hank. There's never been any trouble with you. I got to hand it to you. Getting in with some of those guys at the hotels was genius and we all made a lot of money with your help. Naturally I hate to see you go, but to tell you the truth, I believe in a certain amount of luck myself. I've been in the business a lot longer than you and maybe my time is coming up too. But unlike you, there's nowhere else I want to be. I got a family. Yeah, surprising right? Like all us smart guys, we keep our family safe by not talking about them. You just never know when the information could be useful to somebody, right?"

Hank noticed that was the second time Jimmie mentioned how useful it could be to know about family. He also realized that Jimmie was just getting warmed up with his speech when he ordered another beer. Hank snuck a look at his watch. It was 2:45. He had thirty-five minutes before he had to leave to pick up TJ. Knowing the rules, though, you let Jimmie talk until he was done—otherwise things simply wouldn't go your way if you wanted something from him.

Ten minutes later Jimmie ordered another beer. "You want a beer, Hank? You've only had two, but who's counting?"

"No thanks, but excuse me, will ya? I'm ready to piss. Be right back."

"You don't need my permission for that. Piss away!" Jimmie flapped a small hand with a huge diamond ring on his pinky finger in the direction of the bathrooms.

Standing in the dark hallway outside the men's room, Hank made a call.

Althea answered.

"Althea, I need to talk to Junie."

"Why?"

"I need her to pick up TJ. I can't get away from a business lunch without blowing a deal. Would you please ask your mother to come to the phone?" Hank knew he was on thin ice letting Althea know he needed help with TJ. She could turn it into a disaster if she chose to.

"She's not here."

"Why did you answer her cell phone? Why didn't she take it with her?" Hank was rambling in his hurry to get through Althea to her mother. Time was wasting and he really did need to build in a minute's relief before getting back to Jimmie as fast as possible.

"She's shopping."

Althea was clearly enjoying being uncooperative.

"Why doesn't she have her phone with her?"

"It's sitting here in front of me in its charger. She forgot it. Why does she have to pick up TJ?"

"I told you, *you bitch,* my meeting is running long and TJ needs a ride home."

"I'll do you a favor this time, Hank. I'll go get him." Smugness oozed out of Althea's voice as she told Hank what she'd do for him.

Weighing his options, it was the only way. He couldn't get hold of TJ, who was too young to take the bus and know which stop to get off at, anyway. He'd never done it before. Trusting that his son would forgive him, Hank said. "Okay, Althea. You need to be there at 3:30. He always meets me at the big tree."

"I can figure it out. But pick him up at Mom's condo. I don't want to drive him over to the house."

"Sure. I'll be there as soon as I can."

Hanging up, Hank rushed to the men's room and returned to the volatile Jimmie.

"I don't want to know what took you so long, Hank. It couldn't have been a pretty sight in that toilet."

Hiding his disgust, Hank asked him if he wanted a shot to go with those beers. He needed to smooth Jimmie's impatience and knew a little tequila would do it.

"Yeah, I'll take a shot or two." Jimmie snapped his stubby fingers at Juanita. "I respect what you're telling me about wanting to get out of this town and I'm going to help you. Tell you what I have in mind." Jimmie outlined one last big deal for Hank to pull off for "old times' sake" before leaving the great state of Nevada. "It will make you enough money to buy out everything on fuckin' Rodeo Drive in fuckin' Beverly Hills and never have to work again in your life, Hank. And it will make me even more."

Jimmie's so-called idea of "help" explained his amiable reaction to Hank's desire to extricate himself from years of delivering drugs.

Sneaking another glance at his watch, Hank saw that it was now 4:30. Poor TJ had been stuck with his mother for an hour already. He could only hope that June had showed up and had taken TJ home. He turned his thoughts back to Jimmie's requirement for leaving. Any disagreement with Jimmie usually resulted a dangerous correction in the victim's behavior. Maiming or even death was not uncommon. Hank took the safe road and gave a positive response to the idea. "That's a risky order, Jimmie, but I think our distribution system can handle the load." Hank and Jimmie reviewed the details in a coded language only they understood. Each knew exactly what needed to be done.

"One more shot for the road!" Jimmie yelled at Juanita to join them.

By the time Hank left Jose's, it was nearly time for dinner. He prayed that he hadn't just made the biggest mistake of his life by agreeing to carry out Jimmie's idea for running a huge amount of coke into the usual hotels plus getting a few more establishments "on line." But he had little choice. The threat of retribution was too great should Hank decline to cooperate, especially since Jimmie now knew about TJ.

Calling June's cell phone again, it was a relief to hear her answer.

"TJ's fine, Hank. He's watching cartoons and eating spaghetti. He was alone with her for about an hour and doesn't appear to be upset. Don't worry so."

"I don't ever want him to think I've let him down, Junie. I'm on my way home now."

Ten minutes later Hank walked through the door.

"Hey, Dad." An apparently happy little boy left his dinner to greet his father.

"Hi, buddy." Hank pitched his son in the air. "You're not mad at me?"

"Gramma said you tried to come get me but was gonna be late. Mom didn't try to kiss me or nothin' so it was okay."

Sadness showed in June's and Hank's eyes. It was a terrible thing when a little boy didn't want his mother's love.

CHAPTER 27
DAVID AND HANK

For six months after entering rehab, David woke up at six o'clock every morning. He took his scheduled time for a shower, shave, and teeth brushing before going downstairs to breakfast. By seven o'clock he stood in line with a hundred other men with plate in hand for a pretty decent breakfast. He could select as much as he wanted of any type of breakfast meat—bacon, sausage, ham, and the occasional small steak—plus scrambled or fried eggs, toast, coffee, and three types of fruit juice. There were no exceptions to the routine. No calls were allowed in or out for the first month. Then David could make one call a week for the remainder of his stay. They had confiscated his cell phone on the first day, but that didn't matter. David had no one to call. He once tried to reach his sons, but they weren't speaking to him. One called him a loser before hanging up. The other hung up without a word.

The Lighthouse Rehab Center for men was swanky by most standards. The white-collar "inmates" were being counseled by some of the country's leading rehabilitation experts. David was assigned work duty after a daily session with a psychiatrist. Then he was free for an hour "to contemplate his navel," as the men called their free time before gathering for a two-hour group therapy session. An hour for daily exercise was also part of the routine that had become David's life in upstate New York.

With one week to go before being released, David started making plans for what to do when he got out. Though he was also required to complete 160 hours of community service after leaving, David could be working at the same time. A sponsor had been assigned to him and they got along just fine. David was to call anytime, day or night, when tempted to slip off the wagon and dip into his old habits of using.

David felt strange the day he was released. There was no anchoring responsibility. No routine. No schedule for meals or therapy sessions. He wasn't sure he wanted to go back to his apartment, but with no option other than a hotel, he found the two-lane highway and headed south. It was a five-hour drive from the rehab manor to Manhattan. Alone, with no job or healthy distractions, he wasn't sure he could make a go of it without taking a drink, but he sure as hell was going to try. He knew the rules. They had been pounded into him for six months: Attend an AA meeting and call his sponsor every day until they both felt he was securely on the road to recovery. He knew the temptation to take a drink in particular would be very difficult. The drugs he could do without now and he felt ready to return Hank's calls without asking for a connection.

Hank was at home watching *Finding Nemo* with TJ. Though it was a cartoon, it was a difficult movie for Hank to watch. It was about the great love between a dad clown fish and his little boy clown fish but the little boy had been captured by a scuba diver and ended up in an aquarium in a dentist's office. The dad spent the entire time looking for his son, worried that he'd never see him again. "This is a sad movie, TJ. I don't know if I can get through it without crying," Hank was saying as TJ punched his dad in the arm.

"Daa-ad, don't be a sissy!"

Hank's ringing phone took him away from the happiest part of the movie. He didn't recognize the caller's number and answered, "Hello?"

"Hank? It's David. How are you?"

Leaving TJ on the couch to finish watching the fish dad reunite with his son, Hank said, "David, great to hear from you. Where have you been? Did you get my messages?"

The unlikely friends caught up with each other's recent past. They discovered each had come to a crossroads in his life and laughed that it came at the same time for both of them. But the rehashing of everything that had happened since Hank had left David in New York didn't last long and the men began to discuss the future.

"I'm thinking about moving to California. My son, TJ, and I found a town we both like. I'm making plans now to get out of the business and start over."

David thought moving to California was a great idea for Hank, but feeling at loose ends said, "I'm not sure where I'm going to land now that I'm a free agent. I've put out a few feelers for a job, but my contacts know my history and are uncomfortable working with me again. Jack, my boss, said he'd consider taking me back after rehab but hasn't returned my calls, so I guess that door is closed."

By the end of the conversation, they decided to meet up in San Francisco. David was ready for a change of scene while deciding what the next chapter in his life should be. California was as good a place as any to start over.

"I have some business to take care of over the next several days but we'll meet you at the end of the month," Hank said.

"Well, stay out of trouble, man. I'm glad to hear you're hanging up the old ways. Something will work out. You know what they say..."

"What? What do *they* say?"

"*The ability to make decisions is a sign of strength and intelligence.* And..." struggling to remember the exact quote, David added, "*You are a result of your past decisions...so, decide your future...and...What you think determines your place in life.* I got that drilled into me in rehab. It's in a book they gave us and they made us create a new vision for our lives. What I got out of it all was that I have the ability to take control of my life, one day at a time. No one else can decide how to live my life. So I'm taking responsibility for making some changes for the better and making amends to my kids, Josh and Tim. You're a smart man, Hank, and I'll tell you right now, what you're talking about doing is a big decision, but hang on to what you're thinking. Things have a way of working out."

"Uh huh, thanks. I'll try to remember all that."

"Hey, I heard a lot of stories about how people pulled themselves out of the dumpster, in some cases literally! I'll see you in a couple of weeks."

Huh, David thought to himself after talking to Hank, *I guess all that positive stuff they told us sank in.*

Hank rejoined TJ on the couch. "Who was that, Dad?"

"An old friend who's gonna meet us in San Francisco when you get out of school in a couple of weeks. We'll see him, then go find us a mountain to climb."

"All right!" TJ pumped his little fist the way Tiger Woods always did after making a great shot.

CHAPTER 28

Hank wasn't feeling good about everything he had to do in a very short amount of time. His existing connections had taken months to set up. Not everyone is interested in making big bucks as a drug donkey. That's what the bellmen were called, since they were the ones making the final deliveries. He made a few calls to the guys he'd known for the longest time to ask for any leads on making new connections at other hotels.

"We're expanding," he told them, "and there's millions to be made for the right people who want in." In each case, the voice on the other end said that he'd sniff around and let Hank know.

After a week, no one new had come along to help move an enormous amount of coke. But, everyone involved knew that, if no one screwed up, they'd all be rich.

The surprise came when a long-time donkey took a job at a new resort. As a concierge assigned to a VIP level of the new hotel, the man had a perfect set-up for anyone looking for illegal recreation. The news meant that Hank now didn't need to add anyone to the team. However, Hank had a bad feeling about the whole thing. Fear was mounting as he fought his bout of good conscience. He'd been trying to make a significant change and the angel on his shoulder chose this time to challenge his actions. He knew he'd been living a felonious life and had dodged the law on several occasions. Hank didn't want to risk everything he had with his son. He had promised to be there for TJ and if this last big deal didn't work, he'd be in prison for life.

*Decide your future...*Hank remembered what David had said. *I may be deciding a horrible future for me and TJ if I go through with this*, Hank thought.

As tempting as the amount of money to be made was, Hank was thinking about stepping out. Jimmie could get one of the other guys to set up the pick-up point. The plan as he knew it was that a plane from Colombia was to land at an undisclosed location and transfer the drugs to a prop plane that would shuttle the cargo to a private airstrip outside the city limits. Hank didn't know who owned the airstrip or where the warehouse was; he would have to be told at the last minute.

Conflicting thoughts scrambled Hank's brain day and night: *It's so much money; we'll be set up for life. But it doesn't feel right.* Shanti's voice haunted him, "Get out…do something good with your life." And his own better judgment challenged him with the question of what would happen to TJ if he went to prison?

Hank was getting very little sleep. The day was fast approaching when the call would come in with the address for the pick-up and Hank would be expected to convey the information to his men. The success of the job now rested nearly entirely on his shoulders. He had a choice. To do his job and forward the information about where to collect the packages of white powder for distribution on the street and in hotels, or to walk away hoping to live another day. But that would be unlikely. Thinking, *If I die, what would happen to TJ? Probably the same thing that will happen to him if I'm sent to prison.* Althea would get him back or, because they had divorced and Althea had proved to be an unfit mother, TJ would go to June. Either way TJ would grow up without a father—just as he had. It was a conundrum and it was Hank who had gotten himself into this mess.

More frightening thoughts came to mind.

What if I bailed on the job and Jimmie went after TJ now that he knows how important my son is to me? What did he say at lunch? You never know what personal information could become useful to someone who wanted to hurt you? Hank couldn't continue that scenario: it was unthinkable.

Hank put his face in his hands and said out loud, "What *the hell* am I doing?"

CHAPTER 29
GINA, SARA, AND CARRIE

The morning after Carrie's big evening, Sara, Gina, and Dmitri left San Francisco on La Vie Modeling's private jet. The company had sent a Lear jet to pick up two of their most profitable models to get them back to Los Angeles in time for a photo shoot. Sara hitched a ride and would then wait for a puddle jumper in the commercial terminal that would take her on home to San Diego.

It was a short flight, but gave Sara and Gina a little time to get better acquainted in the cabin's cocoon of plush carpet, leather armchairs, and fluffy pillows. It was a relief to take it easy after weeks, months actually for Sara, of whirling around getting everything ready for Carrie's "coming out" party. That's what Gina jokingly called the extravagant evening.

Dmitri had made himself comfortable at the back of the plane for some shuteye. He looked gorgeous even while sleeping with his mouth hanging open and head tilted sideways.

"He can sleep anywhere," Gina said, glancing at her boyfriend of one year. "We met in Egypt, in the desert. We were on a shoot that started at dawn. When the sun came up, the sand, sky, everything looked golden. I've never seen anything like it. We were on camels. It was hot as hell, but I loved seeing the shifting sand as far as I could see. For the picture, I'm only looking at my watch to see the time. That's what we were selling in the ad, a canary yellow diamond watch. It was a play on the sands of time. We were picked by the client because we have the same dark hair. We look like brother and sister, I guess. When clients want a romantic image and simple contrasts, the director suggests using male and female models with the same coloring. That little trick tends to make the product stand out."

Never far from Gina's thoughts, she began talking about Jake. "Jake and I have opposite looks. He's very tall. Has blond hair, dark brown eyes, and the greatest smile. He's one of the nicest people I've ever met."

Sara ventured to get personal and asked, "So, are you guys serious? You and Dmitri?"

Gina glanced at her boyfriend and determined he couldn't hear them. "He's wonderful. A fun guy and I..." Gina interrupted herself and lowered her voice, "...he's kind of dumb. He's a great escort to parties. Good dancer, but doesn't have much to say. I think he's convinced that just because he's good looking that he doesn't have to make an effort to be interesting. I shouldn't talk, though. I barely got out of high school and only completed two years of college. I've always been kind of directionless until Jake came along."

Grabbing the opening, since Gina had just mentioned Jake's name twice, she asked, "Who's Jake?"

Caught in breaking a promise to herself not to talk about him, Gina started to explain how she got into modeling.

"I was such an idiot that day in Beverly Hills. It was a miracle that we ran into a really nice guy who got a kick out of making three silly, nobody Seattle girls' dreams come true. After I stalked Anne Hartford into a shop on Rodeo, Jake was with her, he invited us to a party that night. It was amazing. My friends didn't want to go. They were too intimidated, I think, about not being glam enough for the party crowd. I went hoping to connect with Jake, but that wasn't going to happen while he was with Anne. That's where I met my now ex-husband Robert. Robert and Jake introduced me to the right people."

"So what about Jake? Do you ever see him?" Sara pushed.

"We used to work together a lot more than we do now. Hey, did Carrie put you up to asking me about him? I may be a model, but I'm not that dumb."

Refusing to lie, Sara said, "Well, since you brought him up and I don't know who he is, I'm curious, but yeah, she did ask me to pump you a little about him. She noticed you hadn't mentioned him this weekend."

"I'm trying to get him out of my head," Gina said sadly. Her bright eyes dimmed at the thought. "He's a good friend and I think that's all we'll ever be."

Letting it drop, since Dmitri was stirring and the pilot had asked them to make sure their seat belts were fastened, Sara quickly offered, "Take a little advice from someone married three times. If you have to push the guy to take it to another level, don't waste another minute on him. Enjoy the friendship and have fun with Dmitri."

Gina smiled at Sara as Dmitri wandered to the front of the cabin to join them before landing. "Hi ladies, how *you* doin'?" The Brooklyn accent was unmistakable. Gina gave him a kiss on the cheek and turned to look out the window to watch the L.A. sprawl rise up to meet them.

◈◈◈

Sara took the next day off to clean her apartment, which had been neglected for weeks while she ran herself ragged over last minute details for Carrie's event. But she found a few minutes to check her calendar. Sara had no idea what Carrie might have in mind for the wedding, but assumed her full attention would be required. Big, small? Ballroom or garden setting? In San Francisco or somewhere else, maybe Hawaii, Sara thought. Already fantasizing for her client.

It had been five years since her third and last wedding. Each ceremony had been very different from the one before. Recommitting that she'd never try marriage again, she did wish for a partner. Someone to snuggle with on Sunday mornings, a ready companion for a movie or dinner. Right now she wasn't seeing anyone. Starting her business and becoming busy with her bookings took up every minute of thought and action, and Sara knew she would stay focused on Dare to Dream Events for quite some time. Her vision for the company was expansive, with multiple offices throughout the U.S. someday. A house, a real home somewhere in the country and then, maybe, someone to share her life with. *All in good time*, Sara thought, as she finished daydreaming at her desk and went to grab a dust cloth.

Karen called Sara at home. "Carrie Kendall called. She wants to discuss a wedding. Do we have another big gig booked with Ms. Kendall?"

Sara filled Karen in on the success of the party, replete with a marriage proposal from Carrie's ex-antagonist, new co-president and now fiancé, Charles Baker.

"I'll call Carrie back right now. Thanks for everything, Karen. You did a fantastic job keeping the office running while I've been gone. After hearing about the kind of wedding she wants, I'll likely bring you in on that project, too." Putting away the cleaning supplies, Sara went back to her home office and dialed Carrie's direct line at Kendall Technologies.

ഏഏഏ

"Can you come back? I like discussing things like this in person," Carrie had said.

Missing the private jet experience, Sara found herself on a commercial plane heading back to San Francisco the next morning. The meeting with Carrie was scheduled for nine o'clock. Sara was lucky enough to find a seat at the last minute on an early flight out of San Diego to San José; then she would rent a car and drive to Carrie's office.

Waiting for only a minute before being invited into the spacious office, Sara noticed that Carrie looked remarkably rested for a woman with so much going on. Carrie gleamed in a light grey pinstriped suit matched with a tailored, cream-colored shirt. Two gold chains draped down the "V" of the single-buttoned suit jacket. Large chunky gold cufflinks twinkled at the slender wrists. Sara felt a little frumpy in her black and white pantsuit from Macy's, sitting across from the soon-to-be-famous global corporate executive who was going to spend the rest of her day being interviewed by *Forbes, Inc.* and *Time.*

"Thanks so much for coming, Sara. I know you have other things to do, but I want to get this thing going. From the looks of my schedule I won't be around much for the next few months. This was the only opening I had to meet with you. Although I'd like you to join Charles and me for dinner tonight. Can you stay the day and leave tomorrow morning?"

Sara told Carrie without sounding obsequious, "Your wish is my command. I'm delighted to be here and will make your wedding perfectly phenomenal!"

After brainstorming for exactly one hour, Sara left knowing a lot more about what Carrie had in mind. Charles and Carrie had set the date over Sunday dinner, just as Carrie had said they would. The wedding was to be in six months. Not a long engagement, thought Sara. And, once again, not much time for organizing the kind of media-worthy affair Carrie intended. The good news was that the wedding would be held at the mansion in Marin. It had been Carrie's grandmother's idea. That left a major challenge off Sara's list for finding a venue at the last minute that would accommodate two hundred guests without a tent. "No tent," Carrie had said, and Sara knew she meant it.

With the rest of the day to herself, Sara decided to check into a nearby hotel, shop for what she'd need for spending the night plus a pair of jeans, a T-shirt and tennis shoes. She wanted to be comfortable for the afternoon drive across the bridge. She decided to try to find this massive mansion Carrie was so excited about.

It was a beautiful day in San Francisco. The sky was sparkling blue; a few fluffy white clouds lingered to the East. The bay was peaceful for a change, and Sara drove north with the windows down and the music up. Charging over the Golden Gate Bridge in her compact rental car, Sara's attention was caught by a massive white building on the hilltop in front of her. It was easily the largest house Sara had ever seen and she wondered if that could be the one. Leaving the bridge, she couldn't figure out which exit to take to find the elite neighborhood. Failing to find the road leading to the top of the hill, Sara felt care-free and continued to drive north until she got hungry.

Sara gassed up the rental car in a small town sixty-five miles beyond San Francisco and decided to look for somewhere to eat. Finding a quaint main street of boutiques and cafés, she pulled into the first parking spot she saw and jumped out. The wooden sidewalks and storefronts with overhangs were reminiscent of the old Wild West. The town certainly had character and obviously attracted tourists. The restaurants were full, and shoppers came and went with colorful bags. Breaking the relaxed, vacation atmosphere, a school bus squealed to a stop a couple of blocks away. Striding down the thoroughfare, Sara noted the calm sense of well-being that had come over her. She felt happy, content. *It's so fresh and clear here*, she thought, while noticing the bright, cleanliness of her surroundings, the smiles of passersby, and a forest-scent mingled with an aroma of fresh baked goods as she passed a bakery. It was past noon and the inviting smells in the air reminded Sara that she was starving.

After lunch Sara drove around investigating the uniquely charming area. She found a little real estate office and on impulse stopped in. The friendly receptionist seemed relieved to have someone to talk to and gave Sara a great backgrounder on the town, its history, general property values, and the type of people who were moving into the area.

"This is a special place, Ms. Collins. People who come here have discovered what's important in life. It's a lifestyle that suits only a few, but everyone I've met since moving here about five years ago has found some kind of peace within themselves. It's a social town, too, always something going on. People are real friendly here. Where are you from?"

Sara left the informative young woman with a feeling of magic around her. *She's right*, Sara thought, *this town is a slice of heaven on earth.*

It was nearly time to return to the city and meet Carrie and Charles for dinner. But Sara wanted to see more. She turned onto a curving road that forked one way down into a valley, the other leading up the mountain. Sara chose "up" and opened all the car windows to breathe in the fresh, cool air tinged with the forest's spicy scent. It didn't take long for Sara to fall in love with the neighborhood. The homes were obviously custom-built. Most were pretty big. Sara caught herself humming, something she never did.

In that moment, she knew she would live here one day. Minutes later, after rounding a bend, Sara came to a stop in front of the perfect house. The one she would have designed and had built if time and money were no obstacles. Sara knew she'd found a very special place on the planet. The house that fulfilled her vision of home was well-tended: a lush green lawn, shuttered dormer windows, and window boxes brimming with red petunias, a wide stairway up to the covered porch that stretched across the front of the house. The front door looked to be made of heavy, carved oak with a wrought-iron handle. The driveway curved into a three-car garage. There were two stone chimneys rising above the steeply pitched roof of composite shake. Loving everything about the front of the house, Sara knew she had to see the inside.

Finally checking the time, her dream bubble burst. She had dallied too long and now needed to hurry back to the city. "Ahh!" Sara said in frustration. "I may be late for dinner." Calling and leaving a message for Carrie saying that she would meet them at the restaurant, possibly fifteen minutes late, Sara pulled a U-turn and sped down the mountain, breaking the dense silence of the forest trees lining both sides of the road.

For the next several weeks Sara couldn't stop thinking about that house. "It's the damnedest thing," she told Karen. "I've never felt this way about anything. It was so beautiful and peaceful there. I loved what little I saw of the downtown area but I've got to have that house! I haven't seen the inside and it's not even for sale." After calling the real estate office and reminding the receptionist that they had met a few days ago, Sara spoke with an agent. "I'm sure I can't afford to live in that neighborhood right now, but maybe something will come along one day. Please add me to your e-mail list and call me if that house on Juniper Drive is ever listed." Though Sara continued to obsess over the house and wondered how she could ever afford to live there, Carrie's wedding began to take shape and Karen was beginning to complain about the work load she had been carrying ever since the first Kendall gala. Business was booming for Dare to Dream. The more events they did, the more the phone rang, all from word-of-mouth recommendations. Sara was facing a new decision about how big she wanted her company to become. The plan was to open offices in at least three cities on the West coast and maybe eventually in New York and Chicago. She needed some professional advice on how fast to expand and what it took to do it right, but there was too much to do to keep up with her current commitments. First she needed to hire three more employees for the office in San Diego.

In addition to Carrie's wedding and managing five other projects in various stages of progress, Sara was cooking up an idea of her own. To create an event to raise money for a new, desperately needed homeless shelter in San Francisco. Since it was to be pro bono work, Sara asked Karen to put out an all-call for volunteer help. High school students were always looking for ways to fulfill their community service requirements, as were others by court order.

CHAPTER 30
GINA

Leaving Dmitri poolside in the hundred-degree heat, Gina said, "'Bye, Babe, we have to leave for the party at six-thirty, so I'll be back around five o'clock to get ready." Dmitri managed a "'bye babe" with his eyes closed against the throbbing hot sunlight. Gina closed the gate to the condo's private pool area and left to meet her friend, another pampered beauty under contract at La Vie Modeling.

Los Angeles was a wonderful city for people with money and Gina was one of them. She was ready to enjoy a spending spree that afternoon. Two beautiful girls were on the hunt for new outfits to wear on La Vie Modeling's twenty-fifth anniversary celebration. It promised to be the hottest party in town that weekend. Literally, since the temperature hadn't dropped below eighty-five degrees at night all week.

Striding down Rodeo Drive, long, tan, bare legs glistened in the high-noon sunlight; tourists glanced and some stared. Sunglasses covered half their faces. Gina's hair was in a ponytail tucked through the back of a ball cap. Her friend Andrea's white blond hair flowed freely in what little breeze was created as they quickly walked into their favorite shop.

A second later the manager, a prettily handsome, obsequious man greeted them with air kisses on each check. "I know why you're here!" His exuberance was infectious and led one to believe that he too would be at the party that night.

"I want something soft and gauzy, Simon. I don't want to suffer the heat any more than I have to while trying to look good." At a glance, Gina assessed everything from the wild to chic and knew the dress for her wasn't here.

"Sweetie, you are the most beautiful woman in town," Simon gushed. "How could you not be beautiful tonight? Especially in one of my dresses."

"Simon, you are such a cheater. You tell every woman that she is the most beautiful in town, and shush, Andrea will hear you." Gina wrapped up her chastisement abruptly when her friend returned from the dressing room.

"Oh, Gina, you are so loyal to your..." He interrupted himself mid-sentence. "Andrea! You gorgeous woman, how did you do my dear? Did you make those gowns look good?"

Wise to his schmooze, Andrea said, "No, Simon, I didn't like any of them."

Done with their first stop, the women left the air-conditioned sanctuary and a disappointed Simon who didn't sell a ten-thousand-dollar dress that time. The girls tried two other shops nearby. An hour later, both had found something they loved, with shoes to match.

Only Jake and Robert knew about Gina's first trip to Beverly Hills. She never talked about it, but would remember being an unpolished, audacious young girl who made a decision right there on Rodeo Drive to stay in Los Angeles instead of finishing college. She had made a life-changing decision with no forethought or worry about potential consequences. If it hadn't been for Jake's invitation, though, she would probably be someone's wife with kids in Seattle by now. Gina always thought about those days whenever she shopped in Beverly Hills. Glad her life was as it was, Gina smiled at her friend and said, "See you tonight." Sans air kisses, Andrea and Gina hugged quickly and went their separate ways to get ready for the party at their boss's Bel Air mansion.

❧❧❧

"Hey! I'm home," Gina called out as she closed the front door of their leased condo. Dmitri didn't answer. Hearing the shower running, she slipped into the master bedroom, hung up her new dress, dumped her other bags on the bed, then quickly took off her clothes. She intended to join Dmitri, and stopped short when she heard voices. One female voice, followed by Dmitri's deep laugh. Leaning against the door before entering, she felt sick to her stomach. She nearly barged in to evacuate her lunch in the toilet. Bending over to take a deep breath, she simply couldn't believe what he was doing where they had showered together just that morning. Gina truly didn't know what to do. Go in and attack them and scream like a banshee or tiptoe back out and call to let Dmitri know she'd finished shopping sooner than expected and was on her way home. She heard the rising moans of the woman and Dmitri's usual, "Oh baby," grunts.

Putting her clothes back on, stumbling into the living room, she didn't want to hear any more. Gina sat on the couch sobbing, "Oh my God," between gulps of air. She was crying so hard she hadn't heard the water turn off. The lovers came out of the bedroom stark naked and stood stock-still when they saw Gina with her head in her hands, shoulders heaving. She felt their presence before hearing the woman shout, "Who's this?" and run back into the bedroom. Dmitri wrapped a towel around his waist before going to Gina.

"Don't you dare touch me," Gina screamed. "I trusted you, you bastard!"

The top-heavy blonde managed to find her bikini pieces and streak out the door before Gina could lash out at her too.

"What the hell are you doing? I thought we had something going together. That girl was at the pool when I left. I saw her. Did you just meet or has this been going on for awhile?" Then Gina spewed the foulest language she'd ever used while crying her eyes out. Dmitri sat and took it, waiting for Gina to stop screaming.

After a minute, Gina stood up in front of her live-in lover of one year with her hands on her hips and finally waited for him to say something.

"Babe. Sorry! I didn't know you'd be home so soon." As if that were an excuse, Gina became all the more infuriated.

"You have no idea what you're doing. I can't believe I've wasted so much of my life on men like you. Get out of here! I can't stand to look at you."

Dmitri tried to reach for her, thinking all she needed to calm down was a hug.

"Are you retarded? Leave me alone! Get out!"

Chastised as if by his mother, Dmitri hung his head. "I have nowhere to go, Gina. I'm really sorry about Toni. I didn't mean to hurt you. Please. I'll stop seeing her if you let me stay."

Gina had one more message for him. "Get out before I kill you."

That got his attention. "Okay. Okay. I'm going. Let me just grab a few clothes."

Sitting back down on the couch while Dmitri went to the bedroom, Gina began crying all over again. Her life was a mess when it came to men. What is it about these guys, she asked herself.

By the time Dmitri left Gina alone with a box of Kleenex, it was after 5:30. They were expected to attend the anniversary event together as the agency's top modeling team for Jean Claude Jeans. All the agency's clients would be there expecting to party with their models. *I can't go!* Gina thought and wondered if Dmitri would still go. *Probably*, she thought, *he's too stupid and unfeeling not to go.*

She called her boss to wriggle out of attending. She explained what Dmitri had done. Ariel, the founding principal of La Vie Modeling, gasped, "That's repulsive darling. How could he do such a thing to our beautiful little Gina?" It was a canned response to something that happened all the time in the industry. "But you must be here. We have a commitment to Jean Claude and he's one of our most profitable clients. We simply can't disappoint him over such a boring situation, sweetie. It's getting late. I'll understand that you won't be coming together, but you must be here," she repeated. "I'll send a car for you in an hour and will make up some excuse to Jean Claude if he arrives before you do."

The repetition of how she "must be there" reminded Gina of her contract with La Vie Modeling. Parties of this importance required models to attend as decoration and added interest.

Now Gina had to pull herself together. She couldn't use the same shower Dmitri and that girl had just used, so Gina transferred some things to the guest bath. *It will be a miracle if I can get rid of this puffiness*, she thought. Gina's eyes were swollen and red. Her usually creamy complexion was mottled; the strain around her mouth threatened wrinkles.

Finding her staple bottle of witch hazel, Gina soaked a washcloth and laid it over her face for several minutes. As she pressed gently on the saturated cloth, the cooling sensation refreshed her senses and soothed her swollen face. Her brain began to clear and Gina shifted into emergency mode for getting ready. Showered, hair dried and curled, makeup on, at last Gina pulled on a swatch of sky-blue satin that matched her eyes. It draped around the neck, leaving her back and shoulders bare, plunged at the neckline and flowed tightly over her hips to stop mid-thigh. Her strappy, rhinestone heels picked up the flash of minimal sparkle in the fabric. She brushed out her hair, leaving it to cascade down her bare back like threads of onyx silk. It was going to be hot. She was thinking she could later regret not pulling her hair up off her neck, but liked the effect as she assessed her appearance in the guest bedroom mirror.

Right on time, the door bell rang. Gina walked through a light mist of Calvin Klein's Euphoria and grabbed her tiny purse. The chauffeur greeted her as 'Miss Severns' and helped her into the black stretch limo. *I hope I can keep it together tonight*, Gina thought to herself, as they pulled away from the curb. She also hoped to just make an appearance and leave early.

It was eight o'clock by the time Gina arrived. The party was well under way, since no one wanted to miss a minute of celebrity presence, gourmet food, and dancing to live music by a variety of famous entertainers. Bel Air was considered even more elite than Beverly Hills. Showcase homes were usually one of several owned by the mega-rich. Gina worked for one of those people, a couple from France who spent little time in California. The agency was the woman's pet project. She ran the monolithic giant she had created by supplying beautiful men and woman from the world over to their clients. It was an elite group of models—only fifty under contract. Gina was one of those in a starring role and she needed to muster up a high standard of charm and wit for the challenging evening ahead.

The place was packed and the atmosphere was magical. The party theme played out the steamy L.A. temperature but with a tropical feel. To the relief of the three hundred guests, the house was, of course, air conditioned, and outside a hundred small fans had been hidden in the fronds of potted palms. It was a wonderland of balmy breezes and thousands of white twinkling lights that provided most of the ambient lighting. Fragrant tropical flowers were everywhere. A light beat of music pulsed in every room. Dancing was outside on the massive terrace. The agency's founder would be presented with a life-size crystal sculpture of Venus and Zeus as entwined lovers. Fortunately someone other than Gina and Dmitri had been chosen to give a short speech and present the sculpture—a gift from the agency's stable of models.

Gina held a blended margarita and stood apart from the ebb and flow of countless small groups of extraordinarily beautiful people. It was unreal to see so many truly good-looking people in one place. But that was the business she was in. No wonder everyone jumped from one person's bed to another with little thought of consequences. It wasn't an emotionally healthy industry, and Gina was just beginning to see that maybe she should think about doing something else. Plus, she was now one of the oldest models at La Vie Modeling. During her time in southern California her heart had been broken twice, by Robert and now Dmitri. *Why start looking for a third heartbreaker?* Gina wondered, as she watched the crowd mix and mingle. She saw Robert across the room. He was married again. Gina checked out the dark-haired beauty on his arm. *I bet Robert made sure she could scuba dive before taking the plunge with her.* Gina smiled to herself at the little pun as she turned her head to see who had just come up beside her.

"What's so funny, my gorgeous girl?" But, noting that something was wrong, he added, "Are you okay?"

Gina's smile widened, seeing it was Jake.

"Jake!" Gina wrapped her arms around the neck of the man she had fallen in love with nine years before. To Gina, Jake was the only thoughtful, caring, sweet guy in Los Angeles. "I'm so glad you're here. I didn't know if you'd gotten back from Paris. How did the job go?"

Jake took Gina's hand and said, "It was great. I always love Paris and I'm glad to be back. But what's wrong? You look sad." Gina knew that he was the only one in the world, except for her mother, who ever noticed anything amiss and bothered to ask about it. She thought she had succeeded in reducing the puffiness around her eyes but Jake usually looked harder at her than most.

Feeling transparent with this man, Gina lowered her eyes.

"It's not about how you look, Gina. But your eyes say it all. Something's happened."

Gina didn't have a chance to explain since the reason she had to come to the party sauntered up and put his arm around her waist. "There's my little cherie. My beautiful Gina. Darling, come dance with me."

Jake understood it was business and that Gina had to play nice with the agency's biggest client, Jean Claude. Stepping away, Jake said, "Have fun. Please don't let me keep you."

Jean Claude monopolized Gina for most the evening. She danced when he wanted to dance. She ate when he was hungry and matched him nearly drink for drink, though Gina was keeping her libation of choice to wine and water, while he drank dry vodka martinis. Jean Claude took her hand to lead her to the dance floor again when Gina saw them. Dmitri and his bimbo du jour. "I can't believe he brought her!" Gina murmured loud enough for Jean Claude to ask her what she meant. "That scum, Dmitri." Gina decided to tell him. "We've been living together for over a year and I caught him with another woman this afternoon and now he's brought her here. I can't believe the heartless nerve."

"Ah. I am so sorry to hear about your sadness, cherie. It happens, though. Is there anything I can do to make you happy?" Jean Claude was already pulling her close to him and nipping at her throat.

"No, Jean Claude. I'm upset. Please stop that."

"Ah well, I am not so drunk as to forget my manners," he said, but left her abruptly in the middle of the dance floor.

Fighting to control another bout of tears from hurt and frustration, Gina walked quickly inside to find the bathroom and nearly ran into Ariel, her boss.

"Gina! I haven't seen you all evening." About to give the expected platitude of how beautiful Gina looked, Ariel began, "You look, well, actually you look terrible! Don't tell me you're still mad at Dmitri. He's just a boy. He'll get over her and come back to you, darling. Don't you worry."

Gina shook her head in wonder that yet another person in her life could be so shallow. "Ariel!" she said, "you look glorious. I'm just headed to do a little touch-up. I'll be fine, though I'm not happy that Dmitri brought that girl with him tonight."

"Ahhh. Jealousy. I know the feeling. I can be very jealous too." The extravagant woman before her still didn't get it and Gina was ready to bolt. Summoning up every ounce of control, Gina managed to say, "Thank you for sending the car for me. It's a beautiful party and I'm very happy to be here."

"Not at all darling. You're one of my favorite little chicks. How are things going with Jean Claude?"

"Everything is fine, Ariel. I better let you get on to your other guests and I'll go fix my makeup."

"A good idea for us both my dear. I'll see you tomorrow at the office."

While Dmitri had the decency to stay away from Gina, he had certainly made a point of lusting after his new friend on the dance floor. Jake noticed and realized why Gina was upset. *The bastard*, Jake thought. He had also noticed Jean Claude's advances and didn't like it. In fact, it dawned on Jake that he'd been keeping track of Gina all evening. It bothered him to see the usual happy light in her eyes clouded over. Clearly she was hurting. Making a decision, he followed her into the bathroom.

"Jake! What are you doing? This is designated as a ladies' room."

"I don't care, Gina. It appears we're alone and I want to talk with you. I know why you're upset. When did you and Dmitri break up?"

"I don't want to discuss it. It's over, that's all I know."

"I have an idea. Why don't I get you out of here right after the ceremony? The presentation is to begin at ten o'clock and it's nearly that now. I have my car. We'll go for a ride with the top down, then I'll take you home. Okay?"

"Yeah. I would love that, Jake," Gina said with a sad smile. "I care about you. Do you know that?"

"Fluff up now. I'll meet you outside near the podium."

Thirty minutes later, the valet brought Jake's car to the front door. Jake helped Gina into his black Porsche Carrera and they took off down the long driveway. Before leaving the city, they stopped at In-N-Out Burger, causing a bit of stir among the casual crowd in the restaurant. Jake had taken off his tie and jacket but it was obvious he wore a trend-setting tux and the woman with him sparkled in an Armani mini dress. Jake made her laugh as they shared a large basket of French fries. Polishing off a strawberry shake, Gina sat back and said, "That's the most food I've eaten in one sitting in years."

"Yeah, me too." Jake leaned over and took her hand and played with her fingers for a minute as Gina watched him.

Silently, Jake stood up and joined Gina on her side of the booth. He picked up her hand again and held it against his chest. "Gina, do you feel my heart? Do you know that I love you?"

It was the most romantic admission of love that ever took place at In-N-Out Burger. Tears escaped Gina's tired eyes for the third time that day. But this time she couldn't be happier.

"I feel it, and you've had mine from the first time we met on Rodeo Drive. But I married Robert and hooked up with Dmitri while you were bouncing between any number of women. I've lost count."

"I was evidently waiting for you. I didn't realize it until tonight when I saw you so sad and that French clown nibbling on your neck. I love you, Gina. It's such a relief to say it."

"I love you too, Jake. I always have. I had decided not to pursue you since that's what every woman you know does, so I settled for being your friend. I wish I'd known sooner how you felt. I feel like we've wasted a lot of time. At least, I did, with Robert and Dmitri. And, that French "clown" is making a lot of money for the agency and me, so I had to be nice to him, that's all. But he crossed the line by trying to turn me into a snack food tonight."

"Sometimes, if we don't know what we want, life will throw stuff, or people, at us to force us to make a decision. Think about your decisions as lessons learned. Maybe we wouldn't have been right for each back then, when we first met. But now, it's not as sudden as it seems, I have no doubt you've just turned me into a one-woman man. There will never be anyone but you, Gina."

They didn't realize how many people were watching them over the rims of their extra-large Coca-Colas. Clearly something had broken through since the attractive couple first entered the brightly lit establishment that smelled of grilled burgers and hot vegetable oil. Gina and Jake couldn't take their eyes off each other and finally shared their first kiss sitting as close as anyone can in the red and white plastic and Formica booth.

They reminisced about the first time they met and the times when their paths crossed while managing their professional schedules and travels around the world.

"I wish you had made a move on me years ago," Jake said. "Remember that club in San Francisco, when we danced all night? I wanted to carry you off that night. But…"

"But I blew it, because Carrie had me on a mission to keep an eye on a guy from her office for her."

"You were scoping for Carrie?" Jake had never met Carrie, but knew she was Gina's best friend. "I thought you were being kind of weird that night, trying to catch that guy's attention while dancing with me."

"I wanted you then and I want you now." Gina's famous smile broke through the memories of their friendship while giving Jake a meaningful, sexy look he'd never seen before.

"Let's go," Jake said suddenly.

"I'm right behind you." Gina knew he was taking her to his house in Malibu Canyon as they roared down the street.

Near the ocean, the air was still warm. The top was down. Gina's hair blew freely back from her face and tangled in the wind. The music was sexy and Jake kept his hand on her knee unless he was shifting gears. He was a good man. One of the few successful models who wondered about the endless amount of money there was to be made on looks alone. No talent required, and Jake never took his situation for granted. He'd simply been blessed with thick wavy hair, a strong square jaw, a craggy smile with a hint of dimples, good bone structure, and wide-set dark brown eyes.

"Life is good, Gina," he shouted, and smiled over at her. Recognizing the joy she felt by the expression on her beautiful face, he'd never felt happier.

Glancing back to watch the road, he took them up Malibu Canyon Drive with the skill of a professional race car driver. There was a turn out that overlooked the city and Jake pulled over.

"I can't wait another minute," he said. "I have to kiss those lips." Jake leaned over and took Gina's face between both hands. He smoothed back her tangled waves and gently pressed his lips to hers.

"I love you. I love you," Gina gasped between kisses. She could feel her heart pounding.

Jake whispered, "You've been my friend and now I've found the love of my life in the same beautiful person."

"Let's go," Gina whispered back.

Jake felt the urgency too, and put the car in gear. They were only ten minutes away from his modern steel and glass home with eternal views of the Pacific coastline. He had bought it three years before, and was always happy to return to its now-familiar creature comforts.

Gina alternately watched the stars and Jake's strong, lean hands on the gear shift as he expertly navigated the way up the windy mountain road. She was imagining what was to come when they got to his house, when her thoughts of making love turned to icy fear.

The driver coming down the mountain took a curve too fast and the old pickup narrowly missed the little sports car, causing Jake to swerve onto the narrow dirt shoulder and just as quickly, back onto the road. Jake had reacted instantly, which saved their lives. The truck kept going and Jake slowed down as he squeezed Gina's thigh.

Gina was sitting up shaken and looking at Jake in horror. "Oh my God. That guy nearly killed us!" she yelled to be heard over the car's engine, the music, and the wind.

"He was probably drunk—it's okay now." Jake risked a quick look at Gina to tell her again, "I love you! I can't stop saying it! I love you, Gina!"

Gina played with his hair as Jake called out his love for her over and over. Both were blissfully aware of what was to come in just a short while: a passionate, exhilarating expression of true love.

❧❧❧

With one mile to go, the anticipation was nearly unbearable. Gina threw up her hands to catch the warm wind, threw back her head, and sang out, "I love you, Jake Harris!" At the same time, a black sedan faltered around the curve. The force of the collision snapped her seatbelt and catapulted Gina out of the car. After a lifetime in the air, her scream ended in the brush ten feet below the road. Jake's side of the car took the full hit on impact.

The young driver crawled out and wandered in shock back and forth across the road. Jake was still in the Porsche, hidden and crushed under the sedan. Gina wasn't found until police and emergency crews flashed their lights down the hill, checking the area for other victims.

❧❧❧

Three days later, Gina barely responded to her mother's voice. Her head and chest were bandaged, one leg was in a hard plaster cast up to her thigh, and both arms and hands were covered in lacerations. Antonella was sitting next to the hospital bed. Red-eyed and drawn, she had arrived hours after getting a call from Gina's boss. Gina's dad came into the room with two cups of steaming coffee. Neither had gotten much sleep, though Gina's brothers had tried to share their parents' vigil over their sister. Hope stirred the mother's heart upon seeing Gina's eyes lightly flutter. Antonella carefully took a battered hand and said, "Gina. Gina. It's mom.

Dad's here too, and your brothers. We're here, sweetheart. Wake up, Gina."

Her mother's voice was getting through, but it sounded so far away. Trying to reach out, Gina found she couldn't move. She tried to speak but her throat was parched. It was too much effort to open her eyes, and she slipped back into the peaceful, black-velvet world of nothingness.

৵৵৵

"Sara, it's Carrie. I need to postpone the wedding."

"What? Oh Carrie, what happened? Did you and Charles have a fight?" Sara had already put a lot of time in on what would have been another lavish affair with Carrie at center stage.

"No. No. It's not that. It's Gina. She…" Carrie choked on the words. "She may not make it. She was in a horrible car accident a few days ago and is still unconscious. The doctors give her a fifty-fifty chance."

A chill crept up Sara's neck, and she shuddered at the thought of her new friend's life hanging in the balance. "I don't know what to say, Carrie. It's so terrible, and you must be deeply upset. Gina was, *is*, your best friend. Was she driving?"

"No. She was with Jake. He was driving." Carrie was clearly devastated and had difficulty sharing what she knew about the circumstances. "Jake was killed instantly," Carrie continued. "Evidently his car was flattened by a sixteen-year-old who'd just gotten his license. It was about midnight and he'd taken his father's car. The roads in Malibu Canyon are winding and narrow. No place for an inexperienced driver showing off by speeding around curves. It's all so senseless. I don't know what Gina was doing with Jake, and where Dmitri was in all this, but knowing her, since she was with Jake she was probably happy during those last minutes. The impact of the crash was brutal. It broke the seatbelts and in Gina's case that was a good thing. She was thrown from the car and landed down the hillside. Someone came along pretty quickly. They thought it was a one-car crash at first. It's dark on that road and Jake's car was so mangled; they didn't even see it crushed under the car that hit them."

Feeling sick to her stomach, Carrie stopped talking.

"Of course I understand about holding off on your wedding." But knowing Carrie had wanted to get the wedding behind her as soon as possible for business reasons, Sara asked, "Will you just go to a justice of the peace now?"

"No. I can't do that. I want Gina to be with me. Charles understands, so we'll wait, though it could be a long recovery time. If she, if she makes it." Barely getting the last sentence out, Carrie abruptly signed off, "I have to go." Carrie hung up with tears streaming down her face. For the first time in her life she prayed. "I can't lose her! Please help her, God. Please let her live."

CHAPTER 31
DAVID AND SARA

David was miserable in New York. He knew no one outside of his old network of business colleagues and none of them extended any hand of friendship. It had been all business in the past. Now he was alone and on edge, wanting a drink. Sometimes he shook so hard to avoid a bar, he would finally call his sponsor, who would talk him down and get him to focus on why he couldn't drink. David was nervous about seeing Hank in San Francisco. He worried about slipping up and having just one little shot of whiskey or line of coke for old times' sake, but he also knew that was not possible. He'd put on weight and craved sugar, a new vice to get under control. His saving grace was a photocopy of his mug-shot from the morning of his arrest. David kept it under a magnet on the refrigerator in his apartment. It served as a reminder of how far he'd fallen and how far he'd come to pick himself back up.

Sometimes he'd call his sponsor several times a day. The poor guy couldn't get any work done. Then there were days that David didn't call him at all, even though he was supposed to. The last time they spoke, David explained that he was going to meet a friend in California. The sponsor strongly advised him to find an AA meeting the minute he got to San Francisco and attend every chance he got.

"It's vital to work the program wherever you go, David," his sponsor told him. "It's a slippery slope back into rehab if you don't. Call me anytime you want. That's what I'm here for."

David was going nuts. He wasn't going to be seeing Hank for another two weeks and didn't want to sit around waiting for the only thing on his calendar to come about. *I need a change of scene now! I can't sit here any longer*, he thought. Two days later David threw a few things into a suitcase and headed West.

It was a good decision. He had always liked San Francisco while there on business in the past. After dumping his bags on the bed in the hotel room, David took off for a walk and played tourist. He jumped on the cable car and rode it down Nob Hill. Getting off at the end of the line, he wandered around Fisherman's Wharf. It was windy and the fog threatened to roll in by late afternoon. He warmed up with chowder in a bread bowl. He stopped to watch the street entertainers he used to ignore, and tossed a few dollars in their jars and open guitar cases. Dodging tourists and beggars, he ran up the steps to the historic Ghirardelli Square and bought a bag of chocolate. He even visited the Maritime Museum across the street. By late afternoon, David was running out of steam and he looked around for a Starbucks. Naturally finding one nearby, he was about to enter when a flyer was shoved into his hand. It was hard not to read it before throwing it away. *Community Service Opportunity...Shelter the Homeless.* The details following the headline about an event to be held in six months included a plea for volunteer help. *One hour—one day—one week. Whatever you can spare.* There was a number to call.

David was not usually someone to offer help, but he hadn't done anything about the court ordered community service. He had four months left to do 160 hours of work. This was something he might look into. While sipping his triple-shot cafe mocha with extra whipped cream, he gave it some thought.

The next morning after breakfast, David decided to find out more about what needed to be done for that homeless event thing. He called the number on the flyer.

The phone was answered on the first ring. "Dare to Dream Events, this is Karen. May I help you?"

"Uh. I ah, I have this flyer here about an event for the homeless...?"

"Oh, great! We need everyone to pitch in. How much time can you offer?"

"I don't know. What kind of work do you need done?" David was uncomfortable and didn't want to commit to anything without knowing exactly what would be expected of him.

"Everything from helping with building construction to serving food or washing dishes at the fundraiser. Do you have any special skills we might tap into?"

David thought a minute. "Special skills. I never thought that what I've done is special but I've been in real estate development. Maybe I could help on the construction project."

"That sounds great! Can you come to a meeting tomorrow evening at seven o'clock? We're inviting everyone we have on board so far to sort out the talent, schedules, and figure out assignments. We'll have beer, wine, and some snacks available."

Thinking how impossible it was to avoid alcohol, David agreed to show up. A sense of purpose and well-being flooded over him. David felt better than he had in a very long time.

The meeting started on time, but David was purposefully late, to avoid socializing with a glass of wine. Coming to the marked door at the end of a long hallway, he listened for a second to make sure the meeting had started before pulling the handle with a loud squeak. All heads turned to see who was joining them.

Sara was at a microphone at the front of the room and invited him to come in and join the crowd, then continued addressing the group of twenty-five people. "With your help, and hopefully others will come along, we will reach the goal of raising five million dollars. Money that will return the old Harbor Building to code, make it habitable, and equally important, comfortable for individuals and families suffering on the streets.

"Now, since there aren't that many of us here this time, let's figure out what kind of talent we have in the room tonight. Would you each please tell us your name, what amount of time you can offer and what you can do to help? I'd like to start creating teams of people to work on specific projects. The first being to deal with the city planners and get an understanding of what needs to be done and how much money it will take for renovation. We figure the five million would be a good first goal, and hopefully enough to finish the building project. Another big piece of this will be to pull off the fundraising event itself. So what have we got here? Who wants to start?"

An older woman stood up and said, "Hi everyone. My name is Alice Mumphry and I used to work in a catering business. I can help with the party food." A woman next to her, maybe Alice's friend, stood up and said she would help at the party too, with decorations. Everyone was focused on the event and no one addressed the other important part, the renovation itself. When it came David's turn to speak up, he'd been wishing he could sneak out somehow, but on the other hand, he had nothing else to do. He had the knowledge and skill to work on the renovation and the little redhead in charge was cute.

Standing, David was used to speaking to be heard by everyone in the room. His voice nearly echoed off the walls and bare floor. "I'm David. I can be here for as long as I'm needed, well, to a point, anyway. I have a background in real estate development and will be happy to work on the building codes and maybe see to the renovations."

The redhead, that being Sara, literally jumped up and down when David finished offering his help on the building. She couldn't believe their luck that someone had come along willing to do so much.

"Thank you, David! Thank you everyone! As I said before, you're going to make this happen for a lot of people in trouble out there. It will also help the city and I know the mayor is very interested in what we're doing. Hopefully, we'll have more people come to the next meeting. My company, Dare to Dream Events, is making every effort to attract a lot of attention and volunteers. If you know someone who can help, please invite them to the next meeting.

"Okay, that's it for now. Thanks again everyone. We'll meet again next week. Same time and place. In the meantime, before leaving please fill out your contact information so we can get hold of you."

Karen was stationed at the back of the room, flagging anyone who tried to leave without providing a phone number. "Mr., uh, David. Sorry, I don't know your last name. How can we reach you?"

"Oh, yeah. Well, I'm in transition right now, but you can take my cell phone number. I actually live in New York, but can be here for a while, like I said."

"We're certainly glad you showed up tonight, Mr. ...David." Sara had come up next to him while he wrote down his phone number for Karen. She was short, but he was six-four, so everyone was short in comparison.

"Not a problem. Sorry, I came in late, so I wasn't able to get your name."

"I'm Sara Collins and this is Karen. Dare to Dream Events is my company and we're donating our services to head up the coordination of the fundraiser primarily, and had hoped to find someone to work on the renovation, which isn't our forte at all. It was a miracle that you found us."

"Well, your flyer caught my eye. A student was jamming them into people's hands left and right down on the wharf. It was hard to ignore."

Smiling up at him, Sara hoped she didn't appear to be flirting, but said, "We'll need to talk soon about the first steps and how to get this off the ground."

David responded, "I should take a look at the building. If you give me the address I'll do that tomorrow."

"Wow, that's moving fast, and it's great." Sara felt a little blush come over her and tugged nervously at her skirt. Karen noticed and made a mental note to tease her boss later about the tall man with reddish-blond hair and quirky grin. "I can meet you there to unlock it if you can make it at noon."

Knowing he had nothing to do but lie around the hotel room struggling not to raid the mini bar, David said, "Sure. That works."

"Good. It's a date, I mean, it's not a date, but I'll see you there, at noon."

Karen nearly laughed out loud at Sara's discomfort.

Cute, David thought as he walked out without further reply.

"What an idiot," Sara said to Karen when she was sure David was out of earshot.

Knowing full well who Sara meant, Karen said, "He's not an idiot. What are you talking about?"

"Having fun, Karen? You know I mean *me*. I sounded like a bumbling fool. The man has important, successful executive written all over him. He's probably a big shot with a little time on his hands for some reason and I couldn't put a complete sentence together."

"Don't worry about it, Sara. You're always so hard on yourself. He seems nice, though. Maybe he'll make it a date and take you to lunch after checking the building."

"Shut up!" Sara said and laughed, but secretly she hoped Karen was right. It had been years since anyone had caught Sara's eye.

The next day, noon came fast for Sara and slowly for David. He wasn't used to having nothing to do and nowhere to be. *This is going to be an interesting project*, he thought. *I might be able to sink my teeth into it.*

David found the Harbor Building in the run-down tenderloin district of San Francisco thirty minutes before he was to meet Sara. *I'm glad I'll be here with her*, he thought. *This is no place for a lady to come alone.* The street was scummy and littered. Iron bars covered the store-front doors and windows. There was a bar on every corner. Drunks, junkies, and the simple-minded lingered or limped along talking to each other or themselves, it didn't seem to matter which. Standing at the front door of the building destined for renovation, David watched the down-trodden pass by. I could be one of them, he realized. I was on my way to living like this. It was only a matter of time.

It was a good experience for David to stand on that filthy street for nearly half an hour. The scene scared and impressed him at the same time. *These people probably blame everyone but themselves for what's happened to them*, he thought. Everyone walking by asked him for money or tried to engage him in some kind of dialogue that made little or no sense. But he knew how to handle the beggars, and held them off until he saw the redhead in a swingy black skirt, red jacket, and high-heeled pumps walking quickly past two men asking for a handout. She side-stepped them and almost ran into an old woman wearing a filthy wool coat in the noon sun.

"Obstacle course!" Sara said, extending a hand for a handshake. "Thanks for meeting me here, David." Sara had recovered the composure she'd lost when they first met.

"My pleasure." Wanting to get her off the sidewalk, David said, "Let's go inside."

Sara fumbled for a second to find her keys and unlocked the giant padlock, as David removed the thick chain that ran through the door handles. He took it inside with them, knowing that even a chain and padlock could somehow be useful to the hopeless and helpless.

Stepping in, the damp, moldy air enveloped them like a ghost's putrid breath. "You'll get used to it," Sara said, as she turned on a flashlight and handed another to David. "Of course the power is off, but as we move into the larger rooms, we'll have plenty of natural light, even through the grimy windows."

"What did this used to be? Looks like it was hotel," David asked.

"Actually, I think you're right. I know that it's 50,000 square feet. Huge for our purposes. Do you think five million dollars will be enough to bring it up to code?"

"Not sure yet," David remarked. He had just entered a familiar world. He had seen hundreds of old buildings that his company, his ex-company, had bought, refurbished, and sold. But this place was in the worst condition he'd ever seen. David asked Sara why it hadn't been demolished.

"I don't know that either. I think the city planners had other, more glamorous things to think about and didn't want to spend a dime on this place even to tear it down. Look! This must have been a restaurant." Sara had wandered into a large wood-paneled room lined along one side by a long stainless steel counter. A gutted kitchen was behind the counter. They continued the tour, checking out the fixtures and water connections before picking their way over garbage and rodent droppings to reach the stairs.

"Must have been very nice in its day," David finally said, after being lost in thought for several minutes.

Coming up next to him, Sara just barely reached David's shoulder. They stood side by side, both fantasizing about what the old building had been like fifty years ago. "Yeah, must have been something special," Sara repeated, while noticing how nice it felt to be standing next to the tall man in his tweed jacket, starched white shirt, and jeans. They explored, checking out every room in the building, until Sara blurted out, "Are you hungry?"

"I, uh, yeah. I can always eat," David replied, surprised that she didn't have to dash back to her office.

"You took a cab here, right? I drove, so let's get my car and I'll take you to lunch. It will be easier for you to get a cab from the restaurant."

"Sounds good," David answered, feeling nervous. He liked this woman. She had a sparkle to her. A lightness and humor that felt good to be near.

"I only hope you fit in my car. It's a two-seater," Sara teased.

Over lunch, David and Sara got more excited about the possibilities the ruined building presented and openly shared their philosophy and ideas about the project as if they were old friends. Sara explained how she'd come up with the idea.

"I drive by the building every day on my way to the office. I see those poor people and wonder how they got there. Why life had been so difficult that they couldn't deal with it. I realize drugs play a large part in their problems, but what drove them to abuse themselves in the first place? Anyway, one day, the idea came together. Like a hand in glove, there's an empty building and there's people needing shelter. It was a no-brainer. But it's going to be a huge undertaking."

While David listened to Sara's ruminations, his own life played out in fast forward and he came to a significant conclusion—that he was fully responsible for everything that had happened over the years: the rise and fall of his marriage and career to the ultimate crash in Central Park. *No one to blame but me*, he thought. What he'd heard in rehab came back to him loud and clear. *It's time to make a difference in life and help others.* This is a golden opportunity to do just that. In that moment, David committed to creating the Shelter as if his own life depended on it.

Sara noticed that she'd been doing all the talking and glanced at her watch. Startled that it was almost two o'clock, she said, "I'd better get back. I have a meeting at three. I'm surprised Karen hasn't called wondering where I am." Actually, Sara rethought to herself, *Karen probably knows exactly where I am, finally having a lunch "date" with an attractive, interesting guy.*

"So can you come to the next meeting, David?" Sara asked before saying goodbye.

"I'll be there. Thank you for lunch, Sara. Next time it will be my treat."

Next time? Sara wondered, then thought, *Cool*!

Returning to his hotel room, David got right to work finding out who to call at the City Planning Department. His old San Francisco contacts from when he was at HGD had moved on. He even called a couple of contractors he had worked with in the past. David hadn't felt this excited about anything in his entire life. When working at his old job, everything had been about money, and making more of it. This project was right up his alley and it would benefit hundreds of homeless people. Rubbing his hands together before opening his laptop to begin a project scope plan, David didn't realize that he was smiling.

CHAPTER 32
HANK

One of the biggest drug deals in Las Vegas history was about to take place.

"Thursday night at eleven. Naturally you'll come alone. What will you be driving?" Jimmie gave Hank the final instructions and coordinates as they walked into Jose's for another casual lunch "between friends." Phones were not used at this point for discussing details, but against Hank's better judgment, he was meeting Jimmie one last time before the drop date.

The two were seated at Jimmie's favorite table before Hank answered. "I bought an old RV from a retired couple. Cash. I told them I wanted to take my wife on little road trip as a surprise."

"Not a bad idea. Though an RV is hard to hide if you have to."

"No worries, Jimmie. Everything's worked out. My guys will drop by the RV Park in Mesquite throughout the night to pick up their share of supplies. This time of year there's no one there. That will be simple, but there's a lot of product to move fast from the plane to the RV. How are you going to manage that?"

"Like you said, no worries. I've got my end set up. Just be there on time. No earlier or later." Changing the volume of his voice Jimmie shouted, "Juanita, come here baby and bring daddy a beer, will you? Your staff is running a little slow today."

Hank left Jimmie still harassing the hostess and wait staff twenty minutes later. He was mad that Jimmie was calling attention to himself. Worse, he had drawn attention to them both while Hank was sitting with him. He didn't want anyone remembering seeing them together, anywhere, under any circumstances.

Walking to his car, Hank reviewed his options. He was tremendously conflicted. In a few days, he would be either financially set for life or running for his life. Whether he bailed out of the plan or did his job, either way he was risking everything, including possibly his son's life. It was a matter of who went after him, the law or Jimmie's henchmen. If he bailed, Jimmie's revenge on Hank and his family would be grotesque and painful. Hank thought, *If I don't go through with it, I may as well kill myself before Jimmie does it for me*. Shaking away the thought, and recalling his resolve to make a better life for TJ, Hank had two days to decide.

≈≈≈

It couldn't have been a darker night in the Nevada wasteland sixty miles outside of Vegas. It was hot and still. A good thing, since winds would have complicated the schedule if the plane had been unable to land. It was a chancy aspect of how Jimmie ran his side of the plan. There were five men at the hangar. Upon landing, the plane was to taxi into the hangar, which was just large enough for a small plane and the two cars already parked inside. Hank was determined not to raise suspicions among Jimmie and his men and would refuse to answer any questions about when the drugs would be transferred from the RV to the various distributors. That's where the money would change hands and there was to be no discussion during the transfer. Hank, being the middleman, was to collect from the donkeys and pay Jimmie. He was one of the most trusted men in the business, and why not? He'd grown up in it. Jimmie had found him on the street when he was sixteen and had taken him under his wing. That was eighteen years ago. It was Hank who had come up with their distribution system in the hotels; since then both had made a very good living.

At eleven o'clock the RV rolled to a stop at the hangar door. If anyone was watching, it would have looked suspicious. But they kept all lights off and the jet-black night shielded them from onlookers—unless of course the watchers had night vision goggles. Everyone except Jimmie wore head-to-toe black clothing, gloves, and sweltering ski masks. No one wanted to be recognized later. No one spoke; even loud-mouthed Jimmie said little while the suitcases loaded with packages of powder were carried from the cargo hold of the small plane to the RV. It all stacked up neatly.

After the cocaine was transferred, a flash of light froze everyone in place for an instant before Jimmie's men scattered and dove for cover. Dust and gravel billowed, filling the air as eight black, unmarked vans filled with men wearing assault protection gear sped up the dirt road and skidded to a stop at the hangar. The hangar lights went on and the RV driver ripped off his ski mask. It was not Hank but someone of Hank's height, weight, and color who happened to be an undercover Drug Enforcement Agent. With his gun drawn, he yelled to be heard by the man cowering in the hangar, "Santiago Benigo, you are under arrest!"

Jimmie, the pilot, and five other men who had just finished loading the RV with two-point-four tons of cocaine, were quickly surrounded by men with M-5s and handcuffed. Five semi-automatic hand-guns found on Jimmie and his men were piled to the side in the gravel.

Jimmie's eyes were wild with hatred when he realized the man he'd trusted for so long had gone over on him. He was pushed into the back seat of the lead car. The others were separated for a discussion about their supplier on the long way back to Las Vegas. The remaining agents secured the plane, RV, and weapons.

Four hours earlier, Hank had left his apartment in a hurry, with TJ in tow. He was finally leaving his life of crime. The life he'd always known and that had allowed him to live extravagantly. Everything would be different now, and he was scared and excited at the same time. Jimmie could have changed the game plan in midstream, but he was a sloppy little man who trusted his protégé.

Saying goodbye to June was difficult.

"They don't know about you or Althea," Hank had told the old woman. "I made sure of that. I think my only mistake was letting them know I have a son, but I don't think they'll ever find him or me if the DEA does its job."

"Never mind. Go make that dream real in California. I'm sure gonna miss you guys. But you did the right thing. You know that."

"You'll come see us, won't you? You might like a change of scenery now and then." Then looking into her watering dark eyes, his heart pounding with wanting to get out of Nevada as fast as possible, Hank took a minute to thank her. "You're the best Junie. I love you."

"Bye Gramma!" TJ cried into her shoulder as June hugged her grandson.

"Bye baby. You be good for your daddy."

An hour later Hank and TJ were on their way to San Francisco. The airplane's steady drone quickly lulled TJ to sleep. He was curled up in a window seat with his head on Hank's arm. Watching his innocent little boy's face, Hank reflected on the past and the future. He checked his watch. It was eight o'clock. In about three hours Jimmie would be arrested, the same time Hank and TJ would be settled in their hotel room. Hank could only imagine what the murderous little man would do, given the chance to retaliate. Hank had set up the man who had found him in the streets and shown him a world of high-stakes fortune. Hank remembered all the deals, all the risks, and of course, the incredible amount of money they had made. But overshadowing any sense of loyalty, Hank remembered that his mentor had killed a beautiful woman for nothing. Jimmie had Shanti killed in spite of Hank's pleading not to hurt her. Shanti would forever live in Hank's memory. He would carry the guilt for causing her death. But in this small way, knowing he had done the right thing tonight, Hank now felt a sense of revenge for her demise. *Maybe, just maybe now, I'll be able to sleep through the night without seeing her terrified face in my dreams. Maybe, I'm on the road to doing something worthwhile with my life.*

Everything had gone as planned—Hank's plan—with the Drug Enforcement Agent he'd given himself up to.

Two nights before they were to transfer an amount of cocaine worth millions to each man in the deal, Hank sat at the foot of the bed watching the slow, deep breathing of his sleeping boy and wondered at himself that he'd ever consider jeopardizing his safety. In that moment, Hank flipped on Jimmie with absolute conviction and called the Drug Enforcement Agency. He spent hours on the phone with someone in the Los Angeles office, then met with a special task force agent who was currently located in Las Vegas. Hank explained to both men what was to happen, involving a tremendous load of cocaine from Colombia, and his role over the years as a dealer. Hank become a confidential informant, a "CI" and gave up his suppliers. In return, the agent made a call to the Las Vegas district attorney's office. It took some doing, but the agent was on Hank's side. The DEA had been after Jimmie for years. Now they had the tough little man by the balls. The district attorney's office guaranteed immunity and the agent told Hank, "When you leave this office, keep walking and I'll forget your involvement. That's all. That's what it's worth to us to catch Santiago 'Jimmie' Valdez Benigo."

Hank told the man before leaving, "I am walking away. Starting over, thanks to you. But, if this doesn't work, I'll probably be dead inside a month. Jimmie, he's a dangerous man. Good luck!"

However, Hank wouldn't be walking away entirely, at least not before testifying against Jimmie in court. Remembering his past was terrible, and having to appear in court would be difficult, but Hank was confident he had made a decision that would result in a new, wonderful life for himself and his little boy. Weeks ago, after touring California with TJ, Hank had made a list of everything he wanted to make happen: Find a safe place to live and create a normal, happy life for himself and his son. *We're on our way*, Hank thought, then dropped off for a brief dreamless nap before landing.

CHAPTER 33
SARA, DAVID, AND HANK

With Carrie's wedding off the books, Sara had more time to devote to her own pet project: the Safe Harbor Shelter. That's what she called it, as a play on the old building's name, The Harbor Building, and what it was to become—a dry, warm, safe, shelter for the homeless.

When David called her with the latest update on how slowly things were moving along with the city planners, Sara told him, "I'll be in San Francisco again next week, since the fundraiser is only two weeks away. I want to be sure we have enough help on hand for that night, and I know there are more people to invite."

David quickly decided to plunge ahead, and asked Sara, "Would you like to have dinner while you're here? I'm getting tired of my own company and would like to hear more about you and your ideas for the Shelter."

"Well, I'm only organizing the fundraiser. Once the money is collected, someone else will oversee putting it to good use with you. But," Sara quickly added, "I would like to join you for dinner. That would be great."

"Great," said David, suddenly feeling at a loss for words.

"Okay. Great," Sara repeated. "I'll be staying at the Monaco near Union Square, arriving on Saturday. I have an appointment with a realtor on Sunday."

"Really? I didn't realize you were moving to San Francisco."

Sara described the magical little town she had discovered by chance. Sincerely interested, David said, "I'll look forward to hearing more about that, too. How is seven o'clock? I've leased a car and will pick you up at the hotel."

David hung up feeling excited. He couldn't believe he had a real, old-fashioned date for Saturday night. *What should I wear?* Laughing at himself over what was typically a female concern, he went back to work calculating renovation costs based on estimates from numerous contractors.

Hours later, he came up for air. Five million wasn't going to cover everything he wanted to see get done, but it would be about enough for retrofitting, new plumbing and electrical, and a new roof. He was still working on finding volunteers to repair and refinish the walls, floors, and stairs, and even replace the elevator. He had no idea where the money for furnishings would come from but that wasn't his problem. Looking at his watch, David realized it was time to leave to pick up Hank at the airport.

David flagged them down in the crowded airport. Hank waved back and stooped to pick up TJ, who looked around curiously for the man his dad had waved at. David was waiting curbside, just outside baggage claim, and had seen his friend through the glass doors. Ten minutes later, they were heading into the city. TJ was acting shy and wondered at this new side of his dad. He'd never heard Hank talk so much or so fast before. And David was obviously excited, too, as he explained what he was doing to renovate an old building that would become housing for hundreds of people, and how it saved his sanity since it was keeping him busy. "But we're going to see everything there is to see while you're here. It's not like I'm punching a clock. Hey, TJ," David continued, "Have you ever seen the inside of a prison?"

It was a joke, of course. David was alluding to taking a tour of Alcatraz Island. Under the circumstances of having set up the felony arrest of Jimmie Benigo only a few hours ago, Hank didn't relish the idea of visiting the infamous facility. However, he wouldn't let the irony of the idea get the better of him. If TJ wanted to see Alcatraz, then they would see it.

"So you must be tired, right?" David asked. TJ's head rested on his dad's shoulder as the men stood in the hotel lobby. "Give me a call in the morning when you want to start the day. We can ride the trolley cars, find some chowder. I even know a great place down on the Wharf that's wall-to-wall candy." TJ's sleepy head came up when he heard that.

The next two days were non-stop for David, Hank, and TJ. They palled around from one end of the city to the other, from the zoo to the promised candy shop on Fisherman's Wharf. They even went whale watching, and on Saturday morning caught a ferry to Alcatraz. On the return ferry ride, David mentioned that he had plans for dinner, but would see them when they got back from their drive up north. Hank and TJ were ready to revisit that little western-style town they'd found during their last trip to California and go hiking again.

❧❧❧

"Hank is a friend," David told Sara over dinner that evening. "His little boy, TJ, is four or five, I think, and the light of Hank's life." Sara noticed a glimmer of sadness cross David's face and wondered what had triggered it.

"Where are they going tomorrow? I know the area pretty well now. I'm heading north myself to meet with a realtor. I think I told you about that."

"Paradise Valley was the town they liked. It would be a very different life for Hank. He grew up in Las Vegas..."

"That's where I'm going!" Sara interrupted. "That's the town I fell in love with at first sight. There's a house I want to see again, and the agent is going to show me some other places. What a coincidence."

David agreed, "Yeah, it is."

During the time David had between meetings on the renovation project, he considered moving to the West permanently. While watching Sara sip her wine, he wondered if he should explain his situation to her. He guessed she'd probably figured out the recovery part, since he hadn't joined her in a cocktail.

Suddenly, without giving it any thought, Sara said, "Come with me tomorrow. It's not two hours from the city and a beautiful drive. That is, if you don't have plans, and wouldn't mind helping me check out the structural bones of the houses I'll be seeing. I would appreciate it if you could," she added, making it sound more like she was asking for a favor rather than a date.

David didn't have to think twice. "It seems like the right thing to do. I'd be glad to add a second pair of eyes and look for cracks in the foundation and such. Sure. What time do we leave?" Feeling at once useful and happy for the excuse to spend more time with Sara, David gave her a big silly grin, causing her to laugh.

CHAPTER 34

By eight o'clock Sunday morning Hank and TJ were already out of the city. TJ had crashed early Saturday night and then got up equally early Sunday morning, rousing his dad from a long-needed sound slumber. Jumping on the bed, bouncing Hank awake, TJ said, "Come on, Dad, daylight's burning." This was a saying his grandmother June used to get TJ out of bed.

Hank had called ahead to reserve a hotel room and signed them up for horseback riding lessons. It was going to be a busy day and he was ready for happy distractions for a change. It was all forward motion from here on. "Hey buddy, what do you say we look around for a place to live today too?"

"Could we live there?" TJ sounded aghast at the idea.

"Yeah, we could do it. I have enough money to get us by and I'll start figuring out some kind of work to do before too long," Hank was explaining more to himself than the five-year-old jumping up and down in front of him.

Hank was not only surprising TJ, he was surprising himself that he'd finally made the decision to move to California permanently.

"And, why not?" Hank asked himself out loud. "We like it. It's a good place."

It was pure coincidence that Hank and TJ were touring around the same small town as David and Sara. The wind was kicking up and the temperature was dropping, but it was sunny out and a good day for everyone to be exploring.

CHAPTER 35
GINA AND CARRIE

"Gina has crossed the line of life and death," the doctor told her exhausted family, who had taken up residence at a motel near the hospital. They spent all their time sitting at Gina's bedside and praying in the hospital chapel. "I'm cautiously optimistic that she'll hold on and stay with us now that she has woken up."

Hearing that her daughter was awake, Antonella pulled away from her husband's protective arm and ran to her daughter's side again. She had been softly calling to Gina nearly non-stop after seeing her eyes flutter for a moment days ago. Antonella was sure that if Gina could hear her, she would somehow find a way back to them.

Gina lay as still as possible but managed to whisper, "I hurt." The nurse fiddled with whatever they were pumping into her veins. "Okay sweetie, I refilled your bottle with something that will make the pain go away. And the doctor just left to get your mother." At that moment Antonella rushed to Gina's side.

"Oh my baby. You're going to be fine. You've come back to us. I was so worried." Antonella lightly stroked Gina's hand.

Her father and brothers came in behind Antonella and surrounded the bed, all trying to choke down their tears.

"Hey guys," Gina said weakly.

Gina didn't remember much of what had happened and she didn't know about Jake. Antonella had insisted that no one say anything until Gina got stronger, but of course it was Gina's first question a minute later.

"Where's Jake?"

It would have taken heroic acting talent to disguise the truth from their faces. Hoping someone else could answer with a lie, her mother turned her head. Tom and Gina's brothers looked at the floor.

"Where's Jake?" she asked again urgently in a gravelly whisper. "I want to know how he's doing." Then it registered, and Gina cried silently while her mother mopped at the river of tears running down the badly bruised and swollen face.

There were simply no soothing words to help Gina through not only the physical pain but now the pain in her heart.

Carrie walked in an hour later with a fresh bouquet of roses. She sat quietly with Gina while the others went to find a quick dinner. "Hey girlfriend," Carrie whispered. "It's me."

Gina opened her eyes. "He's dead, Carrie."

"I know, honey."

"I wish I'd died too."

"I know how much you loved him, but don't say that. It's a terrible, terrible thing. He was a great guy."

"He told me he loved me. He told me I...." Gina couldn't talk any more.

"Oh, honey! I didn't know what happened when I heard you were with Jake and not Dmitri."

"Dim...Dmitri. He cheated on me. But I love Jake. I've always loved Jake."

"I know, Gina, and you always will, but…"

Gina turned her head to face away from her friend. "Don't tell me about time healing everything. I wish I was dead. I don't want to be here without him." And those were the last words Gina spoke for weeks.

∾∾∾

Antonella consulted a psychiatrist. After several sessions with the doctor doing all the talking, she reported back to Gina's parents. "Gina has reached a physical level of recovery that is encouraging, given the short time since the accident. But she doesn't want to live and her health is backsliding. She's given up. I'm sure you've heard that the decision to live or die is very powerful when someone goes through a trauma of this magnitude. A positive mental state can make all the difference in recovery. If this goes on for months or years, Gina could be killing herself as her body wastes away."

"What can we do, doctor?" Gina's dad was a wreck. He'd been strong for Antonella for weeks, but now Gina's deep depression was taking every ounce of his last reserve of energy. He felt so helpless. His only baby girl wanted to die. How could she do that to *them*? To her family who loved her so much.

Two months went by. Gina rarely ate and no one from the family, as hard as they tried, could get through to her. Carrie flew to Los Angeles from San Francisco every weekend to see her, sometimes sitting quietly, sometimes losing patience and yelling at Gina to snap out of it.

"How selfish can you be, Gina? You're tearing apart your family. Your mom and dad are at their wits' end; your brothers and their families are miserable. All because of your self-indulgence. YES, Jake is dead. YES, you've had some tough times, but for God's sake, Gina. You're only thirty years old. Think of your successes! You're incredibly beautiful and smart. YES, you are smart. I know you've never thought so, but I wouldn't have been your friend all these years if you were as dumb as you always thought. You have to decide, Gina. No one can do this for you."

Gina finally spoke, "Shut up."

"What? Did you just tell me to shut up? That's great, Gina. If you can find the spirit to tell me, your arrogant, prideful friend to shut up, then you can tell me to go to hell, too."

"Go away. I'm tired."

"I know you are," Carrie softened. "You have a lot going on." Encouraged that Gina had just completed two sentences, Carrie didn't let up. "But you're not going to get away with this bullshit as long as I'm here and I'll give up everything, and I mean everything, my job, Charles, whatever it takes, to help you through this. I'm here, Gina. You can tell me to go away, to go to hell, to shut up, but I'm staying, so go ahead, curse me. Remember when we were kids? I know I pissed you off all the time, but you always kept your mouth shut and did whatever I wanted. Well, here's your chance now. Tell me what you've always wanted to say to me. Remember when I made you steal those stockings in Macy's and threatened to tell your mother what you did to get you to do something else? It's called blackmail, Gina. I was mean to you and here's your chance to tell me off." Carrie continued to push and berate Gina, hoping that anger would boil up and release what was really causing her friend to withdraw. "Gina, I won't leave until you say something to me." Staring at her battered friend, who was mending from a deflated lung, five broken ribs, and shattered knee and ankle, Carrie waited.

"I loved him, Carrie."

There was simply no fight left in Gina, so Carrie tried a different tactic. At least Gina was responding to her. "Gina," Carrie commanded, "you're not going to kill yourself over a guy. Yes, you love Jake. We all know that. Now you have to decide what's more important and that's living your own life without relying on others to make you happy. You have to take control of your life. It's YOUR life after all, not Jake's, not your mother's, not mine. You can make anything you want happen in your life. You let me tell you what to do all the time when we were kids. Your parents kept you in a cocoon, for God's sake, never letting you make a decision until one day you finally broke loose and ran away. I know you have that fighting spirit in you, Gina, but somehow you've turned all the decision-making about your life over to others. Take it back, Gina. Take control and decide to get better. Decide what you want. Not what Jake would have wanted, or anyone else." It was a long lecture and Carrie finally ran out of words.

Carrie sat silently with Gina for a few minutes. Gina's eyes were closed but Carrie could tell she was awake. "Think about it, get some sleep, and I'll be back in the morning."

Making good on her promise, Carrie was back the next morning for round two. She stomped into Gina's private hospital room and started clearing out the old flowers. She brought two large boxes with her and started packing the stuffed animals with balloons tied to their paws that had piled up on one shelf, boxes of uneaten candy and countless get well cards. After pushing the full boxes under Gina's bed, Carrie taped up one new decoration to the wall where Gina couldn't help but see it all day. It was a montage of photos. Photos of Gina with her mother, father, and brothers. Photos of Gina and Robert at their wedding, and other random shots of people in Gina's life over the years. Photos of friends from the agency, even the double-page ad showing Gina and Dmitri in the Egyptian desert, and one, an old one, of Jake, that Carrie had found in Gina's apartment. Carrie had no photos of herself with Gina, so she had selected one of herself standing with Sara that Gina had taken a year ago during the Kendall Tech gala in San Francisco. Carrie also taped a separate sign above the photo montage but the message was covered.

Gina watched in silence.

Carrie finally sat down in the chair next to the bed and took a sip from her large cup of coffee. She waited for Gina's curiosity to get the better of her, which Carrie knew would happen sooner or later.

Gina didn't feel like playing the game and did her best to ignore Carrie. But in doing so, after ten minutes she realized that trying to wait out Carrie was also a game. "Okay Carrie, you win as always. What are you trying to tell me?"

"This time you win, Gina, if you get the answer right." Carrie replied, jumping up to reveal the message: *Who's in Charge Here?*

"So you want me to answer the question."

"Yup. You've had a lot of success. But you've given your life over to these people in the photos to make decisions for you. Since dying is not an option, I believe it's time to take back your life. Take control. Imagine what *you* want to do and do it." Carrie stood up and kissed Gina on the forehead. "I know you can do it. I'll be back in a few days, but will call you every day until then to see if you want to talk. And you can call me any time, day or night, if you'd like." Carrie left Gina alone, hoping that her tactics would work. At least she'd gotten Gina to start talking again, even if just a little, and while waiting for Gina's curiosity to surface, Carrie had noticed a few chocolate truffles were missing from the one box she hadn't packed away.

Gina had two days to herself, then Antonella entered Gina's room and uttered surprise that all the get well cards and gifts had been taken away. That was her first visual impression that something was different. In the next instant she realized that Gina was trying to smile through her healing lips. Her entire face had been pummeled by the crash and tumble down the steep hillside.

"Are you feeling better, my baby girl?" Her mother hadn't been away long, and wondered at the change in her daughter.

"Hi, Mom." Gina's voice was still weak, but she could get the words out with little trouble.

"You're speaking! Oh, honey!"

"I've made a decision. Look at that poster over there."

Antonella looked at the montage Carrie had put up. She didn't understand the message, *Who's in Charge Here?*

"Staring at those pictures for hours, I got really mad. I realized that all my life, I've done what someone else wanted me to do. I love you and Dad with all my heart, but you guys made all the choices for me while I was growing up. It was stifling, which is why I ran away. But when I got back, it started all over again and it was even worse. I think that's why I left college and ended up marrying Robert. But Robert always told me what to do, too. Carrie was no better, when we were kids. She would goad me into stealing or smoking while threatening not to be my friend any more. Then there's Dmitri. The bastard used me, lied and cheated.

"It's finally sunk in, Mom. I need to take responsibility for my own life and do something I really want to do. I loved modeling, but that's probably over now, so I'm going to decide on my own what to do next. It's kind of exciting. I have to know that I can do something worthwhile and not just jump when someone else tells me to. It feels kind of enlightening, and I want to get well so that I can make something happen."

Gina had just spoken more in five minutes than she had for the entire two months since the accident. Tears trickled down Antonella's cheeks. "I'm so sorry, baby. I had no idea how you felt. We were always trying to protect you and I'm hearing now that we didn't let you fly. Even a mother bird pushes her babies out of the nest to discover their own wings."

"It's okay. I love you and there's still time for me. Time to make a difference somewhere, somehow. I just have to figure that out on my own."

"What brought this about, Gina?"

"Carrie. Carrie scolded me for hours last weekend, until I finally told her to shut up and go away. She wouldn't and didn't. She tried to get me to fight with her, but then she came back the next day with the photos and the sign. She left me alone after that, and I've had nothing to do but lie here and think. One thing I do know is that I want to find love like what you and Dad have with each other." Trying not to cry, Gina continued. "I thought that Jake was my prince charming, like Dad is yours, when he finally told me he loved me." The tears broke through, but Gina controlled them.

"That day will come, my darling girl. You are loved and will be loved by a wonderful man. Just be patient and get well."

Antonella sat with Gina all day. She read her book when Gina dozed off. They watched movies together when she woke up.

When Gina had finished off the box of chocolates, she asked her mother to pull out another box from under the bed where Carrie had stashed everything. Not realizing how gaunt she was, Gina said, "I better not get fat from all of this." The stitches in her lip and chin kept Gina from smiling too broadly but she managed a lopsided attempt. It told her mother that Gina's will to live had finally shown up, her spirit was rebounding, and that she was eager to get out of the hospital.

అఅఅ

Antonella called Carrie late that evening. "Carrie, I can't thank you enough for what you did for Gina."

"Or *to* her, Mrs. Severns." Carrie had never gotten used to addressing Gina's parents as other than Mrs. or Mr. "I couldn't watch her die, and got so mad about what she's been through, it triggered an outrage that I thought might get her attention.

One thing led to another and I pasted together those photos as a last resort. I was so mad that she was giving up and I didn't know what to do. The shrink wasn't helping her. No one could reach her. But thank God, remembering the past and letting it go helped Gina take a first step forward in her recovery. I'm convinced she would have died if she hadn't made the decision to get well on her own."

"I believe that's true, too, Carrie. You've reminded me of something my grandmother used to say about the human spirit and how powerful it is—that it can do anything once a decision is made."

"Gina will be fine now. I know it. I'll be seeing her again next weekend."

"Well, thank you again. I can't tell you how grateful Tom and I are. I hope that you'll come visit us when you're in Seattle seeing your mom."

"I would like that." Carrie hung up with a warm, fuzzy feeling inside. She felt accepted and loved by the people who had once condemned her. Forgiven and forgotten, the past was behind her, and she was grateful, too, that her tactics had worked on Gina.

CHAPTER 36
DAVID AND SARA

David and Sara got to know each other on the drive to the little mountain village of Paradise Valley. While Sara zipped up the highway, David gave her the short version of what he used to do for a living; that he had nine-year-old twin sons; and that he had completed rehab only a month earlier. He also mentioned that his work on the shelter would apply toward community service ordered by a judge and that he was hoping she would provide a written statement of completed hours. Interpreting Sara's suddenly scrunched forehead and downturned mouth as disapproval, David jumped to a conclusion and thought, *She's repulsed. She probably wants to let me out of the car right here and leave me at the side of the road.*

But never being one to beat around the bush, Sara saved him from further self-deprecating thoughts. "So, David. Does that mean when you've completed your community service that you'll be going back to New York? I know this is selfish, but I was hoping you'd see this job through. Maybe we can find some money to pay you to manage the entire project. It falls under urban renewal. The city should be hiring someone at some point anyway, once the big shots see that we're serious. You're doing a tremendous job and I for one would like to see you stay on."

David covered his surprise that he'd completely misread her and relief that she didn't exhibit any judgment. "Sara, I'm back in my niche since finding this project and loving every minute it. I'd even swing a hammer if it helped get the job done. The meetings with the planners and contractors have been typically frustrating. It absolutely amazes me that so few people see the value in what you want to do. But I'm used to all that. This project is, in part, what I used to work on at my old job at Heritage Global Development."

"But," Sara interrupted, getting David back to the question of whether he'd be leaving or not.

"But, nothing. I want to stay. I've never been happier in my life." Seeing Sara's frown turn into a brilliant smile made David's heart take a leap and possibly jump to another conclusion. "In fact, I'd like to see you more often outside of working together on the shelter project."

Sara turned to look at David. Her green eyes bored into his and her smile was inviting. But she was thinking, *I don't believe this. I already have so much going on.* She remembered her resolve not to get involved with anyone at least until she completed the opening of her second office. It would be news to everyone, even to Carrie and Gina, that last Monday she had signed a five-year lease on the office space she'd been renting month-to-month in San Francisco. A branch office of *Dare to Dream Events* was scheduled to open in a month. *But I like him. It's as simple as that. How many chances does one get in love?* Realizing she was ready to test the answer, Sara finally returned her attention to the road ahead. She didn't want to miss their exit.

David remained silent, wondering if he had just made her uncomfortable. For all he knew, Sara probably had someone waiting for her in San Diego.

Sara saw their exit up ahead and signaled her intention to turn. She pulled into the same gas station she'd found by luck the first time she was in the area. The sweet town of Paradise Valley was just five minutes away. Stopping at the pump, she jumped out before David could offer to get the gas for her. Needing a little time, she quickly began crafting what she was going to tell him. In Sara's mind, having been married three times made her a losing proposition for anyone. This was going to be tricky, but David had been up front about his past. It was her turn to come clean, especially now that he admitted that he was interested in her.

Getting back in the car she turned to David before starting the engine. "It's my turn to confess, David, but not now. Let's go have some fun looking at houses and we'll talk over dinner." Then Sara said with another big smile, "I'm happy to hear you'd like me to stick around."

Relief flooded David's male brain. He had thought he'd blown it again by telling her he would like to see her more often. Then thought, *Wow, I was never good at this. I need a drink.* And for the next five minutes, until Sara parked at the real estate agent's office, David berated himself for being a weak, miserable individual reliant on booze and drugs. Wishing he could call his sponsor, he got out of the car and followed Sara into the office.

The agent had lined up five homes within a ten-mile radius of the downtown district of Paradise Valley. The house Sara had fallen in love with wasn't on the market, but it was a great day that left Sara with some tough choices. Rehashing the pros and cons of each house over dinner, Sara finally addressed the promise she'd made to David on their drive up.

"So, David, I should tell you a little about myself before our friendship is jeopardized."

"How could whatever you're going to tell me be any worse than what I've done in the past? You're an angel."

"Thanks, but I've been married three times and haven't kept a job for longer than five years. I felt like such a loser at one point that I'd lost any interest and ambition in life."

Nothing Sara could say discouraged David's fledgling romantic interest. Instead he buoyed her up. "But you have a solid business of your own now. Maybe you just didn't heed the signs over the years to figure out what you truly wanted to be doing. I've only recently learned that when things get uncomfortable in your life it's time to take stock and make a decision to do the same thing differently or to do something completely different. Maybe you just didn't want to get out of your comfort zone—you know regular paycheck and all that."

Sara smiled at David. "You seem to really get it about *daring to dream*. What you're describing was how I came up with my business concept and why I named my business, Dare to Dream. Everything has been going great since I decided to open my own business. In fact, you're the first to know. I'm opening another office in San Francisco. Over the past year I've spent more time there than in San Diego. I've hired five more people for the San Diego office and promoted Karen, who you met at the first Shelter meeting, to manage that 'division.' I call it a division because it will focus on weddings and special events. I'm so excited about the upcoming fundraiser for the Safe Harbor project that I don't want to see it end. I want to do more projects that will help the homeless. Maybe even in other cities. This first event is drawing hundreds of some of the wealthiest people in San Francisco. We'll even see a few celebrities. I feel so good about doing something worthwhile. I'll still manage my friend Carrie's wedding, but I've decided that the San Francisco office will be the main branch for creating fundraising events for non-profit agencies. I can afford to give non-profits and worthwhile city projects a reduced rate and maybe even do a little pro bono work each year."

Sara came up for air. She'd been describing in detail all her plans to an attentive David.

"Sara, I want to be a part of that dream. For years I've dealt with renovations, permits, codes, architects, and contractors, and I have money to keep me going. Eventually I'll need a paycheck, but that will happen at some point. I know it will."

David offered to drive back to the city. They bounced from discussing the houses they had seen to Sara's new office to David's thoughts about starting a consulting company. He would search out urban renewal projects and make them happen. With Sara working on raising money, David would handle finding buildings and managing renovations. Every city needed a team of dedicated individuals willing to slog their way through bureaucracies on behalf of people in need. Sara and David would find plenty of work, and little did they realize on the drive home, they had just decided on a future together.

CHAPTER 37
GINA, SARA, AND CARRIE

Gina is recovering well, considering the extent of her injuries," the doctor told Tom and Antonella.

"When can she come home?" Antonella asked.

"She'll need extensive physical therapy for her leg and shoulder. Her lung looks good and she isn't experiencing much pain from the broken ribs. She was a lucky young woman. She'll come out of this with some scarring on the leg and shoulders, but there will be negligible marks on her face. Now that the swelling is gone in her face, I can see she is a remarkably beautiful woman. I understand she was a model."

"Yes, she is. Since she didn't know until now whether her face would be permanently disfigured or not, she's been thinking about doing something else."

"Well, she's a beauty. We'll know her release date certainly within two weeks." The doctor left Tom and Antonella planning for Gina to come home with them. But Gina had other ideas.

"No Mom, Dad. I'm not going to Seattle. I'll just let you wait on me hand and foot and that's no way to get better. I've been given another chance to do something with my life and I don't want to waste another minute. I'm taking this time to think hard about what I want to do and so far I've decided to move to San Francisco. There are too many memories in Los Angeles. Carrie will be nearby and I'll make new friends. I need to do this on my own."

Gina was adamant, and after her admission that she'd been completely stifled by her mother in particular, Antonella let it go. As much as she wanted to baby her daughter back to perfect health, Antonella knew Gina was making the right decision.

Though Gina's father didn't agree, Antonella told him, "It's for the best, Tom. She's excited about making her own way."

Carrie offered Gina the guest suite in her apartment until her battered friend was able to live on her own. Until then Gina hobbled around the apartment and tried to help Carrie with routine chores. When Sara called to say she was in town, they invited her over for dinner.

They had pizza and salad delivered, since Carrie couldn't cook and Gina wasn't up to the task. Between bites of cheesy pepperoni, Sara announced, "I'm opening an office here." She explained the plan and told them how she had met someone who would scout for available buildings to turn into shelters while she drummed up business for Dare to Dream's fundraiser division. "It's going to be a rather large enterprise. I've already received state funding that was earmarked for social services and the mayor is behind our concept one hundred percent. I hope to hire at least three people right away and then we'll take it from there as the projects develop."

Carrie looked at Gina and asked Sara, "What kind of jobs are you looking to fill?"

"To begin with I'll need a general assistant, a bookkeeper, and a public relations person," Sara replied.

Gina didn't hesitate. "I'm comfortable in front of the camera, Sara, and I can stand up in front of anyone and give a speech. I used to do that for La Vie Modeling's clients at their parties. Of course, I don't have a background in public relations, but I took some communications classes in college and have time now to take some courses. Maybe get my degree after all. Any chance you'd take a chance on a broken-down old model with little experience?" Gina's hopeful smile filled the room. She had instantly recognized an opportunity to sink her teeth into and prayed for a positive answer in the moment Sara took to respond.

Sara looked at Carrie. Carrie spoke out, "She's a good writer, Sara. She's tenacious and people like her. As you know, Gina worked as my assistant for a couple of months at Kendall Tech." Carrie gave Gina a wink, knowing it had been a bogus job with ulterior motives for compromising the company president. Sara was on the spot, but she didn't mind. She liked Gina immensely and considered the idea. Gina was a warm, sweet woman with a new, infectious exuberance for life. She obviously liked people and that's something that can't be faked. The business of public relations could be learned in school and if Gina could write well, that would be key. In this case, they'd both be learning on the job about non-profit work.

After mulling it over for a minute, Sara said, "I think that's a great idea, Gina. Let's talk some more in detail. You would definitely bring energy to the company and will probably get us a lot of attention in the press and even the entertainment circles." As Sara warmed to the idea of hiring Gina, she began selling the concept of Dare to Dream, a company that will strive to rebuild lives. "We'll be finding congregations of poor and homeless and giving them a place to call home, even if it's only a room. At least they'll be warm, dry, and cleaned up. We want to give them a new start and hopefully help them change their lives, get them off the street, give them hope, and something to do that could raise their self-esteem. We already have volunteer consultants lined up to help, including psychologists and medical professionals. It's amazing how many people are willing to help. It just took an organized and focused effort."

After Sara left, Gina voiced her worry to Carrie. "I can't believe I cornered Sara like that. I hope she doesn't back out after giving it more thought."

"I don't think she will. The more I think about it, the more I know you would be a fantastic PR person. You're a natural. But you should follow up on taking some courses."

"I'll look into it first thing tomorrow. There are online universities, and what a great way to fill my day while my body heals. My brain has been going a mile a minute and the boredom is making me nuts. I should have thought of taking classes a while ago, but now I have some direction and a goal."

By the time Sara's new San Francisco office opened for business, Gina had completed her first semester toward a Bachelor's Degree in Communications. David found an apartment in the city and was making inroads on setting up his own company. Hank and TJ had found a house to rent in Paradise Valley. TJ was enrolled in school and had made a new best friend. Hank was floundering around without much to fill his day, but was trying to come up with a long-term plan for making some money in a usual and legal way. He had been called to testify against Jimmie, but the trial had been postponed twice. Hank remained fearful that Jimmie would somehow find him in California. It was a dark cloud over an otherwise beautiful and simple life.

And, Charles Baker was getting impatient about the long-delayed marriage to Carrie.

"I think you're still using Gina's accident as an excuse to continue this charade, Carrie. Are we getting married or not?"

Baker was in Carrie's office. They had completed their weekly meeting, reviewing the project status report and figuring out who would fly to India to assess developments there. One of the first things Carrie had done as the new CEO was to contract with Padma Singh, the brilliant aeroscientist she had met while interning in Research and Development. Carrie ignored her fiancé's question for the moment. "I'll go to India. You stay here and bird-dog the energy project." Then jumping subjects, she added, "And, you know I want Gina to be my maid-of-honor. I've told you that a hundred times. It's difficult for her in that walking cast she's in."

When they stuck to their business relationship, Carrie and Baker were a dynamic team. Personally, Carrie had cooled off on him and resented his nagging about the wedding date. She wouldn't share his apartment before marrying, saying it sent the wrong impression to the Board and their staff, and she wouldn't set a new wedding date until Gina was fully recovered. "Please don't bring this up again, Baker."

CHAPTER 38
DAVID AND SARA

The kiss was long and excited nerves in places Sara hadn't thought of in years.

"I'm finished eating. Are you?" David whispered after moving from her mouth to nuzzle her ear. "I'm full and need to lie down for a while." They were in David's new two-bedroom, two-bath apartment, with a peek of the bay for which the landlord felt justified charging an additional $800. But it was a nice space in a new complex. The open floor plan was sparsely furnished. David hadn't been too worried about getting a couch and rugs. But he had a table and two chairs in the dining room, and a TV and king size bed in the master bedroom. They had ordered Chinese food, and David had found some candles and flowers to decorate the table for their first night together.

"Funny," Sara replied in a deep, sexy voice. "I didn't think Chinese food would make you feel full because they say you're hungry an hour later."

"We won't be thinking about food." Pulling her up from the chair, David led her to his bed and gently pushed her down onto the fluffy white goose down comforter. He told her to lie still and he would take care of everything. Sara's heart sped up and her mind relaxed, ready to enjoy the sensations David was just beginning to impose on her body.

Sara spent the night for the first time with David and wondered upon waking if she might be falling in love with the guy. In fact, she knew it. Rolling over to leave the warm nest, Sara tiptoed out of the room hoping to find coffee and a coffee maker some-where in the mostly empty kitchen cupboards.

"You look great in that shirt," David said as he came up behind her a minute later and wrapped her in his arms. "Did you find the coffee grinder? I only have beans. Come back to bed."

Smiling at how well they fit together despite the variance in their heights, Sara felt protected and safe. David was the first man to "get her," in terms of how she thought and felt. He was very observant for someone who claimed he'd ignored his first wife and didn't know his kids very well. In fact, David truly had changed.

He was no longer the cold, money-obsessed, philandering husband he used to be. David thanked God every day since leaving rehab for his new outlook and concern for others. One of the toughest things he'd had to do during the recovery program was to call his ex-wife and then each son to apologize—to make amends. It was part of the twelve-step program. Lindsey, who had long since remarried, listened for a few minutes to what he had to say, then hung up on him. The twins, Josh and Tim, heard him out and wouldn't commit to a date for getting together. They were still very young, though, and loyal to their mother. But David accepted his punishment and would call them every week to keep the meager line of communication open. He knew one day he would see them again and maybe introduce them to Sara.

Settled back in bed together on a Sunday morning, coffee and paper at hand, Sara said, "I want to go back to Paradise Valley to look around again." It had been months since their first drive up together. Though the few houses Sara saw that day were very nice, she hadn't made an offer on any of them. They didn't compare to the one she really wanted.

"You want to drive past your dream house again, don't you?" David teased.

"Well, yeah, but it looks like a nice day out there. Want to go?"

"Today? Sure! Maybe Hank will be around and I can introduce you."

Hank's answering machine invited David to leave a message. *Maybe he had to go back to Las Vegas for the trial*, David thought. Disappointed that they would miss him again, Sara and David got ready for a day in Paradise Valley.

CHAPTER 39
HANK

David was right. Hank and TJ had left for Las Vegas earlier in the week. Hank was scheduled to testify against his old boss and he was nervous. They were happy to see Junie again, however, and would be staying with her. Althea dropped by to pick up TJ and take him out to lunch. TJ was not happy about that.

"She's trying to make it up to you, buddy," Hank said.

"But she's got other people, Dad. I don't want to meet them. Mom left us and now she's gonna have a baby."

Althea had married a rich widower with two teenage kids of his own and she was four months pregnant. "I get it, son, and I don't blame you for feeling that way. If it's horrible this time, then you won't ever have to see her again. I promise. And you know I always keep my promises."

The trial was in session when Hank walked into the court room. He had been prepped and rehearsed by the prosecution team. Hank had been sorely tempted to bring up Shanti's murder to the D.A.; but he'd been an accomplice and didn't think he would be exonerated in that case along with the drug charges. He didn't want to push his luck, so he swallowed that part of the story and told everything else he knew about Jimmie since they'd met.

Stepping up to the witness stand, Hank swore to tell the truth, the whole truth, and nothing but the truth. He tried to avoid looking at Jimmie, but lost the battle. The men stared at each other for a few seconds, Hank absorbing a silent message of death through the hate-filled glare.

If Jimmie was found innocent or got a light sentence, Hank would be running for the rest of his life. The men who had worked with Jimmie had been tried and found guilty. They were awaiting sentencing, but Jimmie was the set-up man, the boss. He alone knew who to call outside the country for drugs. It would be Jimmie who came after Hank if he could.

The investigators had spent months building their case before Hank showed up on their doorstep. They were getting close to busting the system. Hank had made his decision just in time, or he would have been caught in their net and arrested right along with Jimmie. Hank had confirmed for them that in taking Santiago Valdez Benigo out of the equation, the DEA would have succeeded in eliminating a major drug supply channel in the United States.

He answered every question without hesitation and with full conviction. Though legally safe in the district attorney's promise of immunity, Hank still felt it was risky to come clean on the witness stand. Nevertheless, he gave a devastating account of how Jimmie's business had worked and what he himself had done.

Hank was grilled by the lead defense attorney, Hector Belmont, a short, portly man in a custom-tailored suit. It was Jimmie who was on trial, but Belmont, while trying to discredit the witness, questioned whether Hank was completely out of the "business" and belabored his challenge as to why anyone would walk away from so much money. He couldn't get Hank to budge off his commitment to make something of himself and to be a good father to his son. He described the life he'd led as an orphan and the evil he'd seen and done as a youngster. Hank moved the women in the jury to tears when he explained the depth of love he'd finally found when his own son was born and that he had sworn on that day to always be there to protect him. Hank didn't dare look at Jimmie as he explained the street-life realities of what goes on behind the gloss and glitter of Las Vegas. Hank was able to tell them firsthand about the worst of the worst in the world of child porn in a way that made dealing drugs sound like a step up in lifestyle.

Hank was questioned for an hour. Jimmie's lawyer led him to describe his life in hopes that the jury would understand the level of Hank's involvement. On Hank's final word, Belmont cast an eye on the jury and exclaimed, "So, it wasn't all Santiago Benigo's doing! You, Henry Johns, cooked up their distribution system." Turning fully to get the jury's attention, Belmont raised his voice again to say, "Mr. Benigo should not take the fall for everyone who was involved."

Clearly the defense couldn't hope for a decision of not guilty, but he was setting Jimmie up for a light sentence.

Hank was finally released to leave the courtroom, but told to stay in town in case he was recalled. Exhaustion took over when he got back to June's condo. TJ wasn't back yet from his field trip with Althea.

"How'd it go, son?" June asked.

Hank loved it when she called him son. Over the years he'd come to think of her as his mother.

"I can only pray that he gets a life sentence. I can still feel the hatred while I was testifying. He'll kill me the instant he gets a chance, Junie. I hope he never finds us." Then Hank flopped down on the couch and closed his eyes.

June walked over, put her hand on his forehead, and stroked his hair. "You did good. You're the best father in the world. Now try to rest before TJ gets back."

Hank was required to make himself available, and killed time reading, watching TV, and napping. By the end of the next day, neither the defense nor the prosecuting attorneys had called him back for further questioning. He was free to go. Knowing he wouldn't rest without hearing the verdict, Hank stayed on for a few more days. He sat around the courthouse waiting with everyone else. At eleven-thirty in the morning of the fourth day of deliberations, the jury announced they had reached a decision. Jimmie was brought into the courtroom wearing the now-familiar suit he'd been allowed to wear during the trial. The jury filed in with grim expressions and sat again in their assigned seats in the jury box. The bailiff handed the judge the paper that would in one way or another change not only Jimmie's life, but Hank's as well. If Jimmie got off, he was dead. If Jimmie got out in a few years, Hank would have those few years to run and hide.

The judge asked the jury foreman to announce the verdict. The courtroom was silent. No one coughed, shuffled a foot, or otherwise caused the slightest sound.

The foreman was a heavyset woman wearing a bright green smock. *Funny I should notice what she's wearing*, Hank thought. Then he realized that time had stopped. Her next words could mean a life or death sentence for him, too.

Relishing her moment in the spotlight with all eyes on her, the woman stood up slowly, causing Jimmie to grunt and mutter, "Get on with it."

Having heard him, the woman stared venomously at Jimmie and announced, "On the charges of federal drug trafficking across international borders, the jury finds Santiago Valdez Benigo guilty as charged."

Hank discovered he'd been holding his breath. He hadn't known that Jimmie was being tried on a much larger scale of international drug dealing, which would certainly lead to at least twenty years in prison. Since the man was now about sixty-five years old, Hank figured Jimmie would likely die in prison. But to Hank's surprise, there was more.

The woman was still speaking. "The jury finds the defendant guilty as charged for the first degree murder of Janice Moore; guilty as charged for the first degree murder of Samantha Jenkins; and guilty as charged for the first degree murder of Shanti Lall."

Jimmie's expression was unreadable, though his black eyes bored a hole between the eyes of the woman announcing the bad news.

The judge polled the jury and announced, "Court will reconvene at nine o'clock tomorrow morning for sentencing." The gavel went down and he left his bench.

Hank felt numb, neither happy nor sad. Before he reached his car in the courthouse parking lot, a woman he recognized as Juanita from Jose's Restaurant walked up to him.

"This is your fault!" she spat. "My Jimmie will probably die in that prison, you traitor! You black bastard!" Spitting at Hank a second time, Juanita stalked away.

Damn! Hank said to himself. He hadn't known that Juanita had succumbed to Jimmie's crude advances. *Ya just never know,* Hank thought, shaking his head. Then once again he remembered Jimmie's advice, "Never tell anyone about who you love. You don't know when that information could be useful to someone who means you harm." *Huh, the one person Jimmie probably loved was right under my nose.* Then a feeling of euphoria washed over Hank. He couldn't remember ever feeling this way.

Rushing back to June's, Hank barged into the living room and told TJ to pack. "I'm free! It's over. They're going to put him away!" Hank swung June around in his muscular arms, then picked up TJ and tossed him straight up in the air.

"I'm free, Junie," Hank repeated after settling into a quieter state of joy. "I don't ever have to look back now."

Unlike TJ, June understood the impact this news would have on their lives and shared in Hank's celebration. "I'm so relieved! You'll be safe. TJ will be safe. You made the right decision, Hank. I'm proud of you."

That night Hank and TJ slept in their own beds in the quiet little town of Paradise Valley. It was a cozy and comfortable rental home, but weeks ago Hank had decided to buy a house if everything went well at the trial.

June called him the following day to say the paper reported back-to-back life sentences for Jimmie. The final bust had tied up all sorts of loose evidence the DEA and Las Vegas police investigators had been collecting on Jimmie for importing and selling drugs, and the murders of three young women, one being Shanti.

The next day, Hank began looking around for a job and house in that order. He had plenty of money on hand for a significant down payment and was eager to live a normal nine-to-five life. He called David, who called him right back after a meeting.

"Hank, sorry I missed your call. I'm on a new adventure and it's fantastic!"

Hank recoiled slightly at David's words, thinking they meant more drugs, women, and parties. "Yeah, well sorry I wasn't around this week. I'm all finished in Las Vegas. The trial is over and the guy I knew got double life sentences. And David, I have to tell you something."

David got quiet, hearing the solemnity in Hank's voice. "The charges included Shanti's murder. It was the guy who had her murdered that I testified against."

"You knew him?" David was incredulous that Hank would know anything about Shanti's death.

"David. I have a lot to tell you but not over the phone. When are you coming back to Paradise Valley?"

"Not for awhile. I just drove up with a friend last week. She's house-hunting up there and I had some time on my hands."

"I'm looking around, too. I really like it here. TJ is in school and taking horseback riding lessons."

"Look, I can meet you somewhere, maybe midway. Sounds like we have some talking to do. I want to hear about Shanti and I have some things to tell you, too."

The men agreed on when and where to meet the next day while TJ was in school. Leaving out the rape, Hank admitted to David about threatening Shanti and how he felt responsible for her murder, even though he had tried to stop Jimmie's men from going after her. It was harsh information for David to hear. Though he had no rational reason for it, David had been harboring guilt, too. The men examined their lives, past, present, and future. Realizing they had again reached a crossroads in life, it was time to make a decision to do something meaningful. That's when David told Hank about his new company. By the end of the conversation, David had invited Hank in on his first project. He needed someone who could work with the street people. Talk their language, so to speak, and be comfortable doing it. Hank saw the opportunity to help the same kind of people he'd grown up knowing on the streets of Las Vegas; the junkies, the homeless, and the crazy. Destitution looked the same in any city.

It was a good fit. Hank would drop TJ off at school and drive to and from San Francisco a couple of days each week. He quickly got up to speed on the Safe Harbor Shelter project. Naturally the homeless were curious about what was going on in "their hood." Hank would walk with them down the sidewalk explaining that in about a year, they would have a place to go for food and shelter and help with their addictions and other problems. He told them that lots of people really did care about them and wanted to help—not only with money but with real help to get their lives back on track. A roster of builders, doctors, nurses, lawyers, others who would cook meals, gather and distribute clothes, and give them haircuts after a hot shower was growing.

"There are lots of people who will be donating time to help you," Hank told those who would listen. The natural distrust among the street people, who'd been lied to so often before, presented barriers for Hank. But he knew them. He had been one of them, and after seeing him week after week for months on their streets, they began to accept and believe him. In fact, several down-and-out men who used to build and fix things for a living offered to help. One man among them, named Scott Jacobs, who had lived under a stairwell for the past five years after returning from the war in Iraq, helped Hank mobilize a group of homeless volunteers. The group was dubbed "The Battalion" and the name stuck. As more people on the street heard about The Battalion and what they were doing, it became a matter of prestige to be one of them. Many brought trade skills, others offered to do anything on the project, like sweep up the garbage and pull down the rotting wood paneling and stairs. It was amazing to see useful skill sets nearly lost to mental atrophy, drugs, and apathy come to the surface of the sad individuals who'd given up on themselves. And the more street people joined The Battalion, the more newsworthy the project became.

CHAPTER 40
SARA AND DAVID

Sara's San Francisco office was buzzing with activity. Gina was making progress in her recovery, and though it was slow and tough, she managed to work a couple of hours a day making calls to the media. She even got someone to create a website to provide regular updates to the stakeholders. She was promoting the news and fielding questions from reporters nearly every day. As the media developed the story about the homeless helping themselves and others like them, and calling the Shelter *their project,* money donations toward the renovation doubled in one week. The fundraiser event sold out at $5,000 a ticket. Everyone wanted to be part of the ambitious, innovative undertaking. It was the talk of San Francisco, and other cities were taking notice. The mayor appreciated the nationwide press and positive local attention for a change, and took some unearned credit for the project. Everything was snowballing into something huge and wonderful.

Over dinner at the end of another exhausting day, David updated Sara about his challenges with red tape and Hank's work on the street.

"I have some news, too," Sara said over her wine, while David jangled the ice in his tea. "I heard from the realtor in Paradise Valley." Sara couldn't stop grinning like a fool.

"Yeah?" David was beginning to know her—when it was an important piece of information, at least to Sara, she strung out the anticipation.

"I can't believe it, but *my* house just got listed." Sara now smiled ear to ear, knowing David would appreciate the news that the house she had fallen in love with on her first visit to Paradise Valley was on the market.

"That's incredible! I don't believe it!"

"I know! I was so excited I told the agent to send me every bit of information on the property."

David's first question was, "What are they asking for it?"

Unfortunately that's when Sara's smile faded. "It's more than I can afford. But I'm hoping they'll consider an offer."

"Would you like me to help you through this, Sara?" David was an expert in real estate negotiations but wanted to respect Sara's privacy. They hadn't known each other long enough, David felt, for him to assume she needed or even wanted his help.

"Yes, I would. I'll be going up tomorrow morning to finally see the inside. Can you go with me?"

"I can reschedule my morning, but should be back for a meeting with Hank and the city manager by two o'clock. Hank may be able to tackle the indigents, but he's not ready for primetime with the city planners."

"That will work. We can get there by nine to meet the agent and see the house. If we keep things moving, we can be back by one at the latest."

Sara's dimpled smile returned in full glory, making David's heart leap like it always did when she was happy.

కికికి

On their way back to the city, Sara said, "That house is everything I'd hoped it would be. It's perfect. It's more than perfect. I had no idea it sat on three acres with trees in the back, and a pool, and the massive patio and landscaping." David took Sara's hand as she burbled out the list of everything she loved about the house she couldn't afford.

"I hate to be the voice of reason here," David ventured tentatively. "But they're asking way too much for it. Yeah, it's wonderful and has been well taken care of. The structure and roof are in excellent condition. But a million. Geez, Sara. Can you swing that? And the place is huge for one person."

"I know, I know. I understand and appreciate the reality check. It's over my price range. Don't you think they'll consider a low-ball offer if they know how much I love the house that the owners lived in for twenty years? Won't that mean something?"

"Let's wait to hear what the agent tells us about comps in the area. We could also ask for an appraisal. That usually takes place for the bank loan, but it would be a good third-party opinion to have sooner rather than later." David suspected the house was overpriced, but he didn't want to get Sara's hopes up any higher than they already were. He wanted to see the facts first.

The agent called Sara the next day to say the house was appropriately priced. Sara had come to rely on David for all sorts of advice regarding her business, and now the purchase of a house in Paradise Valley. Located sixty-five miles north of San Francisco it would be about an hour-long commute and the price was more than she could afford. But she felt she'd come home the minute she saw it. She and David talked about the town and that house every time they got together, which was becoming more and more frequent. Neither had told anyone about their romance. They liked it that way. It felt special and protected, free from the opinions of others. Sara in particular thought it best not to flaunt their relationship because of her track record with marriage. Every serious relationship had turned into a marriage that didn't work for a variety of reasons. She knew she was in love with David and wanted to savor how happy they were making each other.

Two weeks later Sara was in tears. As her reality barometer, David was depressing her with his all-knowing advice about not getting herself in a hole buying that huge house. Now, sitting at her kitchen table doodling out on paper as many creative financial options as she could think of within her means, Sara realized how right he was about the high price of the house. The disappointment ran deep.

"I guess you're right, David," Sara said after answering the phone and hearing his voice. "I just can't do it. The house is too expensive. I have to give up on the idea and think smaller."

"Don't limit your dreams, Sara. Keep the house in mind, but keep looking around, too. You haven't seen many places."

Sounding like a spoiled little girl, Sara pouted. "But I want that one. It's the house I've always dreamed of."

There wasn't much David could say on the subject about the house to kick her out of her doldrums, so he switched the conversation to his news. "Sara, this might cheer you up. We got the keys to the building. We can start the renovations."

That did it. Sara snapped out of her petulant self-indulgence. Happiness returned. "That's fantastic! I didn't know you were so close."

"You don't know what happened? I thought you knew."

"Tell me. What are you talking about?" Clearly something had broken loose at David's end. The last time they'd talked about it, David was bogged down in paperwork and red tape at the city's building department. David's hands had been tied. The start date for renovations was threatened, which nearly caused him to lose the window of time the structural engineer and contractor could donate before they got busy on paid projects. That would have brought David back to square one. He would have had to search for other good-hearted souls willing to work on a monster-sized labor of love.

"It seems that one Caroline Marie Kendall is now the proud owner of a ten-story ruin in the heart of San Francisco's seediest, most crime-ridden neighborhood. She bought it, Sara. I knew she had money, but this is ridiculous. Though I suspect the city gave her a deal. Now I understand some of the delays. In spite of the Mayor's tacit support, they didn't want to be bothered. Because of their tight budget, they were worried about the long-term commitment. But Carrie's lawyer negotiated a deal that would keep the city responsible for running the Shelter out of their social services budget as long as she owns and maintains the structure."

"Last time I spoke with Carrie, she asked again how she could help. I didn't want to be crass and say 'give us money,' but that's what I was thinking. I'll have to call her right away."

"It's really taken a load off my desk. The floodgates of work have opened. The Battalion—the volunteers—are gutting the place as we speak, and I expect to begin the rebuild in about four weeks."

"I just got a shudder up the back of my neck, David. I can't believe how good this all feels. The fundraiser is in four weeks. How perfect to be able to show everyone that we're moving on this and that something very special is being created, thanks to you, Carrie, Gina, and your mysterious friend, Hank."

"And you. You started all this. You're the one who dared to dream and dream big." Getting back to the subject of buying the house, David added, "And you shouldn't let go of your dream to live in a home like the one in Paradise Valley. Maybe it won't be that house, but maybe it will be something even better."

They hung up after making a date for dinner that evening, then Sara called Carrie.

CHAPTER 41
GINA, SARA, CARRIE, AND DAVID

Gina was once again helping Carrie pick out a gown. Sara was there, too, looking for advice on her own styling. Gina was walking without a cane now, moving stiffly but unencumbered between the two women. Her own hair and makeup was done. With the exception of the scars at the hairline above one ear and a rather nasty one on her leg, Gina was still a perfect beauty. She wore her hair shorter now. It no longer reached her waist, and without all that weight, the black fall of silk bounced in waves around her face and over her shoulders. Each woman radiated her own style of beauty.

David was to meet the ladies at Carrie's apartment and escort them to the hotel ballroom. Hank wouldn't be there. He didn't want to leave TJ, but had also admitted to David that he wouldn't feel comfortable at the formal dinner, talking with "all those rich folks."

This time Sara was able to enjoy the party. The volunteer caterers, which happened to be the two older women from the very first event-planning meeting, ran the party like clockwork. They hadn't been kidding when they stood up and told those attending that first meeting that they had a little experience with parties. The mayor opened the evening with a touching statement about commitment and dedicated service to those who need our help. The emcee was hilarious. Sexy models from La Vie Modeling scampered between the tables, rousing bidders to a competitive froth to outbid others. A private television production company heard about the project from Gina and sent a film crew and producer. They seemed to be everywhere at once, filming the fun and action for the Dare to Dream documentary about the Shelter, The Battalion workers getting the building ready for renovation, and of course Sara, who had imagined it all from the beginning.

Five hours after the doors to the party opened the last guests left. Four tired friends fell into chairs around one of a hundred now-empty tables. Their volunteer bean counter came over and announced, "I'm happy to tell you that the event raised $5,674,000. That's the total from tickets at five thousand dollars apiece, the silent auction, the live auction, and donations that came in from those who didn't attend tonight but mailed checks."

"We can also expect royalties from the documentary once it's produced and running on TV," Sara added.

"We did it. We exceeded the goal," Gina said quietly, relishing the success. "That's amazing."

"It's astonishing, and our work is just beginning," the ever-rational David said. "It was great to be able to show photos of the work that's been started at the Shelter, particularly the shots of individuals from The Battalion ripping out the rotten wood and appliances in the kitchen. Those people are a great inspiration to the others on the street. Hank told me more and more homeless people are showing up every day to help. They're feeling useful again.

"And thanks to Carrie, we have a leg-up on how to use the money. Since you're the building owner, it will be easier for us to get through each inspection check point, which will save time and money," David added.

"I'm just glad to be a part of something so meaningful," Carrie said thoughtfully. "It can't always be about me and Kendall Tech… can it?" she said with a mischievous grin. In her heart she knew everything had been about her and following in her grandfather's footsteps. Now it felt good to be outside of herself and be with people she could call friends. People with a common cause. The Shelter project had brought them all together. No, Carrie corrected the thought, *Sara had brought them together*, and with the exception of missing Baker, she had never been happier.

A teary-eyed Gina said, "You're incredibly generous, Carrie, and my great friend. And I'm feeling like it's time to go. My stamina isn't a hundred percent yet." Gina took Carrie's arm to steady herself as she stood and stretched, causing everyone to appreciate what the woman had been through that year.

✧✧✧

The next day's news was full of reports on the success of the Dare to Dream's fundraising event for the Safe Harbor Shelter. The reporters name-dropped notable attendees and trumpeted how much money had been raised in one night.

One story in the *Chronicle* stated:

> ...it is a testament to the tenacity of Dare to Dream Events business owner, Sara Collins. She's a force who can make anything happen when she puts her mind to it. The old Harbor building is now the Dare to Dream Safe Harbor Shelter. The project has inspired other cities throughout the U.S. to adopt the model for new homeless shelters and getting their people off the streets. Ours is the first of its kind to involve the help of those who will be living in the Shelter, which will provide a place for rebuilding lives. The city of San Francisco thanks Sara Collins and her dream team: David Hendricks in charge of renovations; Henry Johns, the communications conduit to the homeless and inspiration for The Battalion, the group of individuals who among

hundreds of others will live in the Shelter until they get back on their feet; Gina Severns, supermodel turned public relations director, and Caroline Kendall, Owner/CEO of Kendall Technologies, primary financial backer, and last-minute savior from nearly insurmountable challenges presented by our own city bureaucrats.

The mayor was only mentioned for giving a self-serving political speech at the beginning of the evening.

CHAPTER 42

Sara stood in the doorway of Gina's office. "Gina, I want to get us all together for dinner at my new house next month," Sara told her now full-time public relations director.

"House? Did you find a place in Paradise?"

"YES I DID!" Sara laughed. "Actually the town is called Paradise Valley." Sara winked and ran to her own office to pull up the online images of her home. "It's mine! I signed the papers this morning."

Gina had followed Sara and said, "I thought it was out-of-this-world expensive. I don't mean to pry, but you said you couldn't afford it."

"The owners and I came to an accord, so to speak. They got antsy about moving and reduced the price, I put in an offer and we negotiated, without David's help, I might add, to a point that made it possible. Since all the publicity from the Shelter fund-raiser, business is pushing our limits in both offices. I'll have to staff up again if I decide to keep expanding. In other words, we're making money, Gina!"

"Congratulations, Sara." Gina was happy for her friend, but reflected for a minute on her own life. Carrie was reconciling with Baker. David's business was keeping him on the road, and at that very minute he was back in Boston reconnecting with his sons. And, Sara had just bought the house she'd been obsessing over. *As for me*, Gina's mind rambled, *what do I want to do now*?

"Gina? Are you listening?" Sara asked.

"Yeah, you want to throw a dinner party...and that house looks amazing."

Gina loved her job and was good at it, but sometimes she felt empty. She missed Jake terribly and wondered if she would ever find anyone to love again. Lately she had found herself fantasizing about having a baby or two. It had taken her a full year to completely recover from the accident and now she wanted a very different life.

"...will you come?"

"Of course! Wouldn't miss it for anything."

CHAPTER 43
HANK AND GINA

The Monday following Sara's party, Hank stood alone in his bright, modest kitchen, savoring a first sip of morning coffee. Having finally met Sara, Gina and Carrie, he had been surprised to learn how different they all were: different backgrounds, styles, personalities and yet, they were obviously good friends. Carrie's reserved character, Sara's spunk, Gina's…well Gina's bright blue eyes and the undeniable, immediate attraction he'd felt couldn't be categorized. His thoughts then turned to the quote on Sara's computer that he'd read when he'd called TJ from her office: *Imagination is everything…*

TJ interrupted his train of thought.

"Hi, Dad. Whatcha doin?" TJ's hair was as rumpled as his Spiderman pajamas. The bottoms were twisted nearly sideways, causing Hank to wonder how TJ got down the hallway to the kitchen without tripping.

"Well, I seem to have a standing order for hot chocolate. So I thought I'd get that going for you."

"Dad, were there kids at that party?" TJ had obviously been giving it some thought.

"It was a grownup party. No kids, otherwise you would have gone too, buddy. I didn't want to wake you up when I got home just for a kiss from your old man."

"I wouldn't mind." TJ rubbed his still-sleepy eyes. "Are you gonna be here tonight?"

"Yeah. I sure am. But now that we're settled in our house, I need to make some new friends too. Just like you did at school. That's okay, right?"

"Have you made any friends, Dad?"

"You know David. You met him in San Francisco. He's a good friend. But I met some other people at the party, too, and they're real nice. Real nice," Hank repeated, thinking of Gina.

"Will I meet them?"

"Probably. The house I was at has a great swimming pool. Maybe we'll get to swim there someday."

"Awesome." TJ struggled to the top of the kitchen counter stool to watch his dad make scrambled eggs. He took a first sip of his hot chocolate, which was a perfect lukewarm. "Good job, Dad."

"I'm glad it's to your liking." Hank played it serious, finding it hard to hide his smile.

The exchange had become a ritual between them every morning before TJ got ready for school. But this morning there was a twist to their conversation.

"What's gonna happen to us now?"

The question startled Hank. "What do you mean? Aren't we okay? You asked that Saturday night, too, when I called from the party to say good-night."

"Yeah, we're good." TJ looked up with a milky mustache. "I was thinking if we're going to be here forever. Just you and me."

"Would you like that?"

"Sure! Unless I find a girlfriend someday." TJ checked his dad's expression for a response.

"TJ. Is this about my being gone Saturday night?"

"Well, 'cuz now you have all sorts of friends. Are you going to leave me, Dad?"

"WHAT! Are you nutty? What did I put in that hot chocolate? Oh, it must be the whipped cream that's making you think crazy."

"Aaaw Dad. I have whipped cream all the time."

"And that better stop. You're thinking crazy stuff." Hank taunted as he tried to scoop off the cream that was beginning to slop over the top of TJ's cup.

TJ fought him off. "No, it's not the whipped cream!" Defending what remained, TJ quickly licked it off his cup and fingers.

"Eew. You're all gooey now." Hank laughed and grabbed the towel to wipe his son's face and hands.

"But, I mean, what if you get a girlfriend. What will happen to me?" TJ was clearly concerned about any more changes in his life.

Hank hunkered down over the counter and came face to face to his beloved little boy. "You are number one. Don't you know that? It nearly killed me when you ran off in Vegas. I made you a promise that I not only have to keep, I WANT to keep, because you are my life, my heart and soul. I would die without you. I love you, buddy and if I should be so lucky to find someone else to love, then that will make both our lives better. There's a never-ending supply of love to go around, TJ. Have you noticed that? You love Gramma June and you love me, and I think you still love your mom. You love all sorts of things and maybe even your new friends at school, and you haven't run out of love yet, have you?" Hank wondered where that bit of wisdom came from, but made sure TJ understood what he was trying to tell him.

"TJ, I hope to find a nice lady to love someday. I hope maybe to get you a brother or sister. What do you think about that?" Before TJ could answer Hank went on. "But you will never be any less loved if that happens. In fact, you would be even more loved. Does that make sense?" Straightening up, Hank watched his son's eyes. They were bright. Not with tears but with understanding.

"That's so cool, Dad. So we can love as many people and things as we want and it will never run out?"

"Yup. In fact, I think that the more you give love, the more you get love."

"Coooool," TJ said again thoughtfully. "Hey! Where's my eggs!"

That was the signal that the conversation was over and Hank dished up a large spoonful of his special scrambled eggs with bacon.

"TJ, I want you to tell me if something is bothering you, though, and I'll do whatever I can to fix it. Do you like Mrs. Harper? I'm working more for David now and we're really busy building a big house for people who have nowhere to live. It's good work and I'm happy to be doing something to help those people. But we have a deal, right? You'll tell me what's going on in that little head of yours?"

"'Course Dad. I don't mind Mrs. Harper. She makes cookies and stuff. It's nice here."

"Then it's a promise, right? Now you better go wash up and get ready for school. I'll drop you off today."

While TJ got dressed, Hank decided he would call one of his new friends later.

CHAPTER 44

Gina, there's a guy on line two for you."

"No name?" Gina asked the receptionist.

"No. Sounds sexy."

Gina picked up the line. "Gina Severns, may I help you?"

"Gina. It's Hank Johns. We met Saturday night at Sara's house." Hank didn't need to remind Gina who he was. She hadn't stopped thinking about him.

Sitting at her desk gazing at the summer-time-green maple tree outside her office window, Gina twirled a strand of hair. "Sure, Hank. I've been thinking about you." She didn't play the game of cat and mouse with someone she liked. Having nearly died twice, she had a sense of urgency to live life fully and happily ever after, like her parents.

"You have?" Hank was surprised, considering how remote he'd been, and how he had even put off her flirtation at dinner.

"Well, yeah. You confused me, and I don't like being confused."

"I was a little confused that night myself. It was actually my first dinner party. Can I make it up to you? I was wondering if you would have dinner with me this Friday."

Gina's heart began beating a little harder and her palms got a little sweaty. Suddenly nervous and excited, she blurted out, "Oh! I would like that."

Hank, on the other hand, was experiencing a far greater attack of nerves. His heart was pounding and an adrenalin rush hit him so fast he nearly stammered, but managed to breathe and say, "Great! I'll be working with David until five. Do you mind an early date, say six o'clock? I can pick you up at your office or apartment, whichever is most convenient for you."

Gina chose her apartment and gave him the address.

Each hung up feeling a warm glow of anticipation.

CHAPTER 45
CARRIE

"It's phenomenal!" Charles Baker reported proudly. Baker, Carrie, and seventeen board members were seated around Justice Kendall's table that would accommodate thirty comfortably. Heavy furniture and antiques acquired by the founder himself created an old-world ambiance in the boardroom—a stark contrast to what Baker was explaining as the latest, greatest, energy-producing innovation to come along in the modern world. "The project is in the final test phase and will take about six months. As you know, we received a tax break for the work Kendall Tech has done to date and the feds are accelerating the work by helping to fund Phase IV. We'll have an excellent financial report for the stockholders in the fall." Charles sat down.

Upon hearing no questions and there being no new business, Carrie adjourned the quarterly meeting.

Leaving the board members to catch up with each other, Carrie nearly gushed, "I'm so excited, Baker. My grandfather would be very happy about the direction the company has gone—your work is truly imaginative."

Carrie and her on-again, off-again fiancé walked down the hallway toward their adjoining offices. Though their working relationship never wavered, both driven and dedicated professionally, their personal relationship suffered from lack of passion. But they had grown to love each other and the last time they'd parted, Baker had called her to reconcile. They never showed affection in public, but before turning into her office, Carrie took Charles's arm, "Baker, let's go for a walk. The VPs can run this place for an hour or so without us." She ducked into her office for a moment and returned with a black, London Fog trench coat. Charles helped her slip it on. Waving to the security guard at the reception desk, they left the building and automatically turned right. They were in sync without discussing the destination. Stepping into the foggy drizzle, Carrie exclaimed, "It's actually raining." She opened her umbrella and Baker put his arm around her shoulder.

"Do you want to get coffee?" Though he was enjoying the invigorating temperature at least for now, he wanted Carrie to be comfortable.

"Let's just walk." She smiled.

"You're feeling pretty good about everything, aren't you?"

"Yes, I am. The heart research foundation is well underway, Kendall Tech is doing better than ever, thanks to you and your brainy idea of energy fusion. And I'm particularly excited about the Shelter, Dare to Dream's Safe Harbor Shelter. Sara says it's already nearing capacity, housing over five hundred people. I'm thinking about looking for another building to become another shelter. It's a great feeling to help so many people."

"I'm proud of you. You're an incredible woman, and I love you. I'll never forget that first day we met in the mailroom. You were wearing a black skirt, white blouse, and dorky flat shoes. Your hair was long and straight, and you hadn't opted for contacts yet. Those black framed glasses made you look smart but nerdy."

Impressed that he remembered what she'd been wearing all those years ago, Carrie replied, "So you think I look good now?"

"You were pretty, but unpolished. Now you're a head-turner."

"Well, thanks, Baker. I've never been told I was pretty before." Carrie blushed and closed the umbrella they had shared. She turned her face to the sky. "Grandfather told me my imagination would create all sorts of things—good and bad—and I've finally chosen to focus on the good. I think *we're* good, Baker. Good together. Let's set that wedding date." She glanced over at him.

Charles stopped and turned the woman he loved by the shoulders to face him. It was raining a little harder now. "Do you mean it this time, Carrie? I'm ready if you're sure. In fact, I've never stopped wanting to marry you." Without waiting for an answer he kissed her. Kissed her passionately for the first time in their relationship, as pedestrians flowed around the oblivious pair. Carrie felt her heart open wide to accept his love and warmth. She felt light and happy, and in love.

To love and to be loved. It was the last thing on her current wish list to come true.

CHAPTER 46

Later that morning, Sara asked Gina to meet with her. "Did you know that Carrie and Charles have set a new wedding date?"

"No! I didn't." It was still raining outside. Gina noticed the rivulets of water coursing down the windows outside Sara's office. "When did that happen?"

"Evidently about an hour ago. Carrie wants to pick up where I'd left off on the planning, but now I'm buried with the next Shelter projects in Sacramento and Chicago, and we have several other event contracts. Unless I hire someone else to work with Carrie, I think my option for managing the wedding is you, and who else is better suited than the maid of honor and best friend of the bride. What do you think?"

"I can do it, Sara. I'm up to full time and more now. The press knows about the upcoming event for the next shelter and several reporters will cover it. Though I was planning on going to that." Then Gina remembered to ask, "When's the wedding date?"

"June thirtieth. A Saturday, at five. She wanted a dinner reception with orchestra, more flowers than Hawaii can grow, and Wolfgang Puck or someone of his ilk to cater it."

"Simple Simon!" Gina was confident about her capabilities. "I can call on Karen for help, right?"

"You'll have to, but if you need even more help to make Carrie's wedding the wedding of the century, let me know."

"I'll call Karen right away. This will be a big society event. I know Carrie will expect press coverage. Oh! I have to call Carrie! I'm so excited."

Gina nearly ran out of Sara's office.

❧❧❧

"Caroline Kendall, please." Gina caught Carrie on her first try. "I can't believe you've set the date. What happened? Did he propose again? I want to hear all about it."

Basking in her friend's excitement over the news, Carrie agreed to have lunch with Gina.

Gina arrived first. It was the same restaurant where she and Carrie had first plotted the set-up against Baker seven years ago. This time it was Gina who was recognized by name and given a prime table by the window. Carrie entered a few minutes later apologizing for being late. She looked happy.

"Carrie. I think you're glowing, but brides are supposed to glow. So did you finally take my advice? I said you were being a fool not to marry Baker. I know you love him."

Carrie was wearing a blue blouse and star sapphire earrings. Her engagement ring was back on her finger and reflected in the window as Carrie held the menu. "I am happy, Gina. Yeah, you helped me see that I have a good man in love with me. I have no more doubts about marrying Baker. Let's order, then I'll fill you in on my morning."

"That's so romantic, Carrie," Gina exclaimed, after hearing about the kiss in the rain that sealed the deal. "I couldn't be happier for you. Your wedding is going to be awesome, fit for a queen." The women went over a few ideas, rethinking some things that Carrie had thought she wanted when Charles first proposed.

Then Gina switched subjects. "I have a little news too. It's not a big deal but I'm kind of excited about it all the same."

"Spill it!" Carrie said.

"I have a date on Friday. Hank called this morning and asked me out. I was surprised because he was so distant at Sara's party. I told him he confused me and he asked if he could make it up to me." Gina gave Carrie a word for word account of the conversation with Hank.

Epilogue

It was a sunny afternoon in Paradise Valley. Hand-in-hand, TJ and Gina went ahead of Hank through Sara's now familiar living room. Ever the little gentleman, TJ opened both terrace doors for Gina and said, "Careful, Mom," as her huge tummy led the way.

"Hey there, little family!" Sara called.

David walked over and gave Gina a hug. "How are you feeling? You're getting close, right?"

"Eight months and counting the minutes," Gina replied. "I never thought my stomach could possibly stretch so far." Hank shook David's hand and the two walked over to the bar. David handed Hank a beer and poured iced tea for himself.

"Gina!" Carrie shouted from the pool. "We're down here!"

Gina glanced in the direction of Carrie's voice and saw her friend sitting on the steps in the pool next to Charles and their fifteen-month-old daughter, who was splashing around in her daddy's arms. TJ had already run past the adults and launched himself cannonball-style into the deep end of the glistening water. Josh and Tim, David's sons, tossed the beach ball to TJ when he resurfaced like a rocket. Sara handed Gina a glass of sparkling cold cranberry juice, then walked with her down the path. Hank and David followed closely behind, nervously expecting Gina to pop any minute.

Sitting by the pool, Sara contentedly took in her friends' chatter and the children's play and laughter.

David sat down close beside her. Adding his smile to Sara's happy expression he said, "This all feels like paradise to me."

Sara's gaze moved to the afternoon light changing on the horizon.

"It's everything I imagined it would be."

ABOUT THE AUTHOR

Mary De Groat discovered her passion for writing while working as a marketing communications professional for the past twenty-five years. A student of metaphysics and meditation, she believes in the power of imagination, which she has unleashed with demonstrated results. While written primarily for entertainment purposes, it is Mary's hope to inspire readers to know they too can reset what isn't working in their lives. *Beyond the Last Horizon* is a work of fiction based on the principles presented in Rhonda Byrne's *The Secret, The Power of Decision* by Raymond Charles Barker, and other many works and teachings studied over the years. Mary lives in "paradise" overlooking the vineyards of Carmel Valley, California.

www.ingramcontent.com/pod-product-compliance
Lightning Source LLC
Chambersburg PA
CBHW020336180626
46812CB00001B/237